Courage

Time to Live or Time to Die?

By

Ian Newton

Copyright © *Ian Newton*, 2024

All Rights Reserved

First published: 9th September 2019

Publisher by Ian Newton

The right of Ian Newton to be identified as author of this Work has been asserted by in accordance with sections 77 and 78 of the Copyright, Designs and Patents Act 1988.

All rights reserved. No part of this publication may be reproduced, stored in retrieval system, copied in any form or by any means, electronic, mechanical, photocopying, recording or otherwise transmitted without written permission from the publisher. You must not circulate this book in any format.

This book is a work of fiction and, except in the case of historical fact, any resemblance to actual persons, living or dead, is purely coincidental.

ISBN number 978-1-80558-565-7

To my three children

Table of Contents

Prologue 8
Chapter 1 1
Chapter 2 13
Chapter 3 16
Chapter 4 18
Chapter 5 19
Chapter 6 22
Chapter 7 26
Chapter 8 29
Chapter 9 38
Chapter 10 41
Chapter 11 46
Chapter 12 49
Chapter 13 53
Chapter 14 59
Chapter 15 62
Chapter 16 63
Chapter 17 64
Chapter 18 66
Chapter 19 68
Chapter 20 75
Chapter 21 79
Chapter 22 80
Chapter 23 82
Chapter 24 90
Chapter 25 92
Chapter 26 94

Chapter 27	96
Chapter 28	100
Chapter 29	101
Chapter 30	102
Chapter 31	104
Chapter 32	105
Chapter 33	107
Chapter 34	109
Chapter 35	110
Chapter 36	112
Chapter 37	113
Chapter 38	115
Chapter 39	118
Chapter 40	124
Chapter 41	126
Chapter 42	131
Chapter 43	132
Chapter 44	136
Chapter 45	140
Chapter 46	143
Chapter 47	144
Chapter 48	145
Chapter 49	151
Chapter 50	154
Chapter 51	158
Chapter 52	162
Chapter 53	163
Chapter 54	166
Chapter 55	167
Chapter 56	169

Chapter 57	170
Chapter 58	171
Chapter 59	175
Chapter 60	176
Chapter 61	180
Chapter 62	182
Chapter 63	186
Chapter 64	189
Chapter 65	191
Chapter 66	193
Chapter 67	194
Chapter 68	196
Chapter 69	198
Chapter 70	199
Chapter 71	206
Chapter 72	208
Chapter 73	209
Chapter 74	217
Chapter 75	220
Chapter 76	223
Chapter 77	227
Chapter 78	229
Chapter 79	232
Chapter 80	236
Chapter 81	237
Chapter 82	239
Chapter 83	245
Chapter 84	247
Chapter 85	250
Chapter 86	253

Chapter 87	254
Chapter 88	255
Chapter 89	257
Chapter 90	259
Epilogue	262

Prologue

As adults, we wouldn't consider ourselves to be particularly brave but always hoped that we would be if needed.

Men recognize that as men, there is an expectation of bravery or courage…but all hope never to be tested.

Men also sometimes daydream about being the hero: someone who fights against the bad guy and saves the lady. Yet the irony is largely lost on us all, we want to be the hero, but we absolutely do not want to be tested.

At the cinema, we see many acts of amazing courage, mainly by larger-than-life characters that always appear to have nine lives, and sometimes we hear about true acts of courage, whether it's by a member of the public or, too often by a member of our armed forces.

The question remains.

'If tested, what would I do?'

'Bravery is the capacity to perform properly, even when scared half to death.'

— **Omar Bradley**

'The two most important days in your life are the day you are born…and the day you find out why.'

— **Mark Twain**

Chapter 1

Home is where the heart is

I've always loved this sofa: so soft and two feet longer than average; definitely one of my best investments.

'Have a nice sleep, did you?' Hayley asks me. 'I cannot believe you missed the ending, which means I'm gonna have to watch it again.' Hayley smiles as she strokes my hair.

'I know, but it felt soooo good just closing my eyes and drifting off. Do you fancy a latte darling?' I reply, knowing only too well that Hayley makes the best lattes ever and I wouldn't know where they were in the kitchen. That's not to say I don't cook or get involved in the general housework, but Hayley's the lead, plus she's a better cook. It's also largely her home now since I work over three hours drive away most weeks in Wales, leaving just after tea time on a Sunday evening and returning on Friday. My company's head office is on the same site as the plant that manufactures Christmas Tinsel garlands.

I started the job two and a half years ago and whilst it's been very satisfying, it's also been the toughest job I've ever done. Making the sacrifice to be away all week was never part of my career plan, but the chance to be CEO of a medium-sized business that badly needed a turnaround was so attractive, that I took the post. Another key attribute of this company was definitely the fact that it had its own UK manufacturing. Most of my previous roles had been in sales and marketing and I consider myself very fortunate to have worked in some fairly large organizations, but this role in Wales gave me full accountability for the manufacturing operation which was a great boost for my CV. I initially agreed with Hayley that it would be a maximum 2-3-year role, but life seems to be flying past and I'm already into my third year. I am also conscious that prior to this job, my last 3 positions lasted less than 18 months each, so I needed to stick in this role for a while, otherwise, future employers would start to wonder why I never lasted long with a company...not a great reputation to have. The only great thing about moving around so much has been getting an increase in salary each time.

Most of my earlier career feels like it was preparation for the roles I do now. After leaving school at 16 (without many qualifications), my 1st job was as a sales assistant in a department store, which considering how shy I was, was some achievement. Fortunately, we did not have many customers through the door, so I didn't have to speak to many people. Over the next 3 years in various retail roles, I gradually came out of my shell and became more confident with people. Throughout my 20s, I worked for some multinationals that gave me some terrific training, which helped me build up my all-round management skills. My main motivation for my career was making sure I could look after my family financially and of course, I wanted a nice house, with a white picket fence and garage.

I have three incredible children, but I suppose every parent has the same perception about their children. You may notice that I didn't say 'great or wonderful,' but incredible.

James is 18 now and suffers from a neuromuscular disorder called Spinal Muscular Atrophy (SMA). Basically, he has about 10% to 20% strength in his muscles, both inside and outside his body. His condition is muscular and doesn't affect his brain, so effectively he's a normal young man, goes to college, and works part-time in a graphics studio. He drives an electric wheelchair and we have always tried to treat him as normally as possible. The key problem with his condition is that we must protect him from chest infections. Without sounding too dramatic, they can quickly turn into pneumonia, and if not acted upon immediately, can turn bad.

If you don't have a disabled family member, you won't necessarily know that there is a completely separate world exists, where the most basic of activities need careful planning. For example, is parking close enough to the movie theatre when planning a trip to the cinema? Will there be convenient seating available and will there be a lift that is working completely fine? Thankfully, as James has gotten older, the world has become more accessible and he manages to get around pretty much everywhere now. He even belongs to a wheelchair football team. This again isn't something people would imagine going on around the world, but it's quite big and is regulated by FIFA (the world football's governing body) and James belongs to a really good team. Having seen him play a few times and occasionally even get on the score sheet is pretty damn special!

James is a complete inspiration to me and whilst I have always privately struggled to deal with his condition, I am honoured and privileged to have him in my life.

Our two girls, on the other hand, are not always a shining light in our lives, and as teenagers can be quite a challenge.

All the children had biblical names, which stems from both their mother Linda and I being Christians. The irony is that the youngest (age 13) Abigail's name means 'source of joy' and the eldest (15) Sarah's name means 'princess'. I am not sure who decided this way back in the day, but they definitely got them wrong. That's not to say that I'm not extremely proud of both of them and love them both very much. But when they want to be they are typical teenagers, who, once you throw some hormones in, can be very challenging, to say the least. Abby takes after her mother and Sarah after me. However, other than laziness and some pretty regular telling of 'white' lies, I wouldn't change them for the world, and God help any person (especially members of the opposite sex) who harms one hair on their bodies. Hayley bought me a great T-shirt off the internet that I proudly wear covering off 10 'rules of engagement' for any boys who foolishly think they can get involved with my girls. One of my favourite lines is 'Remember, anything you do to my daughters, I will do to you.' It always makes me chuckle and I made sure they posted the full list on their Facebook pages, just to ensure any potential suitors get the message.

Having said this, my Christian faith is very important to me and whilst I might bluster a bit and sound very protective about my girls, it's just a bit of a laugh.

I absolutely believe in the story of Jesus and know he is my saviour, but living and behaving like him has always been a challenge I constantly fail.

I do pray most days, get to church irregularly (probably eight to ten times a year), and try to behave and make decisions that Jesus would, but I struggle massively. I am a very normal guy, who tries to reduce the number of things I know I shouldn't do and do more of the things I know I should. The children's mother and I always wanted to try and bring them up with these things in mind and without doubt one of the proudest and most emotional days of my life was witnessing my son James get baptised. I even held him in the pool as he was 'dunked'.

Sadly, too many things distract us all these days, and whilst it might not be obvious to other people, fundamentally God is very important to me.

Because of the children and our belief in God, getting divorced wasn't an easy decision for Linda and I. In fact, it probably meant we dragged out our marriage 1-2 years longer than we did. Neither party was really at fault; we just fell out of love with each other over time and ended up unhappy and arguing constantly. Despite our best efforts and trying various strategies - from me living upstairs, in hotels, around my brothers, etc. etc., we couldn't make it work.

That was over nine years ago and luckily for both of us, we have found new relationships and I for one have now been with Hayley for over four years, and whilst we have our own ups and downs, I can honestly see us together forever. Hayley is a little over 5 feet tall with beautiful, long dark brown hair. Ever since we 1st met, she has been building a collection of shoes with heels ranging from 4 to 5 inches. We regularly get comments (I'm 6 foot 2) or double takes from people when we are out together, and it's even funnier when we are on holiday near a beach and she's wearing flat shoes. With soft features and striking eyes, she often gets mistaken for my daughter...something she regularly teases me about. We met on an online dating site, but always told people a different story because around that time, dating sites were not seen as very cool. Hayley often reminds me of our 1st date, when she initially thought I might be an undercover police officer because of my rapid questioning skills. The truth is, I had been on numerous dates and found them very tiresome, and wanted to get into a person's views on things quickly, so as not to waste anyone's time. It obviously wasn't too bad, as our 2nd date was the following day and the rest is, as they say, history. We soon realised we shared the same interests in music, film, and the arts and in particular both loved spending hours wandering around museums and art galleries. In our 1st year together, we visited the Louvre in Paris, the Rijksmuseum in Amsterdam, and of course the British Museum in London.

Hayley has a seven-year-old son called Scott, who can be a real challenge. Scott has a very strong personality and is incredibly bright. Considering his age, he sometimes puts my own children to shame when it comes to playing trivial pursuits. Occasionally we clash a little and I have to keep telling him that I am not trying to replace his father, but because he typically ignores everything I say, I try to discipline him, which doesn't help our relationship. That said, we do spend some quality time together and during most summers I manage to take him fishing over at a local lake. It's pretty rewarding to have seen him go from someone who wouldn't go anywhere near a maggot or worm to someone who can now cast out and catch his own fish.

Hayley's a teacher at a local school and works hard to do a full-time job, look after the house, and be a mother to Scott. Until I met Hayley I had always thought teachers had an easy life, with easy hours and loads of holiday, but she has so much marking and her own homework to do almost daily, that it really is a full-time job. When I say homework, I mean preparation for the following day, which seems to always consist of some arts and crafts stuff, and the living room is normally filled up with an array of different types of material and paint. Whilst Hayley teaches 6-7 year-olds and covers several subjects, she majored in art and in her own right is a very good artist. Not that she will allow any of her work to be visible around the house (too embarrassed), but instead has bags of drawings and paintings collecting dust in the attic. Anyway, I now have a new-found respect for teachers, helped by the fact that Hayley never lets me forget it.

Because my job takes me away all week, I struggle to contribute to the household chores, but I have recently agreed to do the ironing of my work shirts as Hayley hates ironing. For some reason, I enjoy it. I can cover off a dozen items without realising it as long as there's some sport on TV. We did have the luxury of a cleaner for a while, but with us trying to tighten our belts in preparation for the future, we long ago decided to save the money and do it ourselves.

'Thanks for the latte, babe.' Hayley sarcastically comments as she sees me already halfway through the one that she made me.

'Lovely, thanks. Darling, you know you make the best in town.' I replied.

Hayley rewinds the last 30 minutes of the movie (after the microwave, Sky Plus has to be the best-ever invention), so I can watch it and we both snuggle up again on the lovely sofa.

The only thing troubling me is the tiny infection that appeared yesterday on my middle finger. I seem to get simple paper cuts two or three times a year that blow up and easily get infected. I can't seem to escape the throbbing finger and I know the only solution is to let Hayley relieve the pressure by sticking a needle into the skin. As if she is reading my thoughts, 'David, when are you going to let me fix that finger for you?'

'When Hell freezes over.' I said.

'You coward.'

'You only want to see me in pain.'

'You baby.'

'I will do it myself later.'

'No, you won't, and it will keep you AND I up all night.'

'I was hoping you would do that.'

'Naughty. Not in front of the kids.'

'These children have seen more sex on TV or Facebook and are taught about it every day at school, so I'm not sure we need to worry.'

Sarah pipes up, 'Dad, you're disgusting.'

'Yeh, you're disgusting.' Scott copies Sarah's lead. Scott idolises Sarah and treats her like a big sister, so it's never a surprise when he follows or echoes whatever Sarah says.

Hayley tries again, 'Come on, darling, you know it's the only way to relieve the pressure and it won't get better unless you let me prick it.'

'Now it's your turn to be rude,' I reply.

'Daddddddd,' Sarah comments.

I know Hayley's right, but those needles hurt. It's especially worse when someone else is administering the pain.

As it's happened a few times before, Hayley springs into action as if preparing for a medium-sized operation. She dashes into the cupboard for a needle, then into the kitchen to cauterise it with a flame from the cooker. I, in turn, head for the operating room (upstairs toilet), away from the children so they cannot hear the screams and see my contorted face.

Hayley appears soon afterwards, seemingly all too eager to launch at me with what looked like a 10" needle and with a large smile on her face. She is clearly enjoying the prospect of causing me discomfort enormously. Clearly the needle isn't 10" long, but it might as well be as I know the pain I will shortly be enduring. Did someone once say "Love hurts"? Well, I am just about the find out. Truthfully, I know Hayley is only forcing me to do this for my own good. The finger has been a problem I've moaned about quite a few times that day and the only solution is this mini operation.

Hayley takes my hand and presses it down to ensure I don't move (or escape) and sticks the needle in my finger. Before the needle even pierces the skin, I swear out loud. 'That's £1 in the swear jar.' Hayley says.

'What? That's for the girls, not me.' I protest.

'You must lead from the front, darling,' she replied. Sarah recently left her Facebook account open and I couldn't help myself from taking a sneaky look, only to be horrified by the common use of foul language used by their friends and, on occasion, by Sarah. So, I lectured them all about swearing and how it would not be tolerated, and if anyone was caught swearing again, whether on Facebook or not, they would pay a £1 fine into a charity box. Up until that moment, the box had remained empty.

Within seconds of making a tiny insertion, the messy stuff is flowing out and the pressure on my finger is relieved and I start to breathe properly again. Hayley looks up at me, gently dries my eyes which had been watering profusely, and gives me a huge hug.

Operation over; the patient calmed down and happy.

It's Saturday afternoon and it's my favourite weekend because I have my children over. I have them every other weekend and when I do, with Scott at home as well, the place turns into a madhouse.

Shortly after moving into my current house, I had an extension put on the back to ensure I could have James over, and more recently, Hayley and I have attacked the long garden and made it look very presentable. Plus, Haley's overall 'female touch' has turned the house into a nice home.

The children's main home is a lovely 4-bedroom home, which was only built 6-7 years earlier and has a massive garden to house all the children's pets. I've never been big into pets and throughout the marriage, the children constantly begged me to let them have rabbits, then guinea pigs, and a dog, and eventually, I agreed to a single goldfish. It was therefore very predictable that the minute Linda and I went our separate ways and I left the family home, I was replaced by two dogs, a rabbit (who later died due to an incident with one of the dogs), several guinea pigs, and a cat.

It's now nearly 11 pm and the two youngest are in bed, and Sarah and Hayley are on their way. James and I are (as we always do) watching the big Saturday night football show. We spend all day trying not to learn of the scores, so we can watch the highlights on TV as if the teams were playing 'live'. James loves his football, and I'm sure would be into coaching if his disability wasn't so severe. The whole family supports the Blues (Chelsea) and James regularly keeps up to date with the entire goings on at the club throughout the week. Currently, much to our delight, Arsenal, our least favourite club, is 1-nil down, with only 10 minutes to go.

'So what do you recon Dad, 2-1 to Arsenal?' James sniggers.

They have an externally annoying habit of getting goals in the last few minutes to win the game.

'If not 3-1... buggers!' I reply.

Lo and behold, within 60 seconds, Arsenal has scored and it's 1-1, but much to our delight the other team hold out and it ends in a 1-1 draw.

'2 points dropped. Very nice,' James retorts.

'Yep, cracking result for us. That means we close the gap by two points after our smashing up of West Ham this afternoon.'

Whilst we try not to know about the other results, we always watch Chelsea live if they are on TV and they battered West Ham earlier in the day.

'Bed after the next match?' I ask James.

'Two more.' is his standard reply. This means I start putting him to bed around 11.15 pm. Pretty early for an 18-year-old, but it takes around 20 minutes to get him undressed and set up to sleep and this can easily drag on for 40 minutes because it's our time to chat, with everyone else in bed. His night carer, Maria, normally arrives about 11.30 pm and it's always good to catch up with her. Maria's been a carer for James for over 10 years and has proved to be a reliable friend. James tends to need turning in bed around 6-8 times a night, so luckily we get government funding to pay for a carer to be around all night, allowing the parents to sleep. After the next two games, James asked me to place his hand on his gear stick on his wheelchair to enable him to drive to his bedroom. As he passes the kitchen, I call out, 'Damn, I've forgotten your drugs. Hold up, son.' I pop into the kitchen and grab some medicine bottles from the cabinet and fill a few syringes. It's so casual of me to say, 'Fill a few syringes', but James takes his drugs in his stride, whereas most adults, including me, would moan continuously about having to take drugs three times a day.

James parks his wheelchair and briefly, after lifting him onto his bed I start doing some stretches. Within seconds of starting, the front doorbell goes and Maria arrives and I let her in and return to James. The chat continues about the football results and what the game is tomorrow.

I finish putting James to bed (one of my genuine pleasures in life as it's a very one-to-one contact) and put his breathing mask on. After a quick cuddle (for only my benefit I'm sure), I say goodnight.

Part of what humbles me is how James handles his condition. Apart from taking horrible-tasting drugs three times a day, his stretches, and general limitations, he never complains. As I've said to people before, I have always struggled with his condition, apparently, a lot more than James does. I know he gets frustrated with his disability, but his general mannerisms and personality have always been positive. He has good ideas about what he wants from the future and is turning into a very fine adult. He made me incredibly proud by achieving 2 A's levels last year and is now involved in intense computer and overall IT studies.

I hate myself for not being around that much due to my work, but I also suspect he doesn't need me as much as I want him to. Ironic I know, but that's life I guess. You bring your children up, and are desperate for them to flourish, develop their own relationships and activities, and when they do…they cut you loose.

Every other weekend I take on my second job (as all dads will know), as a taxi driver for the girls. This used to be a chore but now I enjoy it (don't tell them this), especially picking them up from a party and bringing them home safely. They are always excited about what's happened that night and it's always nice to have that time with them. Not that I'm always convinced that Sarah's telling me the truth, but as the actor Jack Nicholson once said, I probably couldn't handle the truth anyway. At 15 going on 18, she is, despite my best efforts, turning into a beautiful young lady. For some reason, she doesn't like it when I suggest she wears a long-sleeved top that covers her entire upper body and long baggy trousers. I just hope and pray she stays safe, as she journeys through the ups and downs of life.

Being away all week means the weekends and particularly the nights are special times for Hayley and I. Forgetting the rude stuff, sleeping in the same bed as Hayley is simply brilliant.

It's ironic that I sleep better when I'm alone in bed and Hayley sleeps better when we sleep together. Whether that's a Man thing or not I don't know as it's a great feeling going to sleep with someone you love, but staying asleep is difficult. Every time I feel I need to move, I worry about waking Hayley, so I tend to lie there in an uncomfortable position, not sleeping, rather than risk waking her up.

Sunday comes and goes and I drop the children back off at their mother's at the usual time of 7 pm and return home. Normally I would swap back to the company car (I use the converted family car on the weekends that I have the children, as it caters to James's wheelchair and four other passengers) and get on the motorway for the three-hour drive to Wales. Everyone thinks I'm mad doing the journey every week, but the three hours' peace and quiet in the car has normally followed a pretty hectic weekend, and if I'm honest, I enjoy the drive. Plus, with me renting a cottage only 10 minutes from my office, I'm doing less weekly mileage than I've done in my last two jobs. The only downside to being that close to work during the week is the tendency to work very late, knowing there's only a short journey home each evening.

Tonight's different, as I'm up early tomorrow to get a car to the airport, where I'm flying to New York for some customer visits. I attended a US trade show last season and developed some really good retail contacts that have agreed to follow-up meetings in New York. I have managed to secure four customer meetings and have two dinners set up with other contacts. I expect all the meetings to go well, as the Americans typically like the designs from Europe and see us as leading the way on decorations. I've stuffed two suitcases full of samples and know it's going to be a pain dragging them around from meeting to meeting in the heat of spring, but that's the only way to present how strong our designs are. Anyway, I've not been to NY for over 15 years, so for once I'm excited about the trip and can't wait to see what's changed, visit Central Park again, and try and catch an ice hockey match at the Garden (home to the New York ice hockey team).

New York's also beautiful in the spring time and I only wished Hayley was coming with me.

Chapter 2

Approximately 24 hours earlier, approx. 80 miles away from the south coast of England, a couple had just arrived by car a few miles from the ferry port of Dieppe in France.

Their arrival at Dieppe was the 2nd from the last leg of their 5-week journey that had taken them from a village in Pakistan, through Afghanistan, Kuwait, and Iraq, and then into Turkey. After a few days' rest, their journey continued across the Black Sea by boat into Romania and then on land through Hungary, Austria, and Switzerland. There, they crossed the relatively low-key border into France. About 2 miles from each border crossing, they met a new contact that would only be with them for that leg of the journey. Every different contact was from the country they were entering, therefore fully understanding the customs of that country, and of course the language. The only consistent thing with each contact was that they all spoke English.

It had been decided that the couple would not take any air transport or stay in any normal accommodation for fear of leaving a trail. Therefore, on the first 2 weeks of their journey, they spent all their nights in makeshift tents and thereafter they slept in the transport provided, car, boat, or lorry.

Having arrived near the Dieppe port at close to 11 pm on a Saturday evening, they only had 1 hour to wait until the late crossing over the English Channel into the southern Port of Newhaven, located about 4 hour's drive south of London. To ensure the couple never aroused anyone's suspicion, everything had been planned so they wouldn't stay too long in the same location. Most of the border crossings they came to had fairly small groups of migrants trying their luck to cross, with the occasional large group harassing the local authorities. However, the chances are, if the couple waited around too long at the places, the local authorities might start asking questions. Yes, they had all the proper identification documents, but on closer scrutiny, an alert border guard with the right training might notice their fake passports, as they were travelling under different names. This was always a risk as most EU countries have signed up to various minimum standards of documentation for travelling between neighbouring countries and were wise to how easy it was to buy forged documentation. That's why the couple also carried lots of both Euros and US dollars; to help deal with any 'local' issues of passage. All the US dollars had been used up on entering Turkey; where even the local contact they had met up with needed some extra assistance in getting them past the border guards.

Another vital part of the intense and very detailed planning of this trip was their food intake. Whether hungry or not, both couples and especially the woman, had to ensure they ate more food than normal to compensate for the possible weight loss through the exhaustive travelling. For reasons only known to the couple, they both had to appear very healthy. This wasn't always easy as they were not allowed to eat in public places such as cafes or restaurants, so most of their meals had been prepared by the different contacts they made at each drop-off/collection point. On some occasions, they had no idea what they were eating and most meals or snacks included some form of chocolate or items with high calorific content.

Until they arrived in Hungary, they had travelled in very casual clothes, with rucksacks, and looked like a couple of slightly older students on some sort of gap year travelling around Europe. There they were given a very small suitcase each and slightly more formal clothes to wear. Nothing too bright that would bring attention to themselves, but rather dowdy trousers, shirts & blouses that would mean they should travel largely unnoticed. It would be on this late-night ferry crossing that they would meet another contact who would give them their clothes for the last leg of their exhausting journey.

This particular contact was an Englishman whose name was John Smith. He had come prepared with not only a change of clothes, food, and English currency, but also sea sickness pills for the couple. These pills had been requested a few weeks before after their very difficult sailing across the black sea from Turkey into Romania. They could have entered Romania via Bulgaria, but the security at the Bulgaria border crossing had been recently beefed up after a group of migrants stormed the crossing and practically caused a riot. Armed police shot 3 people, including a 7-year-old girl who was travelling with her parents. Therefore, the route across the black sea was chosen. Because they couldn't travel on any of the ferry lines, they had to make the crossing aboard a small private fishing boat and the weather wasn't kind to them. At an average speed of only fourteen knots, the boat took nearly 22 hours to sail the 325 miles across the sea, and with the heavy swells constantly bouncing the passengers around, it wasn't long before any consumed food or drink had been discarded over the side by both the couple. As they knew the ferry across the southern part of England also had the potential to be another rough trip, their handlers had managed to get the message back to their leaders about the request. They needed to arrive in England fit and healthy.

Chapter 3

After seemingly zero sleep, (despite my finger not hurting anymore), I got picked up at 5.00 am on a Monday morning by a car and headed off to the airport. It's funny that no matter how tired you are, when you have to get up at 'silly o'clock', your body seems to keep waking you up every 30 minutes, and eventually, 10 minutes before the alarm goes off, you fall into a deep sleep.

As my flight is at 9.30 am and the airport is the whole way around the UK's busiest motorway, I have to allow plenty of time for the extremely heavy morning commuter traffic. The journey from Essex to Heathrow can be done in 60 minutes, but typically takes around two to three hours in the morning traffic. I have only ever missed one flight because of traffic and I certainly didn't want to miss this one.

The guy that drives me is an old friend of mine who unfortunately is out of work, so I pay his fuel and typically give him around £60 in cash for his time. Despite being very tired it's always good to catch up with him again and it makes the very tiresome journey go by quickly. The traffic is strangely low and we make the journey in just under 2 hours.

On arrival at Heathrow airport, I check in quickly and head for security. It always amazes me (and sometimes frustrates and makes me laugh), how unprepared people are for security. It's almost as if they have lived their lives in an underground cave and have never read a book, seen a film, or heard about the simple process of airport security. Despite there being several posters and signs up, they are still hopelessly unprepared for passing through security. Today, in three long queues to my right, there's a bit of commotion and a young guy in his late teens or early 20s is surrounded by three security guys. Probably forgot to take out his marijuana from his rucksack!

I go through the drill, taking out my iPad, removing my watch and belt, and after a small delay, because a couple with two children couldn't understand the instructions, I pass through and head for WHSmiths: the only place to get my extra toiletries, water, another book, and the paper. I love reading both on the plane and whilst I'm away. Hotels can be very boring and I'd seen a new thriller advertised and it was now safely tucked away in my bag. I have a relatively small reading range of books and they are all typically autobiographies by famous people. Politicians, sports people, and some biographies of some key people who have shaped history. We all can't help making judgements of famous people from watching them on TV, so it's nice to get the 'inside' track on who they are and what makes them tick. I tend to find a new level of respect for people having known what has shaped their lives and am constantly impressed by how much training or commitment famous people have shown to get where they are. I think somebody once said, 'If you want to know someone properly, try walking a mile in their shoes and you might understand them a little better'. Wise words indeed.

Out of WHSmiths, I head for the business lounge where I can enjoy a light breakfast with the worries of the motorway traffic a distant memory.

Chapter 4

At around 8.30 am, a couple in their 30s and a slightly younger man enter the airport from separate entrances. All three are of Middle Eastern appearance. The couple laugh and joke and appear very much in love, wearing casual Western clothes. Both are a little heavyset and the woman in particular has the appearance of someone who could be 5-6 months pregnant.

The single man, dressed in a pinstriped suit, appears very much the businessman. He has a small carry-on bag and a briefcase. His general body shape was a little heavy, made worse by the fact he had a heavy paunch that looked like a beer belly. Unbeknown to anyone giving this a 2nd thought, this man had never touched a drop of beer in his life.

Whilst the couple had appeared very calm and relaxed, the businessman looked nervous and despite the fact the day was young and the air temperature was only in the late teens, he was already sweating.

All three get into the check-in lines (the single man goes into his own queue approx. 50 feet away from the couple) and they check-in.

The destination on all their pre-booked tickets is New York.

Chapter 5

A little earlier, at 7.55 am, two best friends were going through a familiar ritual of trying to get to work on time.

'We're going to be late if you don't get a move on, Debs.' Laura shouted out as loud as she could without waking the whole hotel up. Both Debbie and Laura were extremely close friends and also had, a long time ago, chosen the same career as air stewardesses. As soon as they met nine years ago at the initial training program, they instantly took a liking to each other and, before long became inseparable. After training they were split up on different routes but tried their best to meet up on stop-overs or move their shifts around so they could catch up, but for the last five years, they have managed to work together for almost 80% of their flights.

Today they were flying the am to New York and were yet to leave their airport hotel to get to Heathrow for the 9.30 am flight. Company policy meant they should be passed security at least 60 minutes before departure time, to ensure they were around to help with pre-boarding. This means they have to get to Heathrow by 8 am to get through security and Laura was getting uptight about Debbie's all-too-casual attitude to company policy.

Laura's own private nickname for Debbie is ditzy, Laura herself simply hated being late for anything and as much as she loved Debbie, Laura often wondered how she passed the security and important health and safety exams they have to retake each year. They include a pretty heavy cross-examination and several role-play scenarios. The second part is a written test and whilst Laura spends some serious time preparing for them and normally achieves a pass mark of 95%, Debbie never swots up and only ever scrapes in just over the pass mark of 80%.

Whilst not jealous in the slightest, Laura is sure the examiners' marking on the first parts of the exams has something to do with the fact that Debbie is 5ft 11" and simply stunning, with long dark hair and a light brown skin tone. The only thing that's stopped Debbie from having a successful career in modelling is her complete lack of self-confidence. She appears to have no idea how beautiful she is. The powers that be have always known this, but have always supported both Laura's and Debbie's requests to work together, citing a good team is much better than strong individuals. Debbie's appearance and likeability also help on the job, as her casual approach and sometimes 'blonde' moments also mean she gets away with basic mistakes and she's popular with the regular passengers and crews. Laura and Debbie make a great team and now typically work in the business class or premium economy section of the plane. Other than in First Class (although some of the customers can be quite pretentious and arrogant in First), the business and premium economy are the sought-after areas to be responsible for, as the atmosphere is normally quite light-hearted and there is plenty of 'down time' for Debbie and Laura to catch up on things.

'Two more minutes. Have you seen my mustard-coloured hair-band?' Debbie calls back in a loud whisper. Laura, standing by the door in her coat, ready to go, simply stares at her best friend and smiles.

'Would that be the mustard-coloured hair-band on your head?'

Debbie races to the mirror and laughs out loud and Laura rushes to her to shut her up and they both hug and giggle. 'C'mon Laura, we don't want to be late now do we?' Debbie smiles at her friend.

Whilst Laura may not be jealous of her friend's looks, Debbie is jealous of Laura's relationship of four years. Not that she's attracted to Michael in any way, but Laura's relationship with Michael is brilliant. Being away from home on the long haul would put a strain on any relationship, but those two seem to blossom more every time they are together. Debbie has grown to love Michael like a brother and whilst Michael always appears quite flushed when Debbie greets him with a huge hug, Debbie is completely oblivious to his reaction.

Debbie's own previous boyfriend left her relationship confidence with men in tatters. She had hopped aboard an earlier flight home nearly two years ago, but instead of surprising her boyfriend with a bottle of champagne to celebrate their second anniversary, she had so nearly missed it, that she nearly killed him with it when she found him in bed with other women. It took Debbie several months to get over the unfaithfulness and betrayal and vowed never to trust another man again.

Both Laura and Michael helped her over the breakup by bringing her along to social gatherings and involving her in loads of things. Occasionally they would be called the Three Musketeers by other friends as they socialized so much together and Laura's best efforts to find her another boyfriend fell on deaf ears. Whilst there was always a long list of eager suitors, Debbie simply didn't want to risk having her heart broken and that was that.

The hotel bus eventually managed to fight its way through the airport traffic and they made it through security with 45 minutes to go before boarding. Laura was extremely relieved, as on previous occasions they had done it with only 15 minutes to board and it can take that long to reach some of the gates at the airport. Heathrow was already a huge airport, but now with the new British Airways terminal 5, it's absolutely massive. Practically every time they travel, Laura and Debbie find themselves tracking down some passengers for boarding who haven't allowed enough time to get to the gate.

Chapter 6

It's a nice perk to be a silver card member with British Airways. You get access to their lounges and are also allowed to go through their equivalent of 'speedy boarding' which means you can avoid the 50-meter-long queue to board the plane and you almost feel like you're an important passenger. I easily find my seat in premium economy and am pleased my secretary Margaret, has booked me an aisle seat. I rarely travel business class due to the cost. The standard flight cost to the US is about £500, with premium economy at £900, but business is around £2000, which is a massive jump. Plus, if I can't sleep anyway, it's a luxury the company cannot really afford and shouldn't be paying for. I have been 'upgraded' three times in the last couple of years, which is a lovely surprise, especially as once it was en route to China, which is an 11-hour flight! Long gone are the days when I worked for a US beer company where we used to fly first class everywhere.

The first time I ever travelled with the beer company, I enjoyed the flight. It was so cool being in the first-class lounge: someone took my luggage away... the real royal treatment. I think I even walked onto the plane three inches taller like I was some kind of royalty. What an idiot I must have looked.

Today, because the USA is five hours behind the UK and with a flight time of around 7.5 hours, it means arriving in New York around 12.30 pm-1 pm. Whilst I tend not to try and get proper sleep on a day flight, I will take one of my 'short naps' after a full lunch and a few glasses of gin and tonic.

The first thing I do on a long haul is put my sexy (Not!) leg stockings on to ensure I don't get deep vein thrombosis. Not that I have a history of the condition, but the amount of space they give 'wellbeing' in the inflight magazine and airline literature, it's scared me into buying a few pairs.

'Glass of champagne or orange juice, sir?'

I looked up and saw a thing of incredible beauty hovering over me with a tray of drinks that turned into an immediate blur as I stared into her brown eyes and froze like a 14-year-old schoolboy.

'Champagne or orange juice?' she repeated.

'Orange juice, please.' I gruffly replied as if my throat was parched after a 20-day trek in the desert without water. 'Yes, orange juice please.' I repeated.

She didn't even seem to notice my red face and offered me a glass, which I took and simply went on to the next passenger. I told myself off for being a complete idiot and hoped I would never have to face her again, knowing only too well she would be popping up every 30 minutes or so with more offers of drinks and nibbles. I immediately wondered why she had chosen a career as a stewardess. Not that there's anything wrong with the job, but surely she had offers of modelling or some other glamorous line of work. Only more recently in my business life, I have come to understand that there are several possibilities as to why people make certain career choices and my thoughts came back to Hayley. Not only was she a terrific person, she was also very attractive; whom I had often thought could have done some modelling herself if it wasn't for her own lowish confidence levels.

As I have grown older and wiser, I have definitely understood that confidence plays a huge part in people's lives and what they can achieve. I know there is a class divide in most communities and countries around the globe, but even a person from a low-income, tough background can achieve great things if they have confidence. Maybe the fact the beautiful air stewardess didn't hold eye contact with me for long was a sign of her lack of confidence around men or probably more likely that she felt repulsed by the vision of a red-faced man in his late 40s, with white stockings up to his knees and who sounded as if he had been a chain smoker for 40 years.

I re-settled myself and browsed through the inflight magazine and importantly the entertainment pages to see what new films I could see to help me through the 7-8 hours. Boredom is not the real problem for me on longer flights. It's the air turbulence that makes me feel sick with fear and always leaves me promising myself I will never fly again. I cannot, no matter what any pilot says (and a few have tried), fully understand how a huge chunk of metal manages to not flip over when the air turbulence strikes. There is simply no logic to it and despite my thousands of air miles around the world, I am always gripped with fear when I hear the captain's voice over the intercom: 'We are experiencing some strong winds, so please ensure your seat belts are on and the cabin staff will not be servings refreshments for a while.' Worse still when he instructs the cabin staff to get strapped into their own seats! That's when I sit there and try desperately to focus on a book or magazine or anything that fights my imagination and tells me we are all doomed.

Sitting one row up and to the left in the aisle seat was a suited businessman. Despite having sat down and buckled up, he still wore his suit jacket, which at the time must have puzzled the passenger to his left as the air temperature on the plane was relatively warm, but as the businessman appeared a little shaky, his fellow passenger probably put it down to a few nerves about flying, plus maybe these Middle Eastern chaps are simply a little uptight.

During take-off, I also noticed the businessman still had his suit on, but it was more a subconscious observation, rather than a conscious one, as he was trying to stay focused on his magazine. Maybe he was also a little apprehensive about taking off?

On boarding and once I had found my seat, my standard practice was to 'take in' the surroundings and fellow passengers. After all, it's going to be a long flight and there's no harm in smiling and saying 'hi' to those immediately around me. If the ice is broken, then those awkward 'personal' moments are easier to deal with. Like complete strangers trying to climb over you to get to the toilet, or my own regular stretching and walking up the aisles, popping into the galley for some refreshments. Plane journeys can be like train journeys, people just sit there, trying to avoid the eyes of those around them and not uttering a word to each other. In fact, train situations are much worse as you have to sit opposite each other.

My fellow passenger immediately to the right in the window seat (in premium economy, there are four seats in the centre row and two seats on either side), was a rather posh-looking woman, in her late 20s, whose initial response from my warm smile was a rather weak nod of the head as if she was acknowledging a servant in her stately home. I immediately thought how funny it would be if I pretended to be asleep for the whole flight, as I doubt very much she would chance 'climbing' over another human being. Although, posh people probably don't use the airline toilets anyway!

Chapter 7

Further back down the plane in economy seats 22 A and B were Mr and Mrs. Anderson (Larry and Betty), en route to Rhode Island in New York to visit their son (Robert) and his wife (Carol), who have recently had their first daughter.

The Andersons have been on a worldwide cruise celebrating their 35th wedding anniversary. They left their hometown port of Portland, which is in the State of Maine, aboard a luxury cruise ship three weeks ago and had been on a two-day excursion in the United Kingdom when they got the call from Robert telling them their granddaughter had come into the world earlier than planned. Apparently, Carol's waters broke yesterday and after a reasonably short labour of eight hours, baby Grace was born weighing a fragile, but healthy 5lb and 10 ounces. Cutting their cruise short, they immediately booked a flight from London and left the very next day. The baby wasn't due for another few weeks, but Robert assured them the birth had gone very well and both Carol and their lovely granddaughter were absolutely fine.

As a nervous flyer, Betty had not flown that much throughout her life and her last flight (a short-haul trip within the USA), was over 10 years ago. Larry, on the other hand, was chalking up close to 1500 flights (although his first for over 6 years), as he is a retired commercial pilot, who also flew for six months in the armed forces at the end of the Vietnam War. Part of Betty's fear of flying has been passed on from Larry, who retired due to ill health (stress), as well as his stories about the many near misses he had either personally experienced or heard of during his career. Larry hadn't been inside a cockpit for over 15 years and had no plans on ever entering one again. Another key problem that he started to have in the latter years of his career was claustrophobia, therefore a cockpit was the last place he ever wanted to see the inside of. Whilst this was a 777; the general set up of the cockpit and its size were pretty similar to the A300's Larry had flown towards the end of his career. At times, he even struggled to be in his wife's small car, so they changed it to an estate. However, they rarely travel anywhere nowadays due to living in a lovely retirement community where the neighbours have become part of a new family and they simply don't need to drive anywhere anymore.

Betty has been a midwife most of her working life and now gets the short bus journey three times a week to the local hospital, where she volunteers in the afternoons as a support assistant to help give the new midwives the skills and confidence to deliver their first few babies. When their son Robert first called them about Carol being pregnant, Betty was thrilled to bits and counted the days down on her calendar in the kitchen with incredible excitement.

Betty now sat there quietly in Seat 22B and focused all her attention on the first pictures of the new baby her son had sent them over the internet last evening. She allowed herself to daydream back to the day Robert was born and felt tears rolling down her cheeks as she recalled the absolute and total joy of bringing him safety into the world. Due to an abscess Betty had on her womb, coupled with some life-threatening surgery that followed the birth, Robert would be her and Larry's only offspring. That's why Larry and her were both delighted when their son and Carol finally announced their engagement (after being together for nearly 12 years), but at the same time were deeply saddened when they said they would be moving to Rhode Island for her job. In Betty's day, women followed their men around the globe (as she had done with Larry due to his job because he had to relocate on several occasions), but nowadays it seems that women can be as successful as men and sometimes that means that their careers would be more important than their husbands. Even though Portland to Rhode Island is hardly the biggest journey in the world, Betty initially rejected and even challenged her son on their decision to move, but soon realised it was a lost cause, not in small part because Robert doted on Carol and she was an amazing daughter-in-law. Being an only child meant getting all his parents' attention, but Robert was also his own man and felt confident his own career wouldn't suffer as his bank repaid his 15 years of loyalty by relocating him to another branch not far from their new home.

Larry spent most of his time attending to their large garden and patio area, both of which he was extremely proud of. Even where there appeared very little upkeep to do, he would be found in his garden or summer house. Betty was convinced he decorated that summer house at least twice a year, just so he could stay outside in the open space. Having said that, the whole garden looked lovely, and twice in the last three years, Larry had won local gardening prizes for his hard work.

Both Larry and Betty gripped each other's hands as Flight BA57 left the runway, soaring like a bird and once it steadied itself, did a casual 18-degree left-hand turn, and then headed for New York, USA.

Chapter 8

Most of the passengers got settled quite quickly in the routine of a long-haul flight and either started reading their newly purchased books or magazines, picked a movie from the onboard flight entertainment, or simply stuck their earphones in and closed their eyes. One couple that caught a few other passengers' interest was the 'obviously' loved-up, Middle Eastern-looking couple in the front section of business class. Because the seats are individual in business, to touch someone else or be affectionate you typically have to stretch over the divider that separates the seats. This is impossible to do discreetly and this couple were acting like newlyweds, which puzzled some older passengers who either felt it was simply inappropriate or considered it unusual for people of Middle Eastern culture to do so. On top of that, the female appeared to be pregnant and some of the more eagle-eyed passengers noticed the woman wasn't wearing any kind of ring on her left hand. Everyone else, including the air stewardesses and senior cabin manager, was instantly disarmed by the obvious affection the two had for each other and, if anything, took joy from seeing people in love.

Which is exactly what Ahmad Suqami and Malika Al-Umari wanted.

Flying under the false names of Sadeem Mostafa and Dannia Yasin and acting like a pair of teenagers in love was exactly the plan; the intention was to make everyone on board feel comfortable and relaxed about the couple. Relaxed enough to allow them to roam freely about the plane, which included the first-class area…which is just behind the cockpit.

Both Ahmad and Malika had spent weeks training for this special day back in Pakistan and had finally gotten used to calling each other by their assumed names. But it wasn't always that way and several times during the training Ahmad had called Malika her real name, much to the frustration of the senior handler that was looking after them.

What made it worse for Ahmad was that during the intensive training, he had fallen in love with Malika. Most nights he went to bed and she was the last person he thought about before sleep and the first name on his mind when he woke up. Malika, on the other hand, was a true professional. Her acting was first class and when in training she handled herself extremely well. On-demand, she managed to act like the besotted girlfriend. Yet as soon as training had finished for the day, she retired to her tent for supper and appeared to spend the rest of her time in prayer. Ahmad on the other hand spent most of his time daydreaming about Malika. Whilst everything about Ahmad was average, his body type, his looks, and his slightly rounded shoulders where he had rarely stood up straight…there was nothing average about Malika. On top of her general confident persona, she had a slim face that highlighted her high cheekbones, very dark green eyes and with long flowing black hair it was obvious that most men would find her attractive. Her striking looks were not lost on the trainers and she was ordered to wear her hair up in a scarf, with absolutely no make-up. This was how she would travel on her mission, to appear very 'normal' and to not bring herself to anyone's attention.

On top of the head scarf, during training, Malika was forced to wear heavy clothes and had an additional set of clothes stuffed under her outfit to give the appearance of being six months pregnant. Temperatures were nearly always in their 90s and she consumed large amounts of water each day, just to keep herself in peak condition.

Ahmad, on the other hand, seemed to wilt under the midday sun and sweated profusely even at night. Growing up, he knew he perspired more than most of his friends, but now that he had the enormous pressure of the training and ultimate mission to execute, things seemed to have gotten worse. No wonder Malika stayed away from him in the evenings as, by the time the training had finished for the day, his clothes were normally dripping in sweat and he looked like he had just taken a shower. Whilst he knew he would never gain her true affection, just being in the presence of Malika and having her pretend to be in love with him in training was like a dream come true. He pretended to himself each night that after a hard day's work, she just needed time on her own. This was better than facing up to the reality that she was completely out of his league.

The Pakistan training camp was based in a village about 6 miles from South Waziristan.

The village had around twenty buildings and one large courtyard in its centre. The day-to-day routine for all trainees started with prayers before sunrise, some breakfast, and then some general cleaning of the whole facility. Then most were given driving lessons and some spent time learning basic English. As it was the start of spring, they could take a short nap after lunch before assembling for afternoon prayers. More training took place in the afternoons, then prayer and evening dinner. Unless there were instructional videos to watch, after night prayers they would go to sleep, as no activity is allowed after final prayers. In addition to the payers' sessions, whether it felt obvious or not to the trainees, every day on at least 4 occasions, the instructors made motivational speeches, quoted the Quran, or chose to pull an individual to one side to encourage them on their journey. This specific camp was for ages +16 only and whilst it was rare, on the odd occasion a trainee would try to flee on his or her own, or their parents would turn up and try to take them home, so it was important that the trainees remained positive and focussed at all times.

The main indoor training facility was an old schoolhouse and the accommodation area was a few houses that had been offered up by the locals. Whilst there were around 30 other people going through various training activities, Malika and Ahmad only worked together.

In one of the rooms in the schoolhouse, there were several rows of chairs, like what you might see on a large coach…or a passenger aircraft. Whenever it was practical, the training took place in this room, so that they both became familiar with these types of surroundings. As the sleeping quarters were based in houses, they had all the usual amenities required to live for a reasonably long period, and on one wall of both Malika and Ahmad's bedrooms were large paintings of flowing rivers surrounded by lush green valleys, depicting paradise. Twice a week there would be a group dinner by the fireside and the instructors would tell stories of past sacrifices (suicide bombers) that had been made by their brothers and sisters and the fact that these people were now in paradise.

Almost 31 years earlier, Ahmad was born just outside the city of Kandahar in Afghanistan, approx. 70 miles from the Pakistan border and was brought up in a relatively modern environment by his loving parents. He loved playing football and at an early age showed signs of promise until a double leg fracture caused by a car crash left him with a limp and ultimately put paid to any dreams he had of a future in the sport. The car crash and subsequent physical impairment also knocked his confidence with people, especially the opposite sex and it wasn't an obvious change in his personality anyone in his family would have noticed. Over time he became more withdrawn and tended to keep himself to himself and spent most of his spare time alone.

Who would want to go out with a cripple? Would any of the local girls be happy being associated with someone who now dragged his left leg a little? Ahmad thought not and tended to avoid being in the presence of the opposite sex on his own. Members of the opposite sex were currently 'officially' allowed to spend time together under strict guidelines, but the laws in Afghanistan were complex. Women officially gained equality under the 1964 constitution. However, these rights were taken away in the 1990s through different temporary rulers such as the Taliban during the civil war. Especially during the latter's rule, women had very little to no freedom, specifically in terms of civil liberties. But ever since the Taliban regime was removed in late 2001, women's rights have gradually improved under the Islamic Republic of Afghanistan and women are once again de jure equal to men under the 2004 constitution. Because of the larger family structures in Afghanistan, the Elders of the families' own views also held some weight on what was or wasn't appropriate.

Because of his lack of confidence and being an introvert, Ahmad threw himself more into his studies as an escape. He also spent a lot of time learning about farming the local land with his older relatives.

The one important distraction he had in life was his favourite football team, the British side Manchester United. His loyalty to United started when his father gave him a secondhand, baggy United football shirt on his tenth birthday, explaining that they were the best club side in the world. His mother always had trouble prizing the shirt off young Ahmad's back to wash it, as for the first two years he seemed to eat, drink, and sleep in it. A lot of his simple childhood was spent daydreaming about things he couldn't have, things he had seen on the television of a neighbour his family always had dinner with on Wednesday nights. Very occasionally he would be allowed to stay up a little past his normal bedtime and watch football. It didn't matter who was playing; as long as they were kicking a ball about, Ahmad still got the treat of his life. He even saw his favourite team on TV once and being able to match some names to the faces of his favourite players only deepened his love for United.

Whilst still living at home and working for a local farmer, Ahmad's life was changed dramatically on his 28th birthday. On a hot sunny day, his family party was in full swing and the local elders in the community were present, as was every living family member he had. Several large tables were set up and filled with several traditional Afghan dishes and over 60 people were entertained by a small group of elderly musicians who played Indian tablas, which are drums made of wood and leather, and long-necked lutes, which are guitar-like instruments.

Just after 2 pm and with no warning, there was a large explosion and a bright light appeared that seemed to cover the whole world. Unbeknown to Ahmad or his family, one of the local elders was a wanted terrorist on the USA's target list and an American MQ-1B predator drone had been circling the region for the past 15 hours as part of an ongoing exercise to track his movements. Originally designed as an aircraft for intelligence-gathering, surveillance, and general reconnaissance, this make of drones were subsequently fitted with deadly missiles and 2 minutes before 2 pm, the US drone had launched a Hellfire missile from around 4 miles away on a search and kill mission. Whilst the drones themselves were always launched locally (this time from a secret location 10 miles north of Kandahar), the drone operators themselves were based back in what effectively was a mobile home inside Creech Air Force Base in Nevada, USA.

Now, increasingly popular, the USA used its 1st armed drone in October 2001, a month after the Twin Tower atrocities. In this 1st attack in 2001, they missed their target, instead hitting a vehicle and killing several of the target's bodyguards. Since then, their accuracy has improved and despite opposition within NATO, they were seen as a useful tool in the war against terror.

By the time they had fired the missile on Ahmad's 28th Birthday, their accuracy had improved to within 20 feet and whilst there was always a level of 'collateral damage' (innocence killed alongside the target), this was seen as 'acceptable' by the US Pentagon chiefs.

Immediately after the bright light had subsided, the screaming started, and the full terror and destruction of the attack became clear. Fallen family members and body parts appeared everywhere. Ahmad himself had been thrown backwards towards a well that had a huge covering to protect users from the sun, which ultimately had given him good protection from the flying debris.

Ahmad managed to gather himself and instinctively looked around for his parents and sister Sebeen.

Sebeen had luckily been in the house collecting more drinks when the drone explosion happened, and the house was remarkably left unscathed from the blast. Only the wooden shutters had been blown away and whilst the side of the house was black from the heat of the blast and debris, the building was intact. Ahmad saw her immediately and felt a huge wave of relief fall over him. His relief quickly turned to horror when he saw his mother's dress among the rubble. With the area around her still smouldering, Ahmad worked his way quickly through the bodies and debris, but as he took each step towards his mother's broken body, his own hope for her survival was draining away from his soul. An arm appeared to be covering her head, but Ahmad recognized his father's jacket sleeve immediately. The very jacket Ahmad had bought for him four months earlier as a present on his father's own 60th birthday. He tore away at the rubble to uncover both his mother and father. His father's back was covered in blood where in the milli-second there must have been before the explosion happened, it appeared he had tried to shield his wife from the blast. Both his parents had their eyes and mouths open as if staring in disbelief as someone does when shocked at a surprise birthday or having heard a loud noise. Ahmad knew both his parents were dead and amongst the screams heard his sister Sebeen screaming as she tried to get close to him. Wanting to shield her from the terror and sight of their deceased parents, he quickly closed their eyes, turned, and scrambled towards Sebeen. He tightly grabbed her and dragged her away, back towards the house, tears streaming down his eyes. His own heart seemingly ripped from his chest. Overwhelming grief quickly surrounded every aspect of his being and he turned his head away from Sebeen so she couldn't see him being sick. People had heard of these attacks by drones and one had even struck and killed several people attending a funeral some 60 kilometres away in another village. That's how he knew the instant the strike happened that it wasn't a gas explosion or an accident. He left Sebeen in the house having firmly told her to stay there, whilst he turned his attention to helping other injured people.

After the funerals of the 11 people who were killed that day, including both his parents, Ahmad's grief started to turn into anger. An anger that grew and grew over the next few months and one he wouldn't lose until he himself departed the earth… or he found a way of avenging his parents. A number of local people were badly affected by the bomb and it wasn't long before people appeared out of nowhere with talks of vengeance and specifically, calling for action. Whilst not initially obvious, these people were recruiters for the Taliban. The attack by the drone on Ahmad's family was a perfect place for them to encourage and develop anti-western doctrine and to look for potential soldiers or even suicide bombers. Ahmad never realized that these people had nothing to do with his local community, but they were talking a lot of sense and seemed to know how to energize those people affected by the terrible destruction and death that happened on his birthday. Before long, with the anger still burning inside his body, Ahmad was turning from a peaceful, family-loving son, into a radicalized Muslim, hell-bent on making someone pay for the deaths of his parents. Within 3 months of the funeral, he started to go to meetings at a mosque near the centre of Kandahar and whilst he and his sister had moved into an uncle's house to live, after a few more weeks, he took up the offer of accommodation from one of the recruiters. He had lost most of his close family members in the blast and was now completely isolated to anyone except his new teachers. Because of his quietish personality, he wasn't initially seen as an obvious candidate to be anything more than just a blunt instrument…someone who could wear a suicide vest, get close to a target and even if he didn't have the courage to blow himself up, another person, within 50 feet, could set the vest of remotely. However, his own anger had developed into a form of strong motivation that his handlers managed to channel into something they felt they could use elsewhere.

The tough part of training in Pakistan was the technical side, which included explosives as well as the handling of a gun. The actual shooting was relatively easy, but it was the gun creation and loading that was a challenge for Ahmad. The gun was made of three types of material and came in loose pieces. All the materials of the gun were designed to pass through the airport security. As individual pieces, they looked like simple parts of a hairbrush, possibly a bracelet or child's toy. Largely made of very strong plastic, only the chamber, the hammer that is needed to strike the firing pin, and the bullets were metal. Any gunpowder was easily concealed in hand luggage on most planes, especially for someone travelling first or business class.

Almost every day both Ahmad and Malika spent at least one hour setting the gun up and dismantling it. Putting all the component parts together in a short space of time was a key part of their future activities. Malika picked the skill up very quickly and was soon able to create a gun from seemingly innocent objects in her handbag from scratch to completion in under just 60 seconds. Ahmad's best time was still nearly twice that long. In his own tent, without anybody else watching, he could achieve success in around 75 seconds, but as soon as he had to complete the task in front of other people, especially the love of his life Malika, he struggled.

This, as well as Ahmad's slow up-take on several parts of the training, was a concern for his handlers and for Malika. Whilst no one doubted his commitment to Allah and to the revenge of his parents, it worried them enormously. On several occasions the senior handler and Malika spoke about Ahmad and whether he was the right partner for her. The saving grace was that Ahmed wasn't expected to use a weapon on the project, but he may need to set one up in case of an emergency. Towards the last few weeks of training the handler (who knew Ahmad was crazy about his phony girlfriend) suggested Malika get closer to Ahmad and pretend to genuinely like him to hopefully settle his nerves and assist the overall operation. As a true professional and completely focused on the mission Malika agreed and became more affectionate to Ahmad, including after the training sessions were completed for the day. Ahmad felt he had already arrived in paradise and amazingly the plan worked and his own performance in training and confidence in himself increased. Not that Malika would go any further than a kiss and a holding of the hands… this they had to do anyway on the mission to be a credible couple. But she lingered a little longer on each kiss and always made sure she kissed him after training when she left him to go to her tent for the night.

Whilst in typical Middle Eastern relationships the man is the dominant partner, in this relationship Malika was definitely the 'alpha male', but knowing all along that she would have to allow herself to become more subservient for the outside world to truly believe in the couple.

Chapter 9

Malika's own childhood had been very traditional and extremely privileged as she grew up in a large house in the city of Sana'a in Yemen. Yemen is, without doubt, one of the poorest and least developed countries in the Middle East, with depleting oil reserves and a recent history of internal conflict. Although the production of liquid natural gas started in late 2009, rampant corruption still holds the development of the country back. Religion in Yemen consists primarily of two principal Islamic religious groups: approximately 60% of the Muslim population is Sunni and 40% is Shia.

Over 2.2 million people squeezed into the capital, Sana'a, which was once a relatively prosperous mining city with rich surroundings. It now has clear class divides with over 25% of the population unemployed.

Her father's successful printing business had been handed down by his own father and continued to prosper as he adapted his machinery and installed up-to-date, computer-based printing. As a result of the new technology, costs were driven down and with a stable selling price, this meant the company's profits followed a steady upwards trajectory. The family was huge and Malika had six brothers and sisters, and four cousins… all living under the same roof. The house was well equipped to hold the numbers, as it had eight bedrooms and three bathrooms and had benefitted from two extensions to cope with the ever-increasing family numbers.

Traditional values were the cornerstone of the family, and the father ensured these were followed with strong leadership and regular family prayer time, which was a key part of the discipline of his Muslim faith. Whilst Arabic is the official language, in highly populated areas foreign languages are taught in most schools from grade seven upwards, and those from privileged backgrounds, who have private education or attend college tend to learn English as a second language. Malika was no different and, as a growing teenager, became fluent.

Whilst Malika loved her family deeply, she was a bored teenager and tended to rebel against the restrictions her father placed on the females of the family. Men were allowed to go out and have social lives, but the women were not. After her time at school, Malika went to college and despite his traditional values, Malika's father allowed her to go to a mixed college. This was largely influenced by the fact that it was barely 2 miles away from the family home, which meant he would be able to ensure that either he or another family member would be able to take her to and from the facility practically every day. Unfortunately for him, and because of Malika's growing independence, the college guaranteed lots of excuses to 'study late' and even the occasional overnight break on study-related trips. Malika sailed through her exams and thoroughly enjoyed playing a full and active part in the college's activities, from the theatre through to the student union. Whilst her father wanted her to work in the family business, Malika had other ideas and at 22 became an assistant political and math teacher in another college. Quite unusual at the time, as fewer than 6% of all teaching roles were held by women. Despite new gender-equal laws being announced every few years, the reality on the ground was that Yemen was a male-dominated country and during this time ranked last in the World Economic Forum's 2014 Gender Gap Report, out of 142 countries. Most of the classes Malika was involved in teaching were only 50% to 60% full of students, as a lot of parents refused to have their children taught by a woman.

Before her 24th birthday, she was promoted to a full-time teacher's role covering both subjects. As she grew older her own views became more radical and without realizing it, by her 28th birthday she was attending evening classes that were supposed to be about advanced political doctrine, but were in fact recruitment sessions for Islamic fundamentalists.

It may sound silly and almost impossible for Westerners to believe that clever, well-educated people from affluent backgrounds could actually be 'conned' or 'brainwashed' in some synagogue or mosque some two thousand miles away. But the reality is that Malika herself was strong-willed and had definite views about the troubles in the region and who was and wasn't to blame. Once she had an idea in her head, she fixated on it and it almost became an obsession. Sometimes the strongest amongst us can be the most stubborn… or end up the greatest, most passionate believers. It was during one of the evening classes that she met the man who would become firstly her friend, then over time, her handler in a mission that would change her life dramatically.

One particular class was about martyrdom and whether any human being would have had the courage to follow through with their beliefs with the ultimate sacrifice. Whilst most people in the class were hesitant and uncomfortable about sharing their own views on the matter, Malika was forthright, stating that she would 'absolutely die' to stick up for her rights and what she believed in. This approach and her general attitude made her a perfect recruitment target for an extremist group that had infiltrated the sessions over two years earlier. Most of those they recruited were weak people who were dissatisfied with their lone and insignificant existence, and who were relatively easy to influence. Becoming a member of a religious group that had a general vision gave people self-worth and made them feel 'special'. Malika would be different, but as a strong and fairly outspoken recruit, it wasn't long before she found herself being mentored by her new friend (handler) in 1-on-1 sessions.

At 29 she was fully indoctrinated into the group calling itself the Sons and Daughters of Allah, which had close links to another terrorist group, which in turn reported into a section of Al-Qaeda. Over the last two years of her life, she had become more and more entrenched in the group and more distanced from her family. However, when she told her family she was soon going on a field trip to better understand the Pakistani political environment, which would help her become a better authority on politics overall, they became concerned and her father forbade her to go. Malika, on the other hand, was already an extremely confident woman now and simply said the trip was part of her destiny to travel. The word 'destiny' puzzled her father, but he felt helpless and watched her leave, worrying about her safety and how she would cope in a man's world.

Chapter 10

ON flight BA57, back in business class, four rows further forward from the Middle Eastern couple, in seat 1B, was Brad Miller. Brad had been an air marshal for nearly two years since leaving the police force, and the UK to New York flight was one of his regular journeys. He also worked on the UK to Denver and Chicago routes. Brad was a good-looking 51-year-old who took care of himself and could easily pass for being in his mid-40s.

Whilst he carried a firearm and had done most of his working life, he had not once had the cause to draw it on a fellow human being. His life as a policeman started at 22 in a fairly small town called Basking Ridge, about 50-minutes drive from New York, and he had slowly worked his way up to sergeant by the time he was 35. There wasn't much action in the quiet town, and most of the activity surrounded traffic violations, where his calming and soft voice was his normal weapon of choice.

Brad had three daughters with his late wife Sandra; two who still lived locally in Basking Ridge, whilst the other had moved to Chicago about three years earlier. Whilst today's trip was to New York, the Chicago route had since become his favourite to work, as he always took a few days off to stay with his daughter and her husband.

His wife Sandra had been in remission from breast cancer for nearly four years when, just over three years ago, it came back. It was much more aggressive the second time around and quickly spread throughout her body, and sadly, she passed two days before their 27th wedding anniversary. Brad was completely devastated and fell quickly into depression. They had been a happy couple with three lovely daughters who were no trouble, and the whole family spent loads of time together. Both Brad and Sandra regularly ran half marathons together and most weekends were taken up with some type of outdoor or sporting activity.

Brad simply couldn't imagine a life that had any meaning whatsoever without his beautiful Sandra. He couldn't escape the pain. Even trying to go through her clothes to give to the charity shop was excruciating. Even his own jogging clothes caused a painful stab in his side as they used to run together. There were pictures on the walls of every room in the house of some part of their lives together.

Everywhere he looked he saw reminders of the wonderful life they shared. Of course, the whole family was affected, and in particular, his eldest daughter struggled to live around all the memories from her childhood, which eventually prompted her to move away to Chicago for a different job. From being an extremely solid family, they were now being broken up before Brad's very eyes. He knew his eldest needed to get away from the pain of the family house. It held so many memories and she had found it as overwhelming as Brad did.

Brad's own work deteriorated and that's when a close friend on the force suggested he try out for an air marshal's role. Initially he point blank refused to consider another role, but softened after a few heart-to-hearts with his girls; they all felt it would be good for him. Within six months, after some pretty intensive training courses and lots of coursework, he became an air marshal. As part of the training he was forced back into the gym and had managed to lose most of the weight he'd put on since he lost Sandra. He hadn't been jogging since Sandra died, but at least he was keeping fit using the running machines in the gym.

He also remained a member of the local police force's gym, which ensured he kept in touch with his old buddies on the force.

Today, on flight BA57 out of the UK, Brad was relaxed and in a good mood. With a brief stopover in New York, he was flying to Chicago to spend a whole week with his daughter Amy and her husband Tony before getting back to work via a trip back to the UK.

A large part of Brad's training involved negotiation or persuasiveness techniques. No one ever wanted to get into a gunfight on a plane full of passengers, so the best thing to do was to try and calm any aggressors down. Plus, it's practically impossible for anyone to bring a gun on a plane nowadays anyway, so whilst he carried a firearm as standard working practice, he knew he would never need to use it. In fact, Brad was quite anti-guns anyway and certainly didn't feel one would be any use 35,000 feet up. However, an ongoing requirement in his role was to go to the range on a regular basis to fire off a minimum of 20 rounds with his 38. Every 2 weeks, he visited the range, which was conveniently located next door to the Police gym. If he happened to be out of the country, he could simply visit a local gun club, show his credentials, and he could use their facilities. Firing the gun wasn't something Brad looked forward to and on his most recent range shoot, he was especially rushed because he was out of town and had a flight to catch. Brad was a stickler for not being late in his role, and on this occasion, this meant he hadn't remembered to fill up the full quota of chambers in the gun with bullets. Most 38 revolvers can hold between 5 and 8 bullets, Brads held 6. After shooting each set of 6 consecutively, you are supposed to refill the gun to its max and then keep repeating until your session has ended. Because Brad only ever shot the minimum required 20 rounds, on this occasion, he left the range in a rush without refilling all the chambers.

Some training that he did very much enjoy was that which covered personal behaviours and body language, which he had a natural ability for anyway, developed through a long service in the police force. You get to know people and can judge their next steps by watching their body language or by looking at their facial expressions, and Brad has been quite successful at that throughout his career.

Part of his job once on board, without anyone being aware, was to casually assess his fellow passengers. It wasn't appropriate to stare or make any type of contact with anyone, but a very casual look around whilst he was getting stuff out of the overhead compartment or stretching his legs would normally suffice. The last thing the airlines wanted was for there to be any obvious police presence on board their planes. Initially, on this particular flight, a few passengers had brought themselves to his attention, including the Middle Eastern couple that was seated fairly close by him, but as most terrorists try to avoid any attention whatsoever, this couple were clearly normal folks as their obvious affection for each overdrew loads of attention to themselves like a bee to honey. Air marshals also receive a passenger manifest before every flight, giving them a full list of all the passengers and crew. On this flight, there were 301 passengers and 15 crew members. In total, the plane could carry 335 passengers, but there were a few spaces in economy, business and first class. Economy plus, or premium economy as it is sometimes called, was full.

Of the 301 passengers on board, there were 176 British passport holders, 54 American, 19 Chinese, 18 Indian, 18 from various African counties, 8 from Middle Eastern countries, 4 Swiss, 3 Italian and 1 German. An important thing Brad had observed, as he reviewed the list in the business lounge before the flight, was that of the eight people from the Middle East, six were from counties that were flagged. In other words, they were countries that had known terrorist groups and were countries that had 'delicate' relationships with the West. However, both his training and the huge amounts of historical data the security services provide air marshals were both a warning and a polite reminder that whilst anyone can be a threat, anyone can also be a law-abiding citizen.

Brad also knew that you would also turn into a complete *crazy* if you chose to assume everyone was a suspicious person.

Something that had bugged Brad a tiny bit (although he couldn't understand why) was the fact that the first-class cabin was nearly empty. When he saw the passenger list before boarding, it was fairly full, but on his walk around ('to stretch his legs') 20 minutes after take-off, he noticed that more than half of the first-class passengers were no-shows! That was pretty unusual, although a few people not turning up for their flight can happen occasionally. Companies that have a team of executives travelling have cancelled trips before, and if they had paid a full fair, they can get up to a 90% refund or a credit on any future flights.

He then understood why they were a little light on crew numbers: the airline must have decided to reduce the numbers at the last minute because of the no-shows. Whilst they still 'bump' (upgrade) people up a class on certain flights, they had clearly chosen not to on this one.

Maybe they were struggling to get a full complement of staff on the flight anyway. Brad made a mental note to ask the co-pilot or pilot (the only two people who knew he was listed as the air marshal on board) if he saw either one and ask them to do a simple check on the first-class no-shows to see if there was a simple explanation.

Regrettably for Brad and the other passengers, Brad saw neither person until about four hours into the flight, and by that time, he had simply forgotten about asking.

Chapter 11

After an hour into the flight, I had started my first in-flight movie. Whilst initially excited about watching 'The Wolf of Wall Street', I was disappointed that the movie was over three hours long. Normally, about 1-2 hours into this type of flight, lunch would be served, and then I would be ready for a nap…all of which would be when I was about halfway through the film.

The main character in the film was played by Leonardo DiCaprio, who plays a rogue New York trader who encourages people to invest in low-priced stocks that have the potential to be huge… only for most people to end up losing their money. Whilst not obviously illegal (people still had the choice whether to invest their money or not), it's still very suspect, as is the way he moves money around to avoid paying taxes.

If you don't get to the cinema that often, a few long-haul flights are an excellent way to catch up on some movies you haven't previously seen. Plus, going to the movies at home normally means someone must compromise a little. You might want to see a thriller whilst your partner is a chick-flick. Worse still if you have three children to satisfy who all want to see different things. So, sitting on a plane with your own personal movie guide and TV is pretty neat and a fairly good way to relax. Anyway, I can't exactly go anywhere 35,000 feet up and air travel is not new to me, as one of the big drawbacks of my job is that it requires a lot of travelling abroad. At least twice a year, I head off to China on product-sourcing trips, and I also look after the Canadian market for my company, which means a minimum of three trips every year to Toronto (one of my favourite places in the world).

I shouldn't really complain about the trips (especially Toronto) as most people would give their right arm to travel to the places I've visited. But when it's on business time, and I'm largely on my own, it gets pretty boring. I have managed some downtime in Toronto, watching the odd baseball or ice hockey game, and even got an afternoon's fishing in on Lake Ontario last summer, what an amazing lake!

Fishing and golf are my two hobbies, but I tend to think and talk about them a lot more than I do, on that special day last summer. I was in Toronto seeing some customers, and the night before the last day of the trip, the customer asked me to pull the meeting forward to 9.30 am instead of 2 pm. As my flight wasn't due to leave until 8 pm, it meant a window had opened up for some leisure time. On all my Canadian trips, I would be accompanied by my agent, Simon, and he quickly called a friend who had a fishing boat. Much to our delight, his buddy was considering taking a day off, and we met at the dock at about 11 am the next day (I think it was one of the quickest customer meetings ever). There were five of us, and we raced out about 5 miles on Lake Ontario and started salmon fishing. Whilst we only caught a couple of smallish fish each, it ranks as one of my top 10 days of fishing ever. The weather was great, the beer ice cold and Simon and his buddies were great fun, and just before the day ended the skipper cut the engine and dived overboard for a swim. After a little encouragement from the guys, I was soon stripped down to my boxers and diving into the very cold but clean, fresh waters of the lake.

Great memories.

The trips I really hate are the China ones. I suffer horrendous jet lag on my trips out and never have a moment to adjust before I walk around some Christmas trade fair or visit factories. Yes, it's great to visit new places, and there's nothing wrong in spending a day in Hong Kong, but as soon as you cross the border into China, its work all the way. The temperature always seems to be in the 80s or 90s, so it's very hot and sticky. Whilst I love the hot weather if I'm on holiday, I would rather it be cold when I'm at work.

Having said this, amazingly, on my fourth trip, the company's China board meeting was cancelled at very short notice, and whilst most of the team managed to get an earlier flight home, I couldn't. They were all flying back to another airport in the southwest of England, and I was heading back to London. This meant I had a free day in Hong Kong, and someone told me to check out the beaches. Beaches in Hong Kong? I had no idea any existed but I took a cab early the next day and managed to spend six hours on one of the island's four beaches. Yes, it's difficult to convince anyone that I'm not away from home on *business trips* enjoying myself, so I have stopped trying.

Chapter 12

After an uneventful couple of hours of flying time, the air stewardesses were preparing for lunch and had started serving the pre-lunch drinks. For some reason, I cannot fathom, I watched to see what the businessman in the row ahead was drinking. Would it be a glass of sparkling water, or would he go straight for the Scotch (whether his religious views allowed it or not !)? Strangely enough, considering all the warnings about getting dehydrated on a plane, he simply shook his head at the stewardess and declined any offers of refreshments. She seemed to offer him just about every available drink she had, but he just politely waved his hand up and shook his head.

I can't say exactly why that bothered me, but it did. Maybe it's my ridiculously vivid imagination, or simply because I've read so many books that involved some kind of bad guy, I don't know.

But whatever it was, one of my eyes was going to be on this guy for the rest of the flight. In the day and age of terrorist plots and post 9/11, I think we have all become aware of the need to 'be involved' in security', even if it's simply calling the police because you see a suspicious package at the railway station. Having said that, how many of us would make the call? We hear stories of people being sued for invasion of privacy or harassed by the police to attend court. Plus, personally engaging with 'wrongdoers' leaves us all open to so many risks, including personal injury, and we have all heard the stories of innocent people being killed when they've intervened in a situation.

Anyway, the most I was probably going to do today was to pour a bottle of Evian over this guy to ensure he doesn't suffer from dehydration.

On a long plane journey, you have so much time to kill wondering what fellow passengers are all about is a good way to pass the time. The rather posh lady sitting next to me was almost squeezing herself inwards rather than touching me in any way, which greatly amused me, as well as meant I had both the armrests to myself. I almost felt like deliberately brushing her arm a couple of times to see if she winced. Maybe I hadn't allowed enough deodorant this morning, or my regular toothpaste had failed me. Whatever it was, she definitely suited the first-class cabin, but it also made me wonder what her 'story' was.

We all have a 'story', and it's unique to us. Our upbringing, our job and family; all these things, as well as the outside world, influence who we are and how we behave. My own upbringing was, by today's standards, very normal. Although I am not sure I know exactly what the 'standards' are today.

For most of my childhood, I had stood in the shadow of my brother Martin, who was 2.5 years older than me. Whilst I was reasonably tall (I shot up to 6 feet rather quickly as a teenager), Martin was 6 ft 5" and twice as broad. Before my teenage years, I was described as a polite, quiet and thoughtful child… which simply translates to shy.

Martin was the opposite and got into his fair share of fights at school. I remember my first day at high school (two months after my 11th birthday); Martin walked me around the school, telling all the other tough-looking kids that I was the strongest in that school year. Luckily for me, they seemed to buy it, and I stayed out of trouble.

I was sportier and played practically all the different types of sports the schools had, and Martin was the cooler, more popular guy who never had any problems getting girlfriends. I, on the other hand, was genuinely frightened to sit next to a potential girlfriend, and my conversation would dry up immediately after the initial 'hello'.

That's until I discovered cider at 15 (but that's another story), but even then, I would go from being sober and speechless to a rambling drunk in less than an hour. Because of sports (particularly football and rugby) and with Martin pushing me to follow in his footsteps, by the time he left school, I had toughened up a bit and (much to his delight) had even been involved in a few small scuffles. They weren't much more than a lot of pushing and the odd punch thrown, but as I always came out of top, it seemed to enhance the reputation Martin had tried to create for me.

He was the stereotypical 'older brother', and whilst on the surface people can think we are very different, as we have matured and closed in on our fifties, we are a lot more alike and would spend half our time together if we could. Martin started working life as a chef and eventually settled working in the building trade as a plasterer. Plastering is a very tough trade, and I have the utmost respect for anyone who chooses it as a career. On the other hand, when I was 21 years old, I didn't last more than two hours as a labourer on a building site (dismissed on my first day), as my hands became sore and my back started playing up.

A bizarre twist of fate meant that, despite my generally shy nature, my first job at 16 was in a furniture shop, dealing face-to-face with the public.

I remember my first-day nerves in that job fortunately, there were very few customers to deal with, and of course, I couldn't sit there drinking cider all day!

Over the next 2-3 years, my confidence grew almost in line with the job responsibilities and at 19 years old, I became a salesperson on the road, selling paint and wallpaper to other shop owners/managers. In this job, I started off accompanying a sales trainer doing customer visits and, on the second week, we came across a store manager who had a very frightening persona. Knowing I had to visit her on my own after training had finished left me with a knotted stomach for the next few weeks.

The following month, on my second day seeing customers on my own, I re-visited her store and sat in the car park for over an hour, trying to pluck the courage up to enter the store. Amazingly on entering, she greeted me with a huge smile and told me to get on with counting the stock. The visit went extremely well and she signed my order off and said she would see me two weeks later. I can honestly say she is one of the women in my life I have thought more about than most. For the whole 10 days before that visit, she was on my mind constantly and I had that feeling of dread leading all the way up to the visit. However, she neither punched me, shouted at me, nor even tried to kill me in any way. She simply smiled, and I soon realized that she hadn't given me a second thought from the previous meeting, and in fact, she was no different to me. We both had a job to do and had more important things in our lives than a *can of paint* to worry about. An important lesson was learned that day. We are all equal, and whilst we have different jobs and come from different backgrounds, no one is better than any other.

It is ironic that sales appeared to be my chosen career, and I seemed to get better results than most… considering my lack of confidence. From about 21 years of age, I realized that my earlier shyness was just part of who I was and, importantly, that it was a load of rubbish. I didn't even understand what I was actually afraid of. There's a saying in sales: 'No one ever killed a salesperson for asking for an order', and that is so true. So, from 21, I just decided to go for things a little more and not worry about the consequences. This approach, even though it wasn't quite who I was, appeared to pay dividends at work. People took it for granted that I was confident and, coupled with my higher energy levels than most, combined to bring ongoing success in whatever role I had.

With a few slices of luck thrown in, I managed to climb the ladder at work and became a Sales Director at 30 and a Board Director at 37.

Whilst I have never been financially well off, I've travelled the world with my various jobs and my career has allowed me to provide for my children and now start my new life with Hayley with some level of security. Yes, I've made some sacrifices to get where I am, but we all have to make choices along the way, and we just hope we can look back and say we have got more right than wrong. My current job does keep me away from home a lot and Hayley and I have agreed that, from next year, I will start looking for a job closer to home. It will be tough to find a similar job, but the experience gained running this company will ensure a few doors are opened, and with any luck, I can find another company with offices nearer London.

Chapter 13

The plane sailed through the air at just over 35,000 feet, and outside was glorious sunshine above the beautiful white, puffy clouds. At about 80% (six hours) of the way through the flight, the whole aircraft seemed at peace. The passengers and crew were at ease, and everyone was either focused on a movie or some form of in-flight entertainment or simply had their eyes closed, dreaming about their return home or what excitement their trip to New York would bring.

The Middle Eastern couple in business class had calmed from their earlier activities and whilst the male appeared to be fast asleep, the female had moved around the plane on several occasions. Walking and stretching at the same time, she largely went unnoticed and hadn't aroused anyone's suspicion. Most passengers simply assumed that as a pregnant woman, she needed to stretch her legs and would, of course, need to use the restroom more than most, which she had.

It was on one of her toilet visits that Malika pulled up her dress and produced a package the size of a small cushion. Picking through the seams (a metal zip would have been picked up through airport security), she opened the package to reveal the component parts of two handguns. Also closely wrapped together was a small string of dynamite sticks. There were four sticks in all and enough string to tie the explosives around her body, which she would later reveal to the other passengers and crew to scare them into submission. They were not real explosives, as Malika and her handler knew; those would have been either detected by security or, indeed, picked up by one of the many sniffer dogs located at Heathrow airport. In a way, Malika would have preferred to transfer from this life into the next by way of a simple and quick explosion of dynamite but had previously come to terms with the fact it would be better if the western world suffered from a larger impact crash into a highly populated area, rather than just destroying the plane in the air.

Malika put the guns together using her unusually shaped bracelets that had been checked by hand at security but not through the scanners.

Inside the bracelets were the barrels of two small guns. To the naked eye, the bracelets looked both metal and ceramic, but once taken apart, most of the components then snapped together to form a barrel that had metal inside, which was vital if they were actually needed for use.

As a woman, she could easily be expected to take a small bag into the washroom, and whilst her bag was slightly larger than the normal *wash bag*, on the assumption of being pregnant, she assumed that most people wouldn't give it another thought. Inside her bag were the handles of the guns. They were cleverly disguised as perfume and *feminine stuff*, and both were identical oblong shapes. They easily clicked together with the barrels, and within 20 seconds, Malika had two guns that, because they have been painted black already, looked like imposing weapons. However, wooden guns, even with a metal barrel, are nothing without some form of additional metal added, as wood will not hold the pressures of a fired cartridge. These key metal components had been cleverly disguised to look like innocent items that anyone travelling may use. The hammer was amazingly attached to her head with two firing pins that looked like a nice, shiny hair clip.

The guns' sears (part of the trigger mechanism that holds the hammer back under the tension of a spring) were part of Ahmad's belt buckle and the triggers were installed inside his larger-than-life headphones that have recently become fashionable. These two components were the handler's biggest challenge, and the idea of the headphones was something he was particularly pleased about; up until he had seen a friend's younger son in the city wearing them, he had been completely lost for a solution. Ahmad had passed these crucial items to Malika during one of their earlier embraces in their seats. Additionally, the springs of the guns were just loosely placed inside Malika's handbag with all her other trinkets and, to the untrained eye, merged into the mess at the bottom of the bag.

Within two minutes, she had created two deadly weapons and chose to carefully hide one inside the trash area of the restroom.

Her latest trip to the toilet had been carefully planned to the exact minute. It was important that her new partner retrieved the gun immediately and equally as important that this all took place exactly six hours into the flight. The planning had to be exact, as the last thing she wanted was to make the guns and do the handover too close to the landing when the captain might decide to turn on the seatbelt sign and announce the restrooms were out of use. Worse still, there was some unexpected turbulence, and this could all happen at any time during the fight and would scupper their plans completely.

On this planned toilet visit, her new partner was now waiting outside the toilet door, dressed in his pinstriped suit. His name was Dalair Alghamdi.

The name Dalair was chosen by his father because he was born prematurely at 3lbs and 3 ounces, and the doctors at the hospital were concerned whether he would survive more than a few hours.

His father felt different, and as each crucial second passed, he saw his fourth-born son fight for his life and grow stronger. Much to the surprise of the doctors, he left the hospital a steady 5lb in weight nearly three weeks later. In Arabic, Dalair means brave or valiant. However, as he grew up, he remained very thin and, as a teenager, weighed only 6 stone. As a result, Dalair became an easy target for the school bullies who made his life hell.

As a quiet and unhappy loner, Dalair followed in his father's footsteps and became a regular visitor to the local mosque in their small town of Faisalabad, about an hour away from the city of Lahore. On occasion, they visit the famous Badshahi Mosque in Lahore, which is the second-largest mosque in Pakistan and South Asia and the fifth-largest mosque in the world.

Dalair didn't attend the mosque because of a deep belief in God, but as a way out from the bullying and at least at the mosque, he felt a sense of belonging. There, he was part of something where people treated him with respect. He had confessed to his father about the bullying, and despite visiting the school several times, his father's intervention only appeared to make matters worse. The bullies were disciplined by the school, but it only seemed to make them more aggressive, and he dreaded attending school. The key members of the group that bullied him came from wealthy families who didn't seem to respect the Muslim faith and, in fact, appeared more like westerners with every new term.

At the mosque, Dalair became entrenched with a particular group of other teenagers and for the first time in his life, he felt happy. Unfortunately for Dalair, he had unwittingly joined a group that was being groomed by a small cell that formed part of a terrorist group who were looking for more martyrs. Dalair wasn't sure when he made the leap from someone who simply didn't care much for the western world and, in particular, the United States of America to someone who felt a strong longing to fight the people who wanted to control the world.

His first assignment, however, wasn't to blow himself up, killing all those around him. As he became a trusted and respected member of the group, his tasks were to assist in transferring packages and information around the area from Mosque to Mosque.

By the time he was in his mid-20s and working as a taxi driver (a job that allowed him to travel around without suspicion), he had managed to become a key member of the cell. At first, he hadn't any idea what he was passing on or what was contained in the packages, but for a while now, the senior member of the cell had been informing him that his work was indeed the work of Allah and that he was playing an important role in defending the nation against the infidels. After several years of *'doing his part for Allah'*, Dalair started to become frustrated and convinced that he was not doing enough. His life had become mundane and almost meaningless. Nearing his 29th birthday, he asked his superior, Fahdr Mohammed, if he could do more.

'I need to play a bigger role in honouring Allah. I cannot see the rest of my life, the next 50 years, driving a taxi and running errands for you. How is that honouring Allah? How is that making sacrifices? You can get a boy to do these things.' He blurted out impatiently

Fahdr smiled. 'My brother Dalair, you are indeed playing a very significant role in helping us fight the American beast. We achieve our objectives in many different ways. Having a trusted member of the group is a powerful weapon. We cannot simply trust anyone. You have become a smart man, a clever man, someone others can look up to.'

'But how can I be smart if all I do is drive a car around the city? I have no wife; I have no children to go home to. All I have is you and the group... and Allah. Surely my life must have more meaning,' Ahmad responded, frustrated.

Fahdr considered Ahmad and remained quiet. After 30 seconds, he moved close to his brother and slowly reached out to give him a hug and then whispered in his ear.

'Brother, if what you say is true, you may be ready to make the ultimate contribution to Allah.'

4 weeks later, in early spring, Dalmair arrived at England's Heathrow airport on a direct flight from Pakistan. As he wasn't known to any of the security forces in any country, he sailed through customs and took a train into London. The freedom of being able to purchase a train ticket without identification allowed him to first travel to the midlands city of Birmingham before returning the same day and taking an overnight sleeper train the Scotland's city of Glasgow. These journeys had been pre-planned in case there he had appeared in any photographs or local suspects list back in his home town. Since 9/11, it has been accepted amongst most Muslim leaders that anyone attending a mosque runs the risk of having their picture taken and appearing on such a list.

On arrival in Glasgow, Dalmair was met by a member of a small cell of *Brothers* and spent the next 7 weeks in a tiny flat on the outskirts of the city. For the first few weeks, nothing much happened except prayer and several long, meaningful discussions about the Koran, and he felt he was going through the same routine as before back home. On the fourth week another man arrived at the flat and pulled Dalmair aside for a personal chat.

'My name is Fareed. I have important news for you about your journey with Allah. Are you ready to serve Allah?

'Yes, I am my brother.' replied Dalmair.

'Good. This is very good. Over the next 2-3 weeks, I will visit you every other day to explain the task you have ahead of you. You cannot talk of the task to any of your other brothers in this flat. A great day is coming, my brother.' Fareed said. This last part of the message was a vital way to find out if Dalmair can be truly trusted. Over the forthcoming weeks, the other men living in the flat constantly asked Dalmair to divulge the subject matter he and Fareed were discussing, but not once did Dalmair break Fareed's trust.

Chapter 14

Malika, still inside the toilet, was busy stuffing hand towels and tissue into the cushion to ensure it was the same size as before, which allowed her to return it under her dress to maintain the image of a pregnant woman. It wasn't the easiest thing to create exactly the same look as before, as she now had the length of string that held the four sticks of fake dynamite around her waist. After a few adjustments, she felt confident enough that her disguise was acceptable and quickly washed her face and then opened the toilet door.

Both Malika and Dalmair had previously been given photos of each other and each other's seat numbers on the plane. On one of Malika's many *walks* down the aisles to stretch herself, she had placed her hand on Dalmair's left shoulder to help her balance as she pretended to stumble a little. He placed his own hand over hers as a pre-planned acknowledgement of each other.

Dalmair was standing very close to the door as another passenger was now waiting behind him. The other passenger, initially quite impatient at the length of time Malika had been in the toilet, soon realised her predicament when Malika came out of the toilet.

'Won't be long before the hot flushes start, my dear.' She said.

Malika, quick on her feet, responded. 'My problem and I'm embarrassed to say, is having to use the facilities too much, almost every hour on the hour. I am so sorry for taking so much time.'

Smiling at Malika, the woman responded. 'Don't worry dear, I've had three of my own, and it gets easier. This your first?'

Malika, wanting to end the conversation as quickly as possible but also not wishing to draw unnecessary attention to herself by being rude, responded. 'Yes, thank you for your understanding. It makes me feel so tired as well; you must excuse me, but I think I need another rest.' She then smiled at the lady and returned to her seat.

No amount of training had prepared her for how she was feeling: nervous, scared, and excited. Did Dalmair remember his part of the plan? Did he remember where the gun was supposed to be and how he was meant to get it back to his seat unnoticed? Had the lady she just spoke to become suspicious? Was she an air marshal? Had other passengers become concerned about her moving around the plane? Was her face too thin to justify her being 5-6 months pregnant?

On returning to her seat, she carefully sat down (the other gun was now strapped to her right leg with a piece of sticky tape) and started to take deeper breaths to help her calm down. She moved her focus onto her mission and her commitment to Allah, and then her thoughts turned to her family.

How on the one hand, she wanted to be close to them and hug them all, especially her six brothers. On the other, she wondered whether they would be proud of her for her actions. She cared that they would be, but she also knew that most of the family was ignorant to the goings on of the real world and were stuck in their 'local' community of friends and family. She had made a short video that they would receive a few weeks after the mission, not begging for forgiveness, but asking - almost demanding - that they understand how important it was that everyone takes a stand against the people of the western world, that they too had a responsibility to speak out against the attacks from America and its allies, against the Arabic world.

She knew it would fall on deaf ears and that, initially, it would bring shame to the family. She hoped her father would forgive her for the impact on his business, but she also knew it was a small sacrifice versus the huge impact she would have this great day.

The people of the western world needed to be shocked into taking action against their own governments to encourage them to stop interfering in the Arab world's issues and way of life. Simple rhetoric and these so-called 'government get-togethers' for peace talks were a sham. It was all about the government of America trying to pursue its own objectives and largely about ensuring it had access to the rich oil reserves held across the Middle East.

By her actions today, she would become a hero, a person of true status and would, of course, please Allah.

Chapter 15

After my second power nap, and I was considering whether to start a new movie. I checked my watch, and it told me I had just less than two hours to arrival time: just enough time to get another movie in.

Having said that, the rather long 'Wolf of Wall Street' had reduced my appetite for another film, and I sat there contemplating reading a few chapters of my newly purchased book.

As I pondered this most important of decisions, the guy in the pinstriped suit was returning to his seat. 'Fair play to him', I thought, 'using the toilets in business class'. They always added a small pot of flowers up there, and sometimes the premium economy ones can get overused by people from the economy. Funny, really, we are all trying to trade up our experience, even when it comes to the toilets on a plane.

One thing still puzzled me about this guy: he still had his suit jacket on. Worse still, he was obviously hot because he had visible beads of sweat running down his face, and whilst he used a tissue or some form of hand cloth to wipe his face, it didn't seem to have any impact. He also appeared to struggle to sit down, as if he had a problem with his leg.

Chapter 16

Dalmair was struggling big time. He felt unwell, extremely hot and was struggling to walk with the handgun stuck down his trousers. Up until five months earlier, he hadn't even seen a gun, let alone used one, and whilst the training he had in Pakistan was useful, he hoped desperately that he wouldn't need to use it. The fake sticks of dynamite he had strapped around his stomach had now started to dig into him, and all in all, he had now started to wish he was somewhere else. Driving his taxi around his home town suddenly felt an extremely attractive alternative to his current predicament. He was extremely thirsty, but had long ago decided not to drink fluids on the plane in case it made him use the toilet too much. He didn't want to keep getting up and possibly bringing attention to himself, which ironically is exactly what he was doing by not drinking.

He tried to relax in his seat, then closed his eyes and prayed to Allah to give him strength to be quiet and still so as not to attract any attention. He also prayed for courage and wisdom to carry out his important task. He recalled the conversations back in Jordan with his superior and friend Fahdr Mohammed. He really did want to be an important person, be someone that actually made a difference in the world, someone his friends in Jordan and strangers from around the world would be talking about over their evening meals that night.

Chapter 17

I couldn't recall seeing this guy take a single drink, and now he looked like he was about to collapse. Everyone else appeared to be ignoring him and minding their own business… or, like me, they've noticed but simply didn't want to get involved. I got my head down and tried to focus on my book.

All of a sudden, a good Samaritan in the seat in front of me leaned across from him and touched him on the shoulder.

'Are you okay, mate?'

He reacted as if he was about to jump through the ceiling of the cabin, but fortunately, his seatbelt kept him strapped to his seat.

'I'm okay. I'm fine. I'm very okay, thank you.'

'Do you want me to buzz the attendant to get you a drink?'

'Thank you very much, no thank you,' he replied again and turned his head away, quickly picking up a magazine from the back of the chair in front to read.

I thought, 'Fair enough'; at least the guy in front had asked the question, which was a lot more than I did. I grabbed my book even tighter and started to read the comments on the back cover, giving the author amazing reviews and telling me how once I started, I *'won't be able to put the book down'*.

Unfortunately, this particular author never really stood a chance, not after my rather uncomfortable observation. Adding my earlier thoughts together with the latest incident had put me on edge. I'm not even sure why I decided to upgrade the refusal of help from one passenger to another into an *incident* … but I had.

I know I was being completely ridiculous, and I had very few… well, actually zero reason to give him more thinking time, but I did.

Why would anyone on a long-haul flight not take his jacket off? Why would the same person appear to dismiss the persistent advances of a beautiful air stewardess and her attempts to get him to take some fluids during their flight?

Why would he appear to be very nervous and uncomfortable? Even worse, on his first trip out of his seat, he appeared to have a hip or leg problem.

However, I never saw him leave his seat to go to the toilet in the first place, so he probably always had that limp. Worse still, maybe he got the limp helping an old lady across the road, and he got hit by a car.

I was now convinced I might need a drink to stop me from adding 2 and 2 up and getting 15!

Get a grip, David; get a grip!

Chapter 18

At about the same time, the air stewardesses Laura and Debbie were taking time out in the galley before the inevitable clearing up and preparation for landing that would start in just under an hour.

'Did you see the skinny guy with the pot belly using the business-class loos?' asked Debbie.

'Yes, I did. Do you know he hasn't had a drink on the entire flight, or any food for that matter? Have you seen him eating his own food?' Laura replied.

'Nope, not a sausage, but that was the first time I've seen him get up to use the toilets. Clearly, he hasn't bothered to read all our company's excellent advice about dehydration and stretching yourself during the flight,' Debbie said, smiling.

'Not that many do, although those two guys in Row 12 in business have certainly taken the advice about drinking very seriously. They've nearly drunk us out of Jameson's.' Laura said.

Debbie laughed, but Laura, who had observed that 1 of these men had tried to make some advances to Debbie, looked solemnly at Debbie and asked, 'Did the guy with the red hair cause you any problems when you were serving lunch?'

'Nothing I can't handle… anyway, stop being so polite; it's not red hair, it's ginger,' Debbie replied.

Now, it was Laura's time to laugh, and Debbie put her hand over Laura's mouth to muffle her laughter.

'Anyway, I'm sure the guy in seat 1B is an air marshal, as I've seen him on loads on flights to New York. Either that, or he's a dedicated *air miles collector*, hoping to become a platinum member. He'll protect me if the ginger ninja starts getting too playful.'

'I had no idea you had become so racist in your old age,' Laura responded. 'Or is it something to do with the fact that *red* was also the colour of your ex-boyfriend's hair?'

'Ouch, caught *RED* handed.'

'Aren't you the funny one today?' Laura whispered.

'So, on a more *important* and much better subject matter, where are we going tonight?' Debbie asked her friend, emphasising the word *important* to make the point that she would rather talk about anything else in the world other than the man who had ruined her life.

Laura replied with a smile, 'Anywhere you want to, my dear. In fact, I happen to know there's a lovely show on at Radio City tonight. It's an American version of our very own 'We Will Rock You.'

'The Queen tribute show?' Debbie asked.

'The very one, and we both know how much you loved Freddy Mercury, even though you were only just born when he was singing at his best.'

'Brilliant. Great shout, partner. Don't suppose you have actually made a booking?'

With a huge beaming smile, Laura produced two tickets from her blouse pocket and waved them in front of Debbie. 'You bet I have.'

Debbie threw out her arms and said slowly: 'You are amazing,' and gave Laura a loving hug. They both sat back down and hurriedly checked out the seating plan on the back of the tickets.

The general banter continued, and they discussed what they were going to wear at the concert as they both enjoyed a slice of cake and a cup of English tea.

Chapter 19

The attack on flight BA57 had been sanctioned over 12 months before, and the people involved at the top were very keen to emulate the success of 9/11.

The total funding allocated to the attack was $275,000, and as the sum was so large, the people accountable also wanted some extra insurance on the plane itself. There was no harm in having a sleeper on board to assist the group if things went wrong or, if required, to take their own action to bring the plane down.

Edward Beech was a 22-year-old political student from Birmingham, England. Whilst he went by the name Edward for obvious reasons, on his recent trip to Pakistan he had recently changed his name to Mohammed Al-Badawai.

Neither of the other three terrorists on board, Malika, Ahmad, nor Dalmair, were aware of Edward's existence. The handlers wanted zero connection between him and the others. That way, if things did go wrong, he could still play a key part in the task without the authorities even considering they had a fourth terrorist on board.

He was seated towards the back of the plane in economy seat number 11B. At 5 feet 8, with mousy brown hair, he looked like a typical British backpacker. Untidy, with baggy clothes, messy hair and at least 3-4 days of facial hair growth, all adding to his persona. However, anyone paying closer attention would have noticed how nervous Edward was. From the moment he arrived at the airport, right up until this moment, he hadn't been able to relax at all. Initially it was because of his very near-miss whilst going through security at Heathrow Airport. His oversized belt buckle had caused quite a stir. To avoid any unnecessary attention, he had taken it off whilst in the queue and laid it on top of his scruffy rucksack (standard luggage for an aspiring student traveller), but as the rucksack also had an unusual metal plated buckle as part of its own design, both items together set the alarm off when they went inside the tunnel on the conveyor belt. Normally, the security guy who looks at the television that scans the cases would make a judgment call to ask a colleague to check a passenger's bag, but in this case, the sizes of both metal objects tripped the physical alarm. Edward didn't help himself much as his face was red and sweaty, and he looked guilty about something. He had been assured by his handler in Scotland that even if Edward was stopped at the airport, he would only have been charged with trying to bring an offensive weapon through security, which at the very worst would get him a fine and maybe a few nights in the cells.

After his belt and rucksack had gone through the system three times, he was then pulled to one side and asked to go through its contents. What was in his favour was his dirty clothes and unshaven look. Again, this type of preparation had been part of his detailed instructions. He had been told not to wash himself or his clothes for the previous 10 days and whilst there are never any guarantees when you go through security, this type of tactic would most certainly assist in his cover.

One of the security guards whispered to another, 'Bet he's got half an ounce hidden up his backside. Idiot should know we don't care about people taking drugs *outside* the UK.'

After several long minutes of searching Edward's rucksack as if he was an international drug mule, they found nothing and let him go.

Two minutes later, Edward was holed up in a toilet, throwing up what was left of the previous night's pizza and chips.

Now, just over five hours into the flight, Edward was 50% drunk (his handler had told him to accept western alcohol to help him remain credible). But this was his first taste of alcohol for over a year, and in hindsight, this was a big mistake. His body had lost all its tolerance for alcohol, and he wasn't feeling that great.

Whilst Edward had gone through his instructions a thousand times in his head, he was now trying to relax and go unnoticed. His plan already included a few trips to the toilet to create his weapon and some prayer time, but due to the alcohol intake, he had already visited it 7 times and had received a few stares from the other passengers around him.

On one of his recent trips, he took his rucksack with him and once inside the toilet, he dismantled the unusually shaped buckle from it. As he knew it would take a few minutes to undo the stitching, as he walked to the toilet, to avoid any suspicion he held his toothbrush and paste in full view so the other passengers would understand he might take longer than usual. Once the stitching had been undone, he slipped the buckle inside his trousers and returned to his seat. As every visit passed, he felt more nervous than before and was convinced the whole plane knew he was a terrorist.

On his last trip to the toilet, he took the buckle he had taken from the rucksack, turned it over and pulled it apart (a similar action to opening a penknife). On one side, the edge was very smooth, but on the other side, it had a serrated edge, about 3" in length. He then slipped the metal casing off his own belt buckle and clicked into place the two pieces. Within 15 seconds, he now had a weirdly shaped but dangerous weapon. Whilst it was never going to help him cut through a solid object, its serrated edge was very visible and, at the very least, would frighten any passengers into following instructions. The main part of his training for the mission was hand-to-hand combat. Edward wasn't a very big man, but he was very nimble, and even that didn't matter too much as his handlers had told him to target young children. There's nothing quite like seeing a man holding a knife to an innocent child's throat to get someone to follow whatever your orders are.

Edward was born in England and had a very normal upbringing. His father was an electrician, and his mother stayed at home and looked after the children. She had previously worked part-time in a doctor's surgery, but since the twins came along, she had stayed at home. Edward was the oldest of three and there was a 12-year gap between him and his two sisters, now aged 10. He knew his parents had tried to have more children a long time before, but it wasn't until they started a course of IVF treatment that his mother became pregnant and, much to everyone's amazement, the twins appeared. Over the last 3-4 years Edward had drifted away from both his parents and no longer spoke to his father at all. There was no *big* family argument or any particular incident, but they just had nothing in common, and Edward felt contempt for his father's lack of interest in anything other than his own career or football. He thought his father was a man of *little imagination* and of *no ambition.*

After school, Edward went to college and studied hard, which actually made him stand out a little bit from the other students because most appeared to have gone to college to improve their social skills and increase the number of friends they could collect on Facebook. The only real friend he had made was a girl about 3 years his senior, called Haifa Sahrian, who was returning to college after a couple of years travelling. Also very bright and seemingly only interested in her studies, Haifa and Edward kept on bumping into each other before and after their lessons in the library of the college and eventually started talking. Despite coming from completely different backgrounds, they got on very well. Haifa was a Muslim, and whilst she appeared to follow her faith pretty much to the book, apparently, her family were quite wealthy and had insisted she spend some time travelling to learn about other cultures, as this would help her grow as an individual. Within a few months, to impress her, Edward even joined the same music group as Haifa so he could spend more time in her company. He quickly became the brunt of the jokes from the rest of the group because not only was he tone deaf, Edward couldn't play a single instrument. After a few weeks, he was discreetly given a role more of an organiser, away from anything remotely musical. Edward (and the whole group) were delighted with his new role.

After knowing each other for over 14 months and now into their final year at college, Edward finally plucked up the courage to ask Haifa out on a date. Confident as she was, she teased him.

'A date? You mean a *study date*. Right?'

'mmm, no, not exactly. I was, mmm, well. I was thinking about a real date. Where we go out to eat together.' He replied nervously.

'So, just like our normal time together. We meet. We eat. And we talk. Right? Haifa continued to tease.

Edward, blushing and sweating, replied. 'Kinda, but on a date as...'

Before he could get the words out, Haifa jumped in. 'Oh, you mean a real date. A proper date, like a girlfriend and boyfriend date. Why didn't you say? Yes, of course. I would love to.'

Finally realising the tease, he looked at her initially in disbelief that she had said yes, but then he smiled like a puppy who had just received a pat on the head from their loving owner. After their first date that very evening, they started to spend more time together, and Edward soon introduced Haifa to his sisters and it wasn't long before she became a big sister to both of them.

A coincidence or not, during college, they also achieved similar results in their A-levels, and because Edward had already decided to stay in the area and attend Birmingham University to ensure he remained close to his sisters, it didn't take Haifa long to decide the same.

It was at the university that Haifa quickly joined the University Islamic Society and it wasn't long before Edward also became a member.

With no apparent interest in sports or physical activities, he now either spent time all his spare time with Haifa and his sisters or attended study with the University Islamic Society.

The society served as a focal point for both Muslim students and staff and also those wanting to find out more about Islam.

Initially, Edward hated the society's segregation policy (outlawed in Britain, where men sit towards the front of the room or stage and women separately at the back) because it meant he couldn't sit next to Haifa, but within a few months, he had not only got used to it, he had also made other male friends, which in turn made him feel more important.

As a very bright political student, he was often involved in pretty heated debates on all the key subjects and both social and political differences between the teaching of Islam and his western beliefs.

On a fortnightly basis, the society would have guest speakers, and during the first term, the speakers spoke only about the Islamic faith and talked about the history of Islam. However, gradually, the speakers started to introduce more hard-line doctrine intent on spreading the news that the Western society and governments were the enemy. How could a society that promotes homosexuality and same-sex marriage be credible? How could a society that is full of people using prostitution and drugs dictate its ideals to Muslims? The arguments were all very sound, and it was difficult to argue against them. On a few occasions, students were asked at meetings to try and challenge these subject matters… to put forward a *westerner's* side of the argument. They even encouraged small groups to do role-plays with one person in the group arguing for the western beliefs and another the Islamic ideals.

On 100% of these occasions, almost by design, the conclusions were both logical and clear. The western societies and countries were encouraging sin and, therefore, were evil.

It was nine months into his first year at university that Haifa first suggested the idea to Edward that he might consider changing faiths. This wasn't a difficult concept for Edward to grasp as he wasn't exactly a God-fearing Christian anyway. Yes, he had attended Boy's Brigade as an early teenager, but the only time he had been to church in his adult life had been to attend a couple of weddings and a funeral.

However, the idea of actually joining a religion, any religion, was not something Edward was going to do lightly.

In discussions about the subject with his male friends and the vice president of the society, he also knew that just converting to a faith wasn't enough… you had to follow that faith properly, which included its doctrine. So far, everything he had heard had made sense, but he was also challenged by some of the practices that the faith and society followed. Segregating women at meetings was one area, as was covering up women's faces. Haifa's own response on the subject was firm. 'I feel a bit insulted by the insinuation that you feel women's views are not considered. Muslim women are all intelligent, and yes, there is patriarchy (a social system where the male is the primary authority figure), and it's an important part of our faith.' Her voice got louder as she went on. 'You cannot just pick out certain parts of a faith and say, I like that bit and don't like that. You're not at a restaurant looking at a menu and deciding what to eat. Faith is 100% commitment.

Edward never mentioned the subject again.

Chapter 20

By the second year of university, the guest speakers had started getting more and more radical. They also introduced other ways of communicating their messages. Leaflets and mini-booklets were regularly handed out, and it was one of these booklets that helped crystallise Edward's thoughts.

The headline was: *'Who are the Terrorists?'*

This was the first time the *'T'* word had been used in literature or ever formally mentioned in any communications by any of the speakers. Yes, the subject matter had come up in some small group discussions, but never in any previous presentation materials.

More recently, the British government had been made aware that several universities and even some grammar schools had been infiltrated by hard-line extremists. These extremists were very clever and very patient. They didn't follow an obvious approach that would easily bring unwanted attention to their activities. As Birmingham had a larger-than-normal population of Muslims already, its university was an obvious target. Even now, in year 2 of his time at university, Edward's own Islamic Society had itself been split into three groups. The first 2 groups were typically following the standard curriculum that allowed people (typically British-born Muslims) to find out more about Islam and its history. The third group, the one that Edward found himself in as the only white British attendee - had been carefully selected over the last three months of the previous year. It contained some very bright students and also some that appeared to hang on to every word being taught. It was in this group that the booklet was being discussed again.

Its main message maintained the same facts that had been repeatedly presented over the last 4-6 months. It looked pretty similar to how people would expect to see the Ten Commandments written down.

There were 10 reasons why the West, and in particular America and its key allies, Britain and France, were not friends of Islam. From prostitution, drugs, indiscriminate use of weapons against people in the Middle East, and the support of homosexuality… the message was clear and concise. How could you NOT be against this evil western society?

On another page it cleverly talked about the key pillars of Islam. Prayer, giving money to the poor, fasting and life on earth are purely a preparation for life after death (Paradise). It was easy to see how one could be convinced, and the last two pages of the booklet featured buildings blown up by the Infidels (America) and a woman carrying what looked like a dead baby in her arms. The headline on this page read the same as the front page 'Who are the Terrorists?'

No one in Edward's group challenged anything they had read, and with their bi-weekly guest presenters also following the same message without even realising it, this group was becoming extremely radical and had pretty much distanced itself from the University's Islamic Society and was going it alone with its teachings. Everyone in the group was sworn to secrecy about what they discussed. Edward did speak to Haifa about some of the sessions and she just stuck with the same message as before. If Edward was serious about Islam, he should covert his faith. She neither challenged anything that he said was going on within his own group nor seemed to be bothered about how much time he spent at meetings. Initially, it was just twice weekly, but over time, this turned into 3 times a week after classes had finished and then 2 evenings. Without realising it, Haifa and Edward were growing apart, and she even appeared to spend more time alone with his 2 sisters than with Edward.

Unbeknown to Edward, with each week that passed, he was getting more and more entrapped into a world he had never previously known had existed.

One thing that did make Edward feel good about himself was that within the society his views seemed to carry weight in the group's discussions. In one late evening session, the discussion came around to a simple question from the Vice President of the Islamic Society, who sometimes attended.

'So, if the Americans are terrorists, what should we do to stop them?' Completely by design, the question was thrown into the group by the group leader to get a response from one person, and that was Edward. No longer could he just sit here at each meeting, casually discussing the issues surrounding the Middle East and the western atrocities without doing something about them. The war waged by America and its allies was unjust, so what *could* or *should* be done about it? Every meeting Edward and the group of students had attended over the last 10 months was designed to get to this very moment.

The moment where, hopefully, the momentum that had been built up over that period would mean that certain people would feel not only obliged to do something but feel like they wanted to. You couldn't force someone to consider the type of action that might be necessary, and they had to want to get involved.

Edward's response to the question was clear and precise. 'Action is needed… action by those that can make a difference.'

No one that night mentioned anything specific, and no one discussed the subject again. The session ended, and the following day, after the university had finished, Edward was approached by the Vice President and another man called Aabzaari Imam. At this first meeting they made it clear to Edward that any future meetings would just be the three of them. The first subject the Vice President talked about was confidentiality. He said several students had failed to keep the contents of the group's meetings private and had been discussing things with other people. Despite wondering how they knew he had spoken to Haifa, Edward blushed throughout this conversation and looked as guilty as charged. Whilst he wasn't threatened, he was left in no doubt how important it was not to discuss his future meetings or their contents with anyone else. Over the next 4-6 weeks, he was treated like a king. Very few students had direct access to the Vice President, and Edward spent several evenings alone with him in his study at the University. Both the Vice President and Aabzaari even joked about what Muslim names he might choose when (not 'if') he converted to their faith. Edward's own ego was being targeted and his own self-importance grew as he was soon invited to return to the main group of students and present on various topics about Islam. At most of the meetings he had on his own with either the Vice President or Aabzaari, they re-enforced the key messages from the previous group discussions and specifically talked about personal responsibilities. 'One man could make a huge impact in changing the society. One man could achieve greatness in the decisions he made,' they both said.

Edward was now a man of importance and he began the steps of converting his faith. Whilst overjoyed at the news, Haifa had become distant and even unfriendly. They no longer held hands as they walked and rarely spent any time alone together. Instead of confiding in her, Edward decided not to discuss anything with her about his own one-on-one sessions with the Vice President and began to treat Haifa like someone who was beneath him and it was these latest actions that added to their lack of closeness. Within a few weeks, Haifa approached him about their relationship. 'It's clear we are not the same people we were who joined the University, and whilst I am delighted you are considering converting, I don't feel we can remain a couple.'

If Edward had heard these words 3 months before, he would have been crushed and practically suicidal. Instead, he only felt embarrassment which quickly turned to anger. Anger that she was terminating their relationship, not him. He was supposed to be in charge and shouldn't be dictated to by a woman. But something stopped him from reacting badly. Perhaps it was the memory of their relationship, but more likely, he simply didn't know what to say or how to react.

The day after Haifa had met with Edward for the last time, she met with the Vice President. 'Well done, my sister. Your work is done. You have performed your task well. Allah is so pleased with you.' He said.

Chapter 21

The following week, Edward went through the full ceremony to convert to the Muslim faith, and an important part of his commitment was to change his name to Mohammed Al-Badawai. Three weeks later, Edward was invited by Aabzaari Imam to go travelling. Edward was told he was going to be an important person in the eyes of Allah. Someone who was earmarked for a special task.

Everything had been provided for, and he was to go on a six-week trip to India, where he would initially spend a week sightseeing to build a realistic story in case someone ever checked up on him before taking a train from Deli to the large northern city of Jaipur, where he was then transported by car onto the town of Bikaner, which was close to the Pakistan border. After a two-day accompanied trek across the desert of Bikaner, he crossed the border and was met by another man who became his handler. Within two weeks, he had formally converted to Islam and was a true believer of all things in Islam. He was soon told of the planned attack on the Westerner's plane and how he could play a significant role. His role would purely be an insurance policy. No one would get hurt, and he would only get involved if he needed to come to the aid of one of his brothers or sisters on the plane. There would be no firearms involved, and assuming the western governments responded positively to their demands (which they historically always do), no one would get hurt.

He did need some training and was introduced to a man who taught him self-defence, then slowly introduced a more aggressive style of training. By the fifth week away from the university, he had become competent in both hand-to-hand combat and the use of various weapons.

Mohammed Al-Badawai was now ready to take the action he had committed to at his university.

Chapter 22

Ahmad had felt Malika's presence as she returned to her seat. He knew exactly where she had been and exactly what her task had been. She gave him a brief smile as she carefully sat down, but she still looked very anxious. As Malika was the strong and confident one, this immediately made Ahmad extremely nervous. Had something gone wrong?

He sat up and desperately wanted to cross over and touch her, more for his own reassurance than hers, but she made no attempt to speak or get close to him and simply sat there with her eyes facing the seat in front. After a minute had gone by, almost as if she subconsciously realized Ahmad's need to touch, she moved over and grabbed his hand. Smiling, she said: 'Don't worry, my brother, everything is in hand. Paradise awaits us.'

'Is everything alright?'

'Yes. I tell you, everything is as we planned. Try and relax.'

Malika surprised Ahmad by leaning further over, almost out of her seat and kissed him firmly on the lips. She wanted to keep up the persona of a loving couple in case anyone had taken in her lengthy recent trip to the restroom and decided to ask themselves any questions. She also knew a contact like that would relieve Ahmad of any nervousness or concerns he might have about how she was feeling.

Ahmad was taken aback but very much enjoyed the warmth of Malika's lips and her breath on his face. It immediately calmed him, and for a moment, he was back in his evening dreams in Pakistan, where, after training, he would lay in his tent imagining life with Malika. Their two imaginary children would take their mother's looks, and he would proudly come home each day after work to a beautiful family and a lovely meal expertly cooked by Malika.

He bounced back to reality as she withdrew from him and awkwardly re-settled herself in her seat. He knew where the gun would be positioned and was extremely grateful he hadn't been asked to carry one. He knew how to use one, of course, but prayed it would never come to that. Their handler told him that he feared that smuggling the components of two guns on the plane would be challenging enough, plus, unknown to Ahmad, they simply didn't feel confident in Ahmad's ability to use one if required when the time came.

Apart from Malika and their *other* partner on the plane, the only other person who would be carrying a gun would be the air marshal, whoever and wherever he or she was. After the analyses post 9/11, it was decided that there would be an air marshal aboard all long-haul flights into the US. The group's own investigations into this role have suggested this role would be taken by a male, aged between 38 and 48: someone dressed casually but not with expensive designer clothes that might attract attention.

Earlier, and without realising it, both Debbie and Laura had been in agreement that the air marshal on that particular flight was indeed sat in business class, in seat 1B.

Malika had also caught sight of him on one of her 'leg stretching' walks around the plane. In fact, he had actually said hello to her earlier when she had passed his row. On her third walk around, she had decided he was the one passenger she had been looking out for and was pleased to have found him four rows ahead of her, close enough to get to him quickly but far enough way for him not to have noticed her and Ahmad too much during the flight. Malika sat back in her business class seat, moved the electric seat out to give herself more room, and allowed herself a brief smile, knowing then the plan she and the others had developed was completely on track.

What neither Malika, Ahmad, nor Dalmair knew was that their superiors were taking no chances that their mission would fail.

Chapter 23

On top of the 'sleeper' on the plane, the people in charge of the planning of this attack also wanted to have a failsafe backup plan. In their experience, many potential suicide bombers either changed their minds or, at times, got talked out of detonating the bombs strapped to their bodies. Most packs carry a single detonator so that the person themselves must detonate the bomb by pressing a single button. This is typically linked with wire to the explosives directly. History has told them that at a crucial moment, even the most committed follower or bravest person can fail to press the button. That was why, with most attacks, they now included a remote device that allowed the handler or another person nearby to remotely detonate the bomb. Clearly, on a plane, some 35,000 feet in the sky, there would be no radio waves or transmitters to allow such devices to work.

On this occasion, the second part of their backup plan was activated eight hours earlier during refuelling and general maintenance at an airport in the United Kingdom.

An incredibly powerful but small device had been strapped inside the wheel arch of the front wheel of a plane. Matched to the exact same colour as the plane's undercarriage, it was almost invisible to any of the team on their last inspection before the plane was given the all-clear. It wasn't large enough to explode the plane in mid-air, but it would most probably take a large chunk of the fuselage out, as well as possibly impact the forward wing on the left-hand side, causing the plane to go straight into a deep dive.

Andrew (Andy) Shaw, a member of the 2-man team that did the terminal's refuelling of aircrafts as well as trucks, had placed the package where he had been told to at around 8.30 am British time that morning.

Andy Shaw was a tall and wiry man with a very pale complexion. At 36 years of age, Andy had now been taking some form of recreational drugs for over 20 years. As a tall 13-year-old, the older boys at school utilized Andy's height by asking him to buy their cigarettes for them at lunchtime and typically rewarded him with a few free samples. He quickly became friends with a few of them and was soon getting invited to parties where the average age of the group was 15-16 years. At 14, he was at such a party when he was offered his first puff of marijuana, which he coolly took in his stride and before long, smoking joints was a regular occurrence for Andy. Whilst being a relatively bright student academically, Andy was inherently lazy. His very strict father had left the family home just before Andy's 13th birthday, and with no father figure around to push him or discipline him, he lost his drive and tended to focus more on ways to get out of school. His father had rather hoped Andy would follow his own career path into local government (he was the number 2 for a local member of parliament) and had always been encouraged by Andy's awareness of general politics and his overall reading abilities. But after one too many affairs, Andy's mother asked him to leave the family home, and he ended up leaving the area altogether because she threatened to expose him to the constituency and his superiors. That meant he moved nearly 60 minutes away, just outside his constituency boundary, and whilst there was initial bi-weekly contact with Andy, it soon faded away. The gap was filled with the older children from the school, and ultimately, that meant bad news for Andy as it shaped the following 20 years of his life. At nearly 16 years old, two years after his first cigarette and once marijuana stopped having the desired effect, he was offered some white powder to snort. The feeling was incredible, and Andy loved it, but as he couldn't afford to buy cocaine himself, he rarely had the chance to take it. That was until he met a much older ex-pupil from his school at a party who offered Andy the chance to borrow some to sell, and as a reward, Andy would get free cocaine to use for himself. This worked for a while, but Andy soon left school and needed an income. At 17, he made a very brave (or very stupid) decision to start adding talcum powder to the cocaine he received, meaning it bulked out by around 20%, giving him his own batch to sell. This worked extremely well for a few weeks until a user complained to the guy Andy was receiving the cocaine from, and Andy had a *visit*. Andy's supplier himself was already watering down the cocaine with talcum powder, so with Andy adding his own, it had become very weak.

Andy spent six days in hospital recovering from two smashed cheekbones, a broken nose and over 20 stitches across his face.

This beating gave Andy a wake-up call and he decided to try and get a proper, full-time job. Unfortunately, as someone who didn't have many qualifications, he had to start at the bottom and take a part-time job at a local petrol station. However, as a relatively bright young man, it wasn't long before he was full-time and was promoted to shift supervisor. This is where he learnt about all things to do with fuel and the difference between diesel and the several different grades of petrol.

Still very much a cocaine-taker with a few other drugs thrown in, Andy's life was now pretty good. He had no dependents and could spend all his money on himself. He had a large contact base of rather 'shifty' friends and became relatively well known as a local person who *knew* people and could put you in touch with someone who can get you *stuff*. One of his other side-lines was dealing in stolen jewellery and some fake watches. One of which he liked so much he wore himself. The only problem was that this particular watch always seemed to go a little faster than it was supposed to, which didn't seem to bother Andy because it meant he always arrived for work early.

Things got even better when, at 26, he got a job at a small regional airport, looking after all the fuel containers that refuelled the aircraft.

It was at this airport that Andy was targeted a couple of years later.

Whilst not a fanatic, Andy hugely sympathized with the cause of the Arab world and hated the British and American political hierarchy (in some way probably fuelled by his own absent father). But his main source of fanaticism was *greed*. Initially, without realizing it, he started passing very low-key and insignificant information over to a guy he had met in the airport's social club for a few drinks and occasionally sharing of cocaine. Some 3 years later, when he got a bigger job at Heathrow Airport, he started providing much more significant information about the goings on at Europe's biggest airport to a friend of his earlier contact he now regularly met in a pub near his hometown of Hayes, in Middlesex.

From flight schedules and changes, general security information to any news on anyone important flying, Andy past it on. He often thought his information was completely useless, but the person who gave him the cash never once commented or complained about its validity.

It also gave Andy's ego a boost that he was providing information that, whilst he didn't think was that important, was still stuff he was clever enough to know he should not be passing on to someone else.

On top of the cash, he also received cocaine, which he was now completely reliant on to help get him through the day.

Despite the attacks in the US on 9/11, he still joked to his friends about how lax airport security was. He easily passed his quarterly drug tests by paying his buddy £50 to let him use his own urine sample. Last year, when they said they would also be taking samples from his hair for traces of certain drugs that stay in your system for a while, he simply shaved his head, and no one challenged him or asked him to supply hair samples from his chest.

Being a refueller wasn't a particularly glamorous job and the fact that you smelt strongly of diesel fuel all day meant few other people paid them and his buddy much attention. It also allowed you access to the fuel caps on the larger aircraft that were above the front wheel archway.

Five times in the last month, he had practised getting down from his truck (the fuel hose was attached to the truck similar to a fire hose) and walking under the plane to pass the wheel to get to the other side of the plane. On none of these occasions did anyone challenge him either there or later that shift, giving him supreme confidence he could repeat this exercise at will. Regular use of the cocaine also ensured he had the arrogance of a man who felt he could achieve almost anything.

When he met his contact, he normally received the cash and drugs in a small white envelope, but when he had met him around six weeks earlier, his contact behaviour was much more serious. He and Andy had felt sure this wasn't a normal meeting.

The guy was carrying a satchel, which he opened briefly to show Andy its contents. Andy was convinced the satchel held over £100,000, and when the man told him to follow him outside to his car, Andy didn't need to ask twice. They drove silently for a couple of miles, Andy's mind racing about the cash and how he would spend it. The car stopped and the guy told him to get out and get into another vehicle, a dark transit van with blacked-out windows. Despite having two grams already stuffed up his nose only 10 minutes before the meet, Andy felt extremely nervous.

There were two other Middle Eastern looking guys in the van, and his previous contact left in the car they had arrived in. One of the guys was in the driver's seat, the other one in the back of the van. He was the one to speak:

'Andy, thank you for taking the time to meet us today. And a bigger thank you for all the very important information you have supplied to us over the years. The people at the top of my organization are very grateful. Now has come the time for you to be greatly rewarded.'

'Am I in trouble? Are you going to let me go?' Andy was still scared and hadn't been taken in what the man was saying.

'Andy, you are amongst friends now. You will come to no harm. In fact, we are here to thank you and reward you for your excellent work.'

Andy calmed down, and as his eyes adjusted to the low light levels in the van, this calming voice had its impact, and he relaxed.

'Errr… just giving you some basic info, no big deal.' Andy replied.

The man continued. 'I know and we are very grateful, but we now have one bigger task that we need your help on. A task that you will be greatly rewarded for.'

Andy perked up on hearing the word *reward*. 'I'm your guy, especially if it's linked to that bag of cash.'

'It is indeed. You get half today if you agree to my proposition and half when it's completed.'

'Trust me, we already have an agreement.' Andy greedily replied.

This angered the man greatly, knowing he was having to deal with someone who was only it for money, but he bit his tongue.

'Andy, this mission is very, very important and comes with a lot of trust. It's also not something to take lightly. Ultimately, it will frighten a lot of people and, however unlikely, could lead to some casualties.'

'Casualties? What d'ya mean casualties?' Andy asked.

'We want to scare the British government a little. Get them to take notice of our cause and also frighten the British and American public into standing up and having a voice. Andy, do you know fully the terror those governments are causing my friends and families back in Iraq and Afghanistan? The torture of innocent men and women? It's time your own women heard and understood what's happening in other parts of the world. The blowing up of our mosques, the killing of children.'

'I know.' Andy cut in. 'Those lousy bastards. All of them are absolutely loaded as well. And they've got the cheek to raise our blooming taxes to help pay for all those bombs.'

Andy continued. 'But let's get back to the word *casualties...*'

Before Andy could finish the sentence, the man continued, 'We need you to place a tiny parcel next to the wheel arch on a plane bound for America. It will be a very specific plane that we choose. There will be a small timer inside the package in a hardened case to protect it against the air pressure at that high altitude.

Straightening up in the van with his eyes widening, Andy cut in again. 'You mean a bomb? A fucking bomb! Are you crazy?'

'No, no, Andy, you misunderstand. It's just a small device that will produce a blowout of the wheel on landing, and No one will get hurt.'

'So it's not a bomb? Or is it? Which is it? Yes or no?' Andy demanded.

'It's not a bomb at all. It's a small device about the size of a 2 large matchboxes that will blow out small spikes into the wheel on landing and cause a blowout. The explosive part that causes it to work is about the size of a large grape. So, it's definitely not a huge bomb. And for completing this simple but very important task, you become rich.' The man explained.

Slightly concerned Andy was getting fixated on the word *bomb,* the man wanted to bring the subject matter back to cash and pushed the satchel towards Andy and opened it.

'How much is in the bag?' Andy asked.

'£25,000 as our gift today, assuming you will go ahead and another £25,000 once you have completed the task.'

'And no one's gonna get hurt?' Andy challenged again.

'Andy, these pilots are very experienced and probably have regular practices on their flight simulators having a burst tyre. Yes, it will shake a few people up and any fool that's not fastened his seatbelt properly for landing may get a shock as they're thrown forward, but we are only talking about minor casualties.'

Andy didn't speak for a while. For how long, he wasn't sure.

Even though he had asked the question, he wasn't thinking about casualties. He wasn't worried if anyone would get hurt. His main worry was getting caught. But he knew the security at Heathrow was pathetic. He himself had even wandered onto a plane once and stolen duty-free cigarettes. He considered the huge amount of cash he was promised and the fact those only inches away from him right now was £25,000.

'Okay, I'm in.'

They carried the friendly conversation on for another 3-4 minutes and then suddenly, much to the surprise of Andy, the guy asked him to exit the van. Andy jumped out, and the man passed him the satchel.

'In three weeks, your normal contact will meet you, and you will provide him with a picture of the wheel archway. A week later he will meet you again to give you the package. Understood?'

'Understood.' Andy replied.

'Andy,' the man said and continued. 'Andy, please can I give you some advice? Andy didn't reply, his mind on the cash.

'Andy.' The man said loudly. Slightly shaken by the man's change of tone, Andy replied. 'Yes, er, sorry.'

'It's important not to bring any attention to yourself before the task is completed. If your friends find that you have suddenly come into loads of money, they might start asking questions. So please be discreet and don't change your spending habits for a few weeks or so afterwards. Please, Andy,' the man almost begged.

Andy replied. 'Yes, got it, understood. Keep a low profile till after the job's done. Got it.'

Andy held onto the satchel very tightly and made his way to the local taxi rank to get a lift home. Full of all things good, he whistled to himself and then sang to himself. 'I'm in the money… I'm in the money…'

Chapter 24

Little did Andy know that he wouldn't get much of a chance to spend the cash.

A month after the meeting in the van, approximately 6.5 hours into Flight BA57's journey to New York, Andy was at his flat and had taken a decent amount of the cocaine he had received from his contact at the pub that afternoon.

Earlier that day, Andy had successfully completed his task of setting the timer and then strapping the package onto the wheel arch of the specific plane they had told him to. Despite being a little nervous, things went smoothly, and no one appeared to see him pass under the giant wing of the plane. He had been given instructions by his contact only a week earlier on how to place the package but had forgotten some of the information minutes after receiving it.

His only recall was the flight number and time. His contact hadn't allowed him to write this information down, but as soon as the contact had left the pub, Andy did grab a pen and wrote this information on his hand.

His shift had finished at 3 pm, and he had been very eager to meet the man who would give him the other £25,000 that he was due. When he did meet his contact, he had been pleasantly surprised when get received another additional reward of a few decent-sized bags of coke. An extra bonus for 'a job well done'!

It was now about 4 pm, and Andy was at home and, having taken three large snorts of his bonus coke, was now bouncing off the walls, really pumped up and ready to party. He kept throwing handfuls of cash in the air, laughing out loud with the music blaring out. Suddenly, he felt a sharp pain in his chest. The pain became very intense. He fell to his knees and then rolled onto the floor. His heart stopped, and within another 10 seconds, Andrew Shaw was no more.

The local police would take ages to connect the dots. It was an unfortunate but simple overdose by a habitual drug taker.

Later that night, Andrew's flat received two visitors. They were in and out in four minutes and left no evidence of their visit. It didn't take them long to find nearly £18,000 of the first payment hidden under the bed and all the final payment of £25,000 that was scattered around Andy's body in the main living room of the flat. The money was needed elsewhere.

Chapter 25

Back in economy row 11B, Edward Beech was trying to focus on his responsibilities. He had been told the plan was to hijack the plane to raise money to fund future activities. His handlers had told him that they could raise in excess of $100m with this type of attack. He was also told a few people might need to lose their lives for the cause (to ensure the authorities took them seriously), but most of the passengers would be fine. He also knew the hijack was going to start very close to American soil and, therefore, would be very close to the end of the flight. He himself would probably not even be needed. There were other, more senior and experienced group members on board who would both initiate and execute the plan.

But Edward was struggling to come to terms with the reality of the situation. Back in the economy section where he was seated, he was surrounded by families and children, and whilst this was very much the plan, the two children seated in front of him were of a similar age to his own sisters. One of the girls was called Juliet and had taken a shine to Edward. Throughout the flight, Juliet and her sister had turned around many times to take a peek at Edward, only to turn away in a fit of giggles every time their eyes met with his.

Suppose the plan did go wrong. Suppose he did have to grab a child and hold the makeshift knife against the throat of a young girl. Suppose he held the knife too tightly, and it cut the girl's throat?

'These innocent children, just the same age as my sisters.' Edward had told himself in the mirror on one of his visits to the toilets.

He sat down on the toilet and prayed for strength. Then he leaned closer to the mirror. 'I must stand firm to Islam. These children are children of the America that kills Muslims and attacks my very beliefs. These young girls will grow up to be infidels themselves.' He threw water on his face as if to try and wash away any weakness or sympathy for the girls he had. 'I am only going to scare them anyway. It's not my job to kill anyone.'

Edward returned to his seat and tried very hard to ignore everyone around him closed his eyes and concentrated on his memorised readings of the Koran.

Chapter 26

Flight time: 6 hours and 45 minutes.

The entertainment system went on to pause.

'This is your captain speaking. I hope you have all had a nice rest and enjoyed the facilities aboard our 777 bound for New York.

'We have approximately 50 minutes before we arrive at Newark airport, so now's the time to have that last stretch and visit of the toilets, as in approximately 20 minutes, we begin our descent. From then, the seatbelt signs will be permanently on and from that time, you won't be able to go to the toilets until inside the terminal. The weather is fine with light clouds and a very nice temperature of 23 celsius, that's about 73 degrees in old money or Fahrenheit. If you want to adjust your watches, the local time on the ground is 11.20 am. Please also ensure your hand luggage is carefully packed away in the overhead compartments.' He continued.

'Cabin crew: 50 minutes until landing, 50 minutes until landing.'

The plane's entertainment system kicked back in, and there was a general rise in activity throughout the plane, people headed for the toilets and began preparing themselves for their arrival in New York.

Typical; I was 30 minutes into my second movie and realized there was no way it would finish by the time we landed. Not that I want to delay landing, of course, but it's a good movie!

I was doubly annoyed with myself as I'm normally more switched on than this and have already used the toilet and brushed my teeth. But now I was going to have to queue to use the toilet.

On arrival, I'd have to go directly from the airport to meet a customer in New York, and I'd been told it was about an hour's drive by taxi, so I wouldn't have any time to stop. I also needed to put a tie on and do a *once over* the pre-meeting notes so I would be fully prepared. I could have done this in the taxi, but I get travel-sick reading anything in a car. I just hoped I wouldn't have to queue for too long to get a taxi so I could arrive a little early and grab a latte somewhere. My first meeting (and the one I was most excited about) was with a large US retailer that had over 300 department-sized stores. Their spend on Christmas products was reported to be over $15m, so if I could secure just 10% of that, it would be a dream. Plus, once I was supplying one big retailer, my company's reputation would grow and it would surely lead to more business elsewhere in the US. I had already gone through the presentation about 10 times, but there was no harm in going over it a couple more.

Chapter 27

Malika checked her watch again and also asked Ahmad for the time on his. She was running through the plan over and over in her mind.

Things were nicely in place. She had taken several walks around the plane and felt she knew where the Air Marshall was and had the gun and fake explosives strapped tightly, as did Ahmad and Dalmair. As there were only three of them on board, she knew she needed an area she could both control and see along the plane in case any brave passengers felt obliged to try and be a hero. The area that had been long ago nominated to be her *'control centre'* was the first-class section. This gave her good visibility as well as made sure she was close to the cockpit. Her colleagues back in Pakistan had done a good job ensuring the first-class area was practically empty.

They had booked several seats on the flight through an agent and, as they had no intention of using them, ensured the area was only a quarter full.

Part of her preparation included checking out the cabin crew, looking to identify the possible weaker individuals from the stronger ones. This would help her pick the exact moment to take control of the plane and also who she would use to assist her in getting into the cockpit. It's amazing what someone will do when they have a gun to their head or see a load of dynamite strapped to someone's chest. Apparently, according to her superiors, you do sometimes come across someone who has the courage to stand up and face a gun threat down. They were typically from the armed services or maybe a policeman who may feel an obligation to be brave. However, 99.9% of people, when being told they must follow someone's instructions or be shot, go into survival mode and will do whatever it takes to stay alive.

The trouble was, if that 0.1% of people happened to be on that flight, the whole plan could go up in smoke. Yes they could bring the plane down, but a key part of the plan was the destination it came down. That's where Plan B came in. If a *hero* refused to obey a command, then you turned the gun on to another innocent civilian and threatened their life. Being brave surrounding your own life is one thing, but allowing another to be killed is something entirely different, especially if they were your partner or a relative.

The other big worry they had was whether people would believe they had any chance of survival, even if they did follow the terrorist's commands. Were they all doomed to die anyway, therefore they should ignore the threats, and this could lead to a kind of mutiny on board, similar to the Flight 93 incident in 2001. Having said this, the bottom line was that people *want* to believe they will be safe, and despite most governments and security forces around the world's view that any hostage takeover involving a plane would only lead to disaster, the general public would prefer to cling to the hope that they would be freed to return to their families.

Part of Malika's planned charm offensive was to encourage the passengers to trust that they would ultimately survive and that this was a hostage situation where a large ransom would be paid by the governments for the safe return of the plane and its passengers. That way, they would cooperate, and none of them would risk their lives trying to overpower her or her two partners. Before they realized any difference, the plane would be in her control and diving at a speed of around 500 miles an hour into their planned target on the ground… Harvard University in Boston, Massachusetts.

Impact time was expected to be 12.40 pm. That was five minutes before the morning sessions ended, thus ensuring a full campus.

There were a number of reasons for this target. Firstly, it holds over 6,400 of the country's (and possibly the world's) brightest students and over 250 of the best teachers ever assembled. Typically, Harvard is a good breeding ground for many of the biggest jobs in both the political and private business world around the country. Secondly, if a child was lucky enough to go to Harvard, then the parents come from either wealthy or influential backgrounds, many from both. Therefore, the impact would be across several generations of very important people. Those very people who can influence policy and their country's Middle Eastern policies. It's easy to sit in an ivory tower discussing the Middle East and making decisions about people some 6,000 miles away that make no difference to your life, so bringing the problems directly close to home would guarantee some change. Whilst reasonably popular, the current American president would come under enormous pressure to try different methods of resolving the conflict in the Middle East. Simply sending in more drones to kill innocent civilians would not satisfy the millions of Americans who would be calling for a complete withdrawal from Iraq and Afghanistan. And with over 30% of the president's own Republican party already supporting this type of action, this attack should speed things up.

The fact that it wasn't seen as an obvious target for the American government meant it gave some credibility to the group's story that this was a simple hijack and that there was no target on the ground. The other important factor about Harvard University was that approximately 11 from its own border was Boston's regional airport, with a runway just about long enough to cope with a 777-plane landing. This would be where Malika would try to convince the authorities that she would be happy to land, assuming, of course, the negotiations had gone well. The plane would take an 18-degree right turn around 10 to 15 minutes before it got to the East Coast of America, proving to the people on board and on the ground that their intentions were not to destroy the plane. This was crucial because the terrorists' group's own intel told them that if there was a possible threat to the ground from a passenger airliner, once it came within 12 minutes from land, it would be shot out of the sky. The US government wasn't going to allow a repeat of 9/11, no matter what the cost.

After the short right-hand turn, the plane would then travel the 250 miles relatively quickly to Boston. Because there's no offensive military or political target on the route, that would leave time for negotiations to continue before those on the ground realised it was too late.

Malika had decided that Debbie would be her 'weak' crew member. A tall and extremely attractive female was deemed more interested in her own appearance and well-being and, therefore, would easily crumble under pressure. And if for some reason she didn't, a threat on her life would ensure somebody else did. During the flight, Malika had chatted to Debbie on a few occasions to ensure she could get really close to her when the time came for action. Debbie seemed so lovely and kind and even asked about Malika's pregnancy and whether she wanted a girl or a boy.

Chapter 28

30 minutes later.

The aircraft's entertainment system froze again.

'Hello again, this is your captain again. I hope everybody's now refreshed and prepared for their arrival in New York. The toilets are now closed and everyone should return to their seats where you will have noticed the seatbelt sign is now on and will be until we are safely at our destination. We have approximately 20 minutes until we land at Newark Airport in New York. We hope you have enjoyed the flight and I look forward to flying with you again.

'Cabin crew, 20 minutes to landing, 20 minutes to landing.'

Seconds later, the senior cabin purser, Brendon O'Leary, spoke in a friendly Irish accent.

'Hello again, everyone, and on behalf of British Airways and all the cabin crew, I wanted to thank you for flying BA and hope you're enjoyed the flight. As the captain said, please ensure you return to your seat and ensure your seats are back up and tray tables are put away. If you have any electronic items in use, please ensure they're switched off for landing.

'On arrival and once in the airport, if you happen to be connecting to another onward flight, please ensure you follow the bright blue flight connection signs in the terminal. Lastly, we at British Airways hope you enjoy your stay in New York and hope to see you back on board in the near future.'

After a brief crackle, the entertainment system came back on.

Chapter 29

At exactly 4.51 pm UK time and 11.51 am local New York time, all of the passengers were strapped into their seats whilst the cabin crew made final preparations for landing.

The aircraft was silent as everyone contemplated their onward journeys: who they would be meeting up with, old friends, new ones, work colleagues, or simply just returning to their home to their loved ones.

An attendant light came on in business class, and Debbie was closest to react. The pregnant Middle Eastern lady probably needed the toilet again. What happened next took Debbie and the rest of the passengers and crew by complete surprise.

As Debbie put her head down to speak to the pregnant lady, she noticed she wasn't strapped in her seat.

Malika jumped up, grabbed Debbie's hair, and pulled her close to her own body. Waving a gun in her other hand.

'Everybody must see that I have a gun. Everybody must see that I am in charge of this plane.'

Part of the first sentence was drowned out by Debbie's scream, and part of the second sentence was also drowned out by the screams of other passengers as both Ahmad and Dalair jumped from their seats. Ahmad tore his shirt off, revealing a waistcoat full of dynamite and Dalair the same, and he was also brandishing a gun.

Within a few seconds the scene on the plane had changed from calm to absolute panic. Despite all the passengers not being able to see what was going on from their seats, the sudden noise and screaming in the forward cabin area quickly spread with a domino effect throughout the plane.

Chapter 30

I was sitting silently one row behind the businessman and, a few minutes earlier, had noticed he had removed his business jacket. Having a plane full of passengers being completely silent as we started our descent had concentrated both my senses and my imagination. Why on earth would this guy, who had suffered the whole flight in high temperatures but kept his jacket on, refusing any fluids, all of a sudden decide he was uncomfortable? With my attention focused entirely on him, what happened next left me with both my eyes and mouth wide open and my whole body frozen still in my seat. I could neither comprehend what he was doing nor react in any way. Now dripping with sweat, this guy stood up from his seat and hurriedly undressed his shirt, revealing a small waistcoat on his bare skin, as well as holding a gun in his left hand. A split second before, a lady's voice had broken the silence, followed by a high-pitched scream. More screams followed as the businessman turned and shouted, 'In the name of Allah, we are taking over this plane'.

Worse was to come as he turned around the face the rest of the people in the seats around him... he had dynamite strapped to his waistcoat. 'Everybody must stay in their seats. You will not be harmed, you will be safe to go home to your families, but you must not resist.'

Almost paralyzed with fear, I was woken from my trance with more screams from inside my head. Only they weren't coming from me; and they were coming from the lady sitting next to me. She just sat there screaming at the top of her voice. I had to stop her, and I had to be quiet. For some reason, I placed my hand over her arm as if that would make any difference... and much to my surprise, it did. She brought her other hand up and placed it over her own mouth as if to *shush* herself up. From being complete and utter strangers whose paths were never ever going to cross again and who would never have spoken to each other... we became instant comrades of sorts. Thrown together by fate.

More shouting came from a female voice in the next cabin, followed by a third person, also in business class, shouting but then trying to calm people. Because the plane was preparing for landing, all the curtains that separated the different cabin classes on the plane were drawn back so I could just make out another Middle Eastern guy standing up in business.

The businessman terrorist in my cabin walked behind me and into the economy and shouted the same thing he had in my cabin. More screams followed, but then he did the same as the other guy in business did; he started to use a different, much softer voice tone to try and calm the passengers.

Chapter 31

Debbie was dragged by her hair into the first-class cabin. Her back was arched as she tried to walk forward without bumping into all the seats. The pregnant lady then released her with a shove into an empty seat and shouted the same message again.

'Everybody must see that I have a gun. Everybody must see that I am in charge of this plane.'

There were only six passengers and three members of the crew in this cabin, and they all sat up to pay attention.

'You will all move to the back of the plane right now. Do not look at me or come towards me in any way, or I will shoot you where you stand. Do as we say, and you will all survive to see your families again. This is a hijacking, not a terrorist plot. We want money for our cause, and when your governments pay us, you will all go home safely.'

She pointed at another female member of the crew. 'You will sit down on the floor and wait until I tell you to move.'

Malika hoped the better educated passengers in business and first class would help her get this message to the other passengers to reduce the chances of any trouble.

The eight people quickly followed her instructions and almost jogged out of first class, passed both Ahmed in business and then the Dalair in economy. Malika looked down the cabin to check that both Ahmad and Dalmair could see her. Both saw her and acknowledged everything was alright with the pre-agreed signal of holding up their right hands.

Malika had control of the crew and passengers.

Chapter 32

Nobody has any idea how they would act in a situation like this. Somehow, my own brain was sending me endless pictures of my children, particularly my son James. Memories of our holidays in Spain, around the poolside, in the hotel bar playing cards. Earlier shots of my smallest daughter on my shoulders in the swimming pool. More recent pictures of my parents' faces, my brother and sister and Hayley.

I realized my heart was beating so hard it felt like other people could have seen it sticking out from my shirt. I gripped the arms on the seats and tried hard to pull myself together.

I whispered under my breath. 'Come on David, you're supposed to be a senior guy, a man that runs a company, a guy that's responsible for hundreds of employees; pull yourself together. Breathe easy, breathe easy.' Within 10-15 seconds, I had re-focussed and felt I had at least regained control of my own body. Without bringing any attention to myself whatsoever, I made a very slow head turn to try and survey the surroundings.

So far, I had seen two male terrorists but had also heard a female voice from the front of the plane. Assuming they were taking over the whole plane told to me there must be at least four or five in total. I tried to recall what I had heard and unless my memory was playing tricks on me, the guy I had been watching for most of the flight had said we would all survive to see our families again. Whether or not it's a basic instinct to hear those words, but I couldn't recall anything else. This could be a hostage situation, so if we all sat tight, we would get through it. I also recalled how he was sweating and extremely nervous, so maybe he was as frightened as I was. I hadn't heard any explosions and whilst there was still some noise coming from the front of the plane, everyone just sat still in their seats. Some children were crying softly, and I could now hear a Terrorist talking again to a mother and her daughter, telling them it would all be alright. He was stuttering the words out and kept repeating the same message. 'Everyone will be okay. Don't be worried, everyone will be okay.'

Chapter 33

Back in economy seats 22 A and B, both Larry and Betty were woken from their daydreams when they first heard the commotion near the front of the plane and then, seconds later, saw a man entering their section of the plane holding what looked like a gun. Around the waistcoat he was wearing was a small string of what looked like dynamite sticks. Both had the exact same thought: that at any second, the plane would explode in mid-air. Larry took both of Betty's hands and took a strong grip and they both closed their eyes and prayed that they would live to see their grandson. Larry quickly whispered quietly in Betty's ear, 'I love you, my darling wife, and I always will.'

Betty could feel Larry's hands shaking with fear and gripped his hands even tighter and somehow, with a calming voice, said 'It's going to be okay, husband.'

As the seconds passed and the plane hadn't exploded, Betty and Larry looked into each other's eyes, and each managed a nervous smile. There was some feeling of initial relief, but as the seconds turned into a minute and the man with the gun repeated his message that everyone must stay in their seats, Betty knew Larry would be feeling more and more claustrophobic. From what they had seen in movies, terrorists don't allow passengers to move around the plane, and that meant Larry's regular 30-minute walks up the aisles would cease. It was not just the fact he physically wouldn't be allowed up to stretch his legs, it was more that he wasn't allowed to and that meant he was being *forced* to sit in a relatively small space. Larry hated and was extremely embarrassed about his fear of small spaces. He was supposed to be the 'man' of the house, a man that had risked his life in a war, who had flown around the world. Being an airline pilot had meant the general public revered you, and throughout his working life, he always felt proud and somewhat special. Yet little did people know the truth, and right now, at that very moment, he was completely useless and more afraid than he could remember.

In an effort to get some sort of control over his emotions, Larry bit his own lip and tasted blood. He even tried to open his eyes, although he kept his face away from Betty to avoid the shame he was feeling.

Despite the terror, despite knowing the terrible feelings her husband was going through, Betty's mind suddenly became very clear, and she looked at her husband with incredible pride and told herself how lucky she was to be his wife and at that moment how she would marry him again and again if she could.

Then, as did most of the other passengers, Larry and Betty simply bowed their heads, trying to ensure they made no eye contact with the people who appeared to be threatening their entire existence.

Chapter 34

Local time 11.53 am.

Malika felt a surge of confidence as everything had gone to plan without her having to use any unnecessary force. It had taken less than 90 seconds to move the people from the first-class area and gain control of the cabin. Ahmad had control in the business class, and Dalair was leaning against the toilet doors in between economy and premium economy, talking to some passengers. She had let go of Debbie and told her to strap herself into a first-class seat. Her next job was to disable the air marshal. He needed to know *she* was now in charge, and she also wanted to get his gun off him. With her gun pointing forward, she walked straight into business class and pointed the gun straight at Brad Miller.

Chapter 35

Less than a couple of minutes had passed since the Middle Eastern female passenger had taken a member of the cabin crew hostage and taken over the plane. This had all happened only a few feet away from where the onboard air marshal Brad Miller was sitting and he felt both helpless to intervene and also stunned by what was happening. Airline protocol also meant he wasn't to involve himself directly unless he could do so without risking the lives of other passengers. As this lady and the other guy in business, both had straps of dynamite around their waists, it was clear he was helpless to act. He also hoped by acting like any other passenger, maybe another opportunity might arise that would allow him to surprise the terrorists.

This plan worked for only a very short time until the woman brandishing a gun came face to face with Brad.

'I know you are an air marshal, so please hand me your weapon. Do not move too fast.'

Brad responded. 'Sorry, I don't know what you're talking about. Please don't hurt me, and I'm not an air marshal.'

Brad did have a weapon on him: his old trusted 38 revolver. Relatively small and easy to conceal on his body.

'If you don't give me your weapon, I will shoot this lady in the stomach. You have ten seconds.'

Malika pointed the gun at a fellow passenger in a seat in the opposite aisle to Brad. Right on cue, Malika's plan worked. Brad raised his hands.

'Okay, okay. Don't harm her. My gun is strapped to my leg.'

Malika retrained the gun on Brad. 'Lying will get you in trouble, Mr Air Marshall. Reach down very slowly, unstrap your weapon, and throw it between my feet.'

Brad followed her instructions, and a split second after he released the gun, he felt a sharp pain on the back of his head, and he passed out. Malika had wanted to inflict some physical violence on someone to re-enforce her superiority over the passengers, and the air marshal was an obvious target. They needed to know that they had to follow her instructions immediately, or they would suffer the consequences. Once he had released the gun, she brought her own weapon down as hard as she could onto Brad's head. She knew the blow had to be with extreme force, as the gun wasn't made of the usual hard metal a normal gun would be made of. She then picked his gun up and checked the chamber and, with some delight, found it only had two empty spaces, meaning she had four more bullets. Whilst her superiors couldn't be sure the air marshal would be armed, they told her it was possible but not something they wanted to rely on. Now, with a real gun in her hand, Malika placed her own gun into the belt of her jeans. She smiled as her own intelligence was spot on about Brad, and this gave her a feeling of even more power and supreme confidence.

Chapter 36

I could hear this going on but not see it as it was happening almost diagonally across from where I was seated and in the cabin ahead of me. The female voice sounded very strong and confident, and I wondered if she was the leader. I instinctively named her T1 and the third person I had briefly seen in the business class section, T2. That left my friend, the sweaty businessman, as T3. Where were the other terrorists? Were they up and about? Were they sitting down, pretending to be normal passengers, ready to come to the aid of the terrorists if there was a problem? I looked around, and everyone who had the faintest appearance of being sun-tanned or had a Middle Eastern completion or dark hair became a potential terrorist. In my cabin, that meant 5 other people were of concern.

The thing was, 2 of these suspects were an elderly couple who seemed pretty harmless to me. But maybe that was the plan…

Paranoia had kicked in, and I knew it.

'Get a frigging grip, David.' I told myself again, angry with myself for a complete lack of intelligent thought.

Chapter 37

Malika's next task was to get access to the cockpit. She knew how difficult this would be and realized it may take a loss of life to get it open, but she had prepared herself for that very eventuality.

Debbie was still whimpering, not from the pain from having her hair nearly pulled out of her head but from the fear surrounding the situation she found herself in. She had briefly turned around and had seen the terrorists strike the passenger she thought was an air marshal, and knowing he himself had been exposed made Debbie feel more distressed. She looked around for Laura and realised she must be in the business class section. Other than one other crew member (Jenny) who had been told to sit down on the floor, she was alone in first class. They both looked at each other and both had streams of wet tears still splattered all over their faces.

'What do we do now?' Whispered Jenny.

But before her colleague answered, Malika stormed back into the first-class cabin, waving the gun in the air. 'Do everything I tell you to. Do you understand?'

'Yes,' Jenny and Debbie said at the same time.

Then, looking at Jenny, Malika demanded: 'Now you two sit in a seat and strap yourselves in and don't talk to each other.'

All the other crew members had been bundled towards the economy section and Dalmair ensured they found the 20 empty seats that had also been booked by the group's superiors to guarantee enough spaces were available in this section of the plane.

Debbie wondered how her friend was, and at the same time, Laura was desperately waiting for signs of Debbie to make sure she was okay. She had initially heard Debbie's screams, then saw her being dragged towards the first-class section just as another terrorist has waved a gun in her face and told her to sit down. Laura remembered talking to both this man and the women who were now terrorizing the passengers and hurting her friend.

Laura recalled that they had recently got engaged, and she was pregnant. She was definitely appeared to be the more confident of the two, which is unusual for their religious background, but at the time, that just made Laura laugh. It's about time men were put in their place.

Now, she understood the situation. The female was definitely in charge, and they probably hardly knew each other.

Malika turned to Debbie. 'Stop your whimpering. You will ask the captain to open the cockpit door and I will explain what our demands are. No one will get off this plane alive unless our demands are met.'

Debbie, still shaking and struggling not to cry, knew this was one demand that wasn't going to happen. Since 9/11, cockpit-door entry was by way of an electronic code system and there was no way the captain or co-pilot would allow access under any circumstances. Even the door frame was made of reinforced steel which meant it would cope with a small explosive charge and also the impact of being rammed by the heaviest item on the plane, a food/drinks trolley. Debbie knew it wouldn't be long before she was shot.

Malika repeated her demand with more venom. 'Shut up making a noise and ask the captain to open the cockpit door, or I will blow this plane up with every passenger on board.'

Chapter 38

Both the captain, Michael Turner and his co-pilot, Dale Stanton were quietly watching with astonishment the entire event take place from the relative safety of the cockpit. Hearing Debbie's initial scream alerted them to a possible situation, and they quickly turned on the in-cabin monitors that cover each class. They had a single 22-inch monitor that split into four smaller screens, giving them a reasonable picture of what was happening on board. Within seconds of witnessing the drama that had unfolded, the captain had reported the incident to the air traffic controllers on the ground. He only told them everything he knew and didn't second guess anything. Guessing at this stage could easily lead to misunderstandings and loss of life. Anyway, it wasn't the captain's job to offer advice or any opinions until asked, as there were experts on the ground with many years of experience who would be better positioned in this situation. Newark was the destination airport in New York, and head of airport security Todd Williams and the on-site negotiator Paul Garcia were sitting in the air traffic control tower waiting for more feedback from the captain.

Unbeknown to everyone on board, including the crew and the Terrorists, four minutes from the captain's first contact with the ground, two F14s had left the runway from the Stewart Air National Guard Base some 60 miles northeast of New York City.

Back in the cockpit of the British Airways flight, both Captain and co-pilot sat still, eyes glued to the small 22" monitor.

Captain Michael Turner, aged 42, had over 10,000 hours of experience flying large commercial aircraft and had been with British Airways for nearly six years. Whilst not an arrogant man, Michael was very confident in his own abilities and also enjoyed a good reputation with the air stewardesses, having dated several over his tenure at BA.

Dale Stanton, aged 35, on the other hand, was a relative 'newbie' on long-haul flights and, having got just celebrated his seventh wedding anniversary a week earlier, was also now an expectant father for the third time.

Whilst this was only the fourth time they had flown together, they both knew of each other's background. Whilst Dale was new to long haul, Michael was very aware that Dale was a very accomplished pilot who had been flying short-haul with BA for over 6 years. They both continued to study the monitor as Michael slowly descended the plane a few thousand feet per minute, which was part of the standard protocol in these circumstances.

'Can you believe this?' Dale asked. 'Has she got a gun? Was that explosives she had around her?'

Whilst on the small monitor, they could get the general picture of events, with the screen split 4 ways, it was impossible to see the details.

Michael responded. 'Not sure, I guess.' As he peered forward, screwing his eyes up to get a better focus on the screen. 'Looks like a gun to me. She's certainly waving something around that's got everyone scared.'

They were both jolted when the cockpit phone buzzed, and Michael Turner grabbed it. He could make out from the monitor that Debbie was on the other end.

'Hi Mike, it's Debbie. Please can you open the cockpit door so this lady can speak with you?'

'Debbie, are you okay? You know that's impossible. We have our pre-determined responses to this type of threat and there's no way we will open the door. Please put the lady onto the phone.' Debbie handed Malika the phone.

'I take it you are playing games, Mr Captain? A game with your passengers' lives. I merely want to talk to you about our demands so you can translate them to your government. This is not a polite request; it is a simple demand. Failure to allow me entry will result in loss of life.'

'Why don't you give me your list and I will forward it on to our people on the ground?' Michael responded.

'It's important we speak face to face so you can understand my demands are serious and to avoid any confusion.' Malika calmly stated.

'I am under strict orders and have very clear instructions in a situation like this and will not be opening the cockpit door,' said Michael.

'Then every two minutes you do not, one of your passengers or members of your valuable crew will die. This is not a threat; this is a promise. My watch is set for two minutes.'

Michael interrupted her, 'How can you convincingly say you only want to talk when you're threatening lives on board?'

Malika responded. 'Your job is not to think, Captain, it is to do as I ask. You need to know how important it is that you obey my instructions. Without the threat of life, you have zero incentive to act.'

Local time 11.56 pm. 5 minutes had passed since the attack.

Chapter 39

Two minutes earlier I had slowly leaned to my left to try and engage with the male passenger across the aisle. 'Can you see anything?' I whispered.

With only the slightest turn of his head, the guy gave me a flash of eye contact. 'Not a thing,' came the reply.

'We must consider doing something,' I stated desperately.

'Like what?' he answered.

'Do you think they're really going to ask for a load of demands, get them agreed and land the plane?' We then all get off and return to our loved ones safely? I said and then continued. 'When was the last time you heard a government, especially a British or American one, caving in the terrorists' demands?'

'Never. Or certainly not for years, possibly 30 or 40.' he replied.

'So what's gonna happen here? They crash the plane into a building, killing us all and everyone on the ground.' I said.

'Maybe, possibly, probably… don't know. They did say they have a list of demands, and once they've got them, they will let us all go,' the guy responded.

'Really. You think that's gonna happen?' I replied.

We both sat back in our seats and contemplated the point. This key point may well define the rest of our lives. We both looked at each other, both frowning, both waiting for the other to answer. We knew the answer to the question, or at least we thought we did.

He asked, 'What should we do?

I replied, 'What's your name?'

'Robert, or Bob, call me Bob.'

'Well, Bob, I'm David and I have no idea.'

My body started to heat up again, and my mouth started to produce lots of saliva. I shivered, even though I was hot. We have to do something! But what could we do? If I tried anything, I would surely be killed, and worse still, other passengers could get hurt. What's the point of risking my life, when there's a good chance we will be saved? Yes, there might be some negotiations but ultimately we would survive. I just had to sit back and not make any sudden movements that bring any attention to myself. Under no circumstances make any eye contact with the terrorists, and everything would be fine. Yes, I'd have a story to tell my grandchildren, but that's about it.

I closed my eyes and I immediately saw my children again. I saw us all in the new house having a summer barbeque. Hayley and I were relaxing in our new loungers and James with I were sharing a cold beer.

I was frightened… very frightened. I opened my eyes. Who was I kidding? Governments do not negotiate with terrorists, full stop. Both Bob and I knew that. Everyone knows that; even the terrorists must know that. There's more chance of the US government blowing us out of the sky than them giving in to the ransom demands. There must be 100 protocols for this situation and none of them allowed for any demands to be met. That would open up the floodgates for every terrorist in the world to start kidnapping and hijacking anything that moved.

Did this mean the terrorists were not planning on anything other than directing this plane into a major government building or a hospital?

Did this mean we were all going to die, and many more would perish on the ground?

Surely, it pretty much guaranteed that the plane would explode at some stage? Either because the terrorists achieved their objectives, or the US government theirs?

The reality of my thoughts and logic brought tears of fear to my eyes. The salt from the tears stung, and I clasped my hands over my face. Why was I on this plane? Why had God chosen today as the day my life on earth would end? Would he look after my son James and my two beautiful daughters, Abby and Sarah? Would he comfort Hayley and the rest of my family?

I never claimed to be a great father, but my children had the right to expect me to be around to guide them into adult life. James needed me. Life and other people can be so cruel and I needed to be there to protect my daughters, keep them out of harm's way. I wanted to buy them their first cars. I wanted so many things. My life was only halfway through and I still had so much to do.

David, pull yourself together! Get a grip, for Heaven's sake. Pray. Talk to God.

I wiped my eyes once more and closed them to talk to our Heavenly Father. I begged him to look after my children and watch over them as they grew up. I asked him to keep James away from any serious illnesses. I asked him to console Hayley and hoped that someday she may know him as her Father. I prayed my own parents and Hayley's would live a long life. I prayed for my siblings, Martin and Julia, that they will live happy and healthy lives.

I then prayed for everyone else on the plane that in dying, none of us would know the fear that we were going to die. That they would be encouraged by what the terrorists had said and feel confident they would see their families again.

I have often felt sick at the thought of a planeload of passengers in air disasters, having minutes to contemplate their forthcoming deaths. Simply crashing into a mountain or being blown up must protect them from that horrible feeling that you know death is coming.

Lastly, I prayed for strength and wisdom. Strength to face my passing without the fear of its coming and the knowledge that I would see my family again in the next life. I also prayed for wisdom to help me find a way out, however tiny the possibility may be. That everyone on the plane would survive, and if the plane was to crash, I prayed for people on the ground.

For the first time in seemingly ages (even though the drama had only unfolded less than 10 minutes before), I felt a little peace. God *is* great. His promise that prayers would be answered, all be it in his timeframe, gave me some comfort. God would look out for my children and the rest of my family.

The rest. Could I do anything right now on this plane that would make a difference? I had no idea.

'Bob...'

'Yep?'

'We can't just sit here. At some stage, we have to try something.'

'What can we do? They all seemed to have guns and explosives strapped to them. Don't forget they said they had some demands, and once satisfied, we would be okay,' Bob replied.

'I don't know, but we cannot just sit here and wait to die. Are you with me?'

'To do what?' Bob asked.

'I don't know yet, but I need to know I'm not alone.'

Both Bob and I were in exactly the same position. We were both terrified by the prospect of having to take action,...action that would surely prove to be fruitless and possibly result in getting everyone on board killed.

A man sitting in front of me, who must have heard us talking, turned around and looked at Bob. 'You heard what they said. Don't try anything, and we'll be alright.'

'Do you honestly believe that?' I said.

'Yes... no... yes. But they haven't blown us up yet, so they must be planning on landing the plane and getting away.'

'Do you really believe they have smuggled loads of explosives and weapons on board, and they're simply going to hand a list of demands to the pilot, get a few million quid and escape in a private jet already waiting for them fully fuelled?' I argued.

'I don't know, but let's at least give the authorities a chance to negotiate,' the man said.

'Negotiate,' Bob replied. 'Since when does the US government negotiate with terrorists?'

'Since never,' I piped up.

The man continued. 'Well, we shouldn't try anything that's going to compromise a rescue mission. Starting trouble can only lead to people getting shot at, and I'm sitting close to both of you, and I don't fancy getting shot.'

I looked at the lady next to me. Her hands were clasped together, and eyes closed. She was mumbling, probably praying.

The man returned to face forward, and I felt a little stunned by what he had said.

After a few moments, I asked Bob, 'How many terrorists do you think there are?'

'Don't know. I've seen two, but I've heard a third. A women's voice, right at the start.'

'Could there be more?'

'Definitely. We can only see into the business from here where the one guy is, but first class is another 30 to 40 feet away.' Bob had wondered the same thing about their numbers.

I replied, 'I'm pretty sure there's only one back in economy. If there were more, surely they would keep one in our premium economy section as well?'

'From what I've seen, our man, who was sitting just ahead of us, might be in charge of us and the economy, as he keeps popping his head in checking in on us,' Bob reasoned.

'That leaves three known, but possibly more in first.'

'Agreed,' Bob nodded. 'What can we do? They all seem to have guns. Let's let it go. I bet there's an air marshal on board, and he and the crew will have a plan for this sort of thing.' he begged.

'I don't know,' I replied. 'I don't know.'

Chapter 40

Bob (Robert) Wilson was a 42-year-old divorced financial controller. He worked for a large international corporation whose head office was in New York but that had operations in several European countries such as, England. He had been in the UK for just over six weeks, helping them implement a new management information system. His job was largely the reason he was divorced, as he spent over half his time travelling around the US states and, from time to time, Europe. It was on return from such a trip nearly four years ago that he came home to find his house virtually empty. His then-wife Susan had finally lost patience with him and his trips away. So she had packed most of the house up and moved away to be nearer her parents. Subsequently, he found out that she had been having an affair for the last year of the marriage, but at the time of their divorce, that relationship had also ended. He wasn't bitter or twisted that she'd left him, but he was angry that the large black sofa bed they had in the downstairs front room had gone with her. Bob had fallen asleep on that sofa so many times and felt he had lost a long-time friend. Bob didn't even blame her for leaving him or the affair. His closest friends had constantly warned him that if a man spends so much time away on business unless the relationship was really strong, they would always find sustaining a marriage very difficult.

Bob had always been a simple man with only one hobby: bass fishing. Even when he was living back home, he spent most weekends getting up early and going fishing either on his own or on a small boat with his friends. Being divorced hadn't changed his life much, other than the anniversary or birthday sex he now wasn't getting. He had been pretty much a loner growing up, with no other siblings, and that was probably why he was so attracted to fishing. He could fish on his own and not speak to anyone else for hours on end.

He and his two buddies he now fished with were all members of a local fishing club. They were not at all like Bob. They both loved the American hunting and fishing scene and spent most of their time fishing together, bragging about their exploits with either a big gun or fishing rod. On several occasions, they had asked Bob to join them on a hunt, but he always politely refused, choosing instead to enjoy the relative peace and tranquillity of the open space of a lake and the challenge of finding that perfect specimen of bass. Shooting an animal for pleasure seems like cheating, and Bob never did or ever considered doing anything that wasn't fair. That's why his career in finance suited him perfectly. You can't hide or change the numbers… they are what they are.

Right now, Bob was trying to do the maths. The guy sitting across the aisle called David had posed a number of very serious questions, but frustratingly, there were no logical answers. There were no facts or figures to contemplate, but there were lots of what-*ifs* and *maybes*, for which all the answers appeared to be terrifying.

He tried to consider the options, even though he hated even thinking about them:

1. Would the terrorists let them land and leave the plane safely? Possibly, probably. He didn't know.

2. Would the governments give in to the terrorists' demands? No. Probably not. No, definitely not. How could they?

3. Could he and this other passenger really make a difference? No, what could they do? After all, the terrorists had guns and explosives.

After going over these options 3 times, his conclusion was that his best hope was to not make any more eye contact with the other passenger who called himself David across the aisle and hope he wouldn't try anything.

Chapter 41

I now started to contemplate getting shot. What would it feel like? I've heard on TV it's like a burning sting and the force pushes you back. At this close range, it would make one hell of a mess, although that depends on the gun used. How do I even know the guns are real? How the hell did they get them on the plane? Plus, that dynamite: why didn't it set off the alarms or sniffer dogs in security? Maybe they had a guy in security or maybe somebody had planted them on board before take-off and they simply retrieved them from a hiding place. If they fired at me and missed and the bullet penetrated the fuselage, would that bring the whole plane down with the loss of cabin pressure? Would I be responsible for killing loads of people who otherwise may have walked free after some tough negotiations with the authorities?

I had some serious thinking to do… and zero time to do it. My business life is all about making decisions, most of which are already ordained because the problems you're trying to solve have already happened hundreds of times before and there's typically a solution. In most cases, there was a right and wrong action. Yes, you needed to take some calculated risks and even needed the courage of your own convictions when making bigger ones, but ultimately the solution to all problems was out there somewhere.

However, in this situation what could I really do? What could both Bob and I do? Would any of the other passengers come to our aid? At the very moment of any action, would I freeze myself? I wasn't strong enough to take on gun-wielding terrorists with dynamite strapped to their waists who probably wanted to die. I don't want to die, but they do: hardly a fair fight and that's even if the opportunity presented itself. Plus, how much force could I use?

This question became a huge one and allowed me to at least focus on one key factor for a few seconds. How much force could I use? Am I allowed to cause significant injury or even death? Surely not? That goes against the whole fabric of my existence. 'Thou shalt not take another man's life'. It is a pretty clear commandment and is not open to interpretation. Especially as I would be the attacker. It's not like I'm defending myself against an attack and then using deadly force to protect myself.

But would I be? Were these people going to kill us?

Suppose they were telling the truth and eventually they would let us go. Maybe I was looking at this all wrong? Surely that's the first question that needed to be answered, and then I'd come back to the bigger question. Were they going to fly the plane into a building, killing us and people on the ground?

Bizarrely I started acting as if this was a business problem, that would eventually bring me a solution, or at the very least answer my question based on the laws of probability.

Firstly, what exactly did I know?

There were three terrorists and at least one had dynamite strapped to their waists. What was that for? Simply to scare us? Why bother; surely the guns would be enough? What about the first terrorist: did she have explosives strapped to her or just a gun?

I kept coming up with more questions and no answers. The important question was: 'Are these guys genuine and would the government really give in to demands and let them land safely without blowing up the plane? Surely the answer was no on both accounts. So, David, what exactly does that mean and are you of a sound mind and judgment in making that decision? Is my answer to these questions probably correct… or is it beyond reasonable doubt? Which one? This was so difficult, so out of my comfort zone. This wasn't a movie or a passage from an article I'd read somewhere, this was real life!

Louder in my head: 'Are these terrorists going to let us live or are they going to try to crash the plane, killing us all? And in trying, will the US government protect those innocent citizens on the ground by blowing the plane up before it was allowed to achieve its objective?'

I felt like I was on trial, in a witness box, trying to answer a billion-dollar, live-or-die question: would the government give in to the terrorists?

My brain was frazzled up and to give myself a breather I leaned across to Bob.

'Are these guys going to kill us all?' I whispered.

He didn't reply. 'Bob, we both need to take action.' I said slightly louder.

He continued to ignore me.

'Bob. Please speak to me.' I begged. 'Bob!'

Bob slowly turned his head and faced me.

I asked him again: 'Are these guys going to kill us all?'

Bob looked at me solemnly. He had been thinking of nothing else. After a few more seconds had passed, Bob replied softly. 'Yes, I believe they are.'

On hearing his answer, I inhaled a huge amount of cabin air and then replied. 'So do I, Bob, so do I. No government can afford to give in to demands. Why go through all the trouble of hijacking a plane only to give up after some tough negotiations? Unless we do something, we are all going to die.'

After a few seconds, Bob responded again in the same tone as before. 'Yes, I think that's probably true.'

Question asked *Milord* (as if still in court) and question answered. In a way, it was both refreshing *and* terrifying to have come to a conclusion; Trouble is, it meant that we were most certainly going to die!

Both Bob and I had a very personal moment together. He reached out to shake my hand, but we ended up holding hands. We gripped each other tightly.

Now that someone else had helped me validate my own thoughts, we had other, terrifying decisions to make. What do we do now? Unfortunately, the answer hadn't changed one tiny bit since I last considered the question. We had to take a step forward into the situation. We had to do something! We couldn't sit there and hope and pray someone else would. The trouble was, action meant going on the attack. How the hell was that going to happen? I had nothing. No weapon, no skills, and no plan.

Plus, of course, there was he question of what action was acceptable to take. How much force can be used to overpower the terrorists? I somehow already knew the answer and simply put, it was 'deadly' force, but whilst that might (only just) have been right for this situation, isn't it better if I can just overpower them and tie them up without hurting him. Plus, I've not even scowled at someone for nearly 25 years, let alone wrestled for my life with a gunman with dynamite strapped to his body. Will I get the time to tie them up? Yes - with Bob's help. But what would I use for rope? Plus as soon as I charge at this first one, if he doesn't kill me with the first shot, his buddies will be all over me in a flash.

I knew I had to use brute, quick, and if needed, deadly force. It had to be over in seconds, as I could not afford to spend time tying a guy up. Perhaps if we raised our voices the terrorist who we think is covering the economy and premium economy section would come over to investigate and tell us to shut up. Then, when he turned his back, we could jump him. But suppose we initially knocked him out and then, just as in the movies, when our backs are turned he wakes up and detonates his dynamite?

My thoughts came crashing back to *deadly* force. I popped my head up again and looked around the cabin and peered back into the economy section. Surely there were other passengers thinking the same as me. I tried to make eye contact with some other men, but they just turned away or put their heads down.

My knees were banging together and my mouth was full of fluids. My pulse had quickened and I felt physically sick with fear and expectation.

How do you disarm or even kill someone in a pre-meditated way anyway? In fact, how do you kill someone full stop?

Chapter 42

The fourth and youngest 'sleeper' terrorist Edward Beech was trying his best to casually look down the aisle. It appeared as if everything was going to plan. 'Praise be to Allah'. He whispered to himself. He had heard a female voice shouting earlier and knew there was one of the group standing at the end of the economy section. He wouldn't be needed after all. After the initial attack and once the screaming had stopped, it all felt surprisingly calm. He guessed there was some negotiation going on with the people on the ground and at some stage an announcement would be made. He silently thanked Allah again for the success of the mission thus far and the fact that it had appeared to have gone without incident.

Chapter 43

Local time 11.57 am.

Captain Michael Turner was on the phone to the ground and was giving feedback on the situation to a senior member of the security services as well as Paul Garcia the hostage negotiator. 'It doesn't look good. She's made threats and still insists she has a list of demands but wants to give them face-to-face. That means opening the cockpit door.'

'Which under no circumstances are you going to do,' came the reply from Todd Williams, the airport security chief. The FBI and Government Counter Terrorism departments had been notified and were en route to the airport. However, the FBI were already connected three-way to the call and could hear the captain talking.

FBI special agent Harris spoke: 'Captain, in your opinion, are they bluffing or do they really mean to negotiate? Sorry, I'll rephrase: in approximately one minute's time, will they kill a hostage?'

'I simply don't know the answer to that. They must have prepared for this and know they have to follow through on their threats otherwise we won't take them seriously,' the captain responded.

Negotiator Paul Garcia Harris spoke. 'We must stall for more time. Tell them you have asked for authority to open the door from your boss and are waiting for a reply. Tell her it's not your call to make. We need time to identify these guys, so at least we know who we're dealing with.'

Agent Harris then diverted his next question to Todd: 'Do we have the flight manifest and can we get the on-flight video footage of where these terrorists were sitting?'

'The last 30 minutes of footage is being downloaded to your office as we speak and it will take around five minutes to download. You should have the email covering the passenger list already.'

There was some movement and noise from the FBI's end. Agent Harris came back to the line.

'Passenger list received. You've sent us footage from all cabins?'

'Yes,' came Mike's reply. Without the passengers being aware, Mike had been reducing the plane's height since the attack had started. Standard protocol told him to get to 25,000 feet where the plane's own internet wireless system allowed communication with the ground. This allowed the on-board videos to be streamed to the tower. This could happen 'live' at 15,000 feet, but at 25,000 feet it can only be sent through as a recorded message. Reducing the height to only 15,000 feet would alarm the terrorists, and also not give enough time for them to react if intervention was required. Without knowing this, another upside of this move was that the F14s could fly comfortably for a much longer time at 25,000 feet versus 35,000.

The captain pressed the call button and Debbie answered, clearly terrified and still sobbing, only too aware that two precious minutes had passed since the terrorists had made the threat. 'Debbie, this is Mike. Please pass the phone to the lady.'

Malika grabbed the phone. 'Do we have agreement Mr Captain, or will you stand by and listen to your crew member dying outside your door? Her life is in your hands'

Mike responded, 'I have asked the ground for permission to open the cockpit door, and they are getting permission, but I need more time. It's standard protocol, I'm not authorized to open it myself and need the big boss to give permission. Please, I am not stalling, I just need permission.'

Aggressively, Malika responded, 'You are lying Mr Captain. Any second now one member of your crew will be lying dead and her blood will be on your hands.'

'I promise I'm not deceiving you. Please, I beg you, please give me more time. Let me know some of your demands and I can get things started.'

'Where are your superiors and how long will they be?' Malika asked.

Relieved about the possible breakthrough and knowing the team on the ground were listening, Mike took it upon himself to answer. He had several years of training for this type of situation and whilst he couldn't remember every single protocol exactly, his general persona gave him the confidence to engage. He had no idea what another 10 minutes would give him or his fellow passengers, but it might allow everyone to consider another plan or at the very least keep Debbie alive for the time being.

'Five to six minutes only. He's been contacted and is rushing to the tower as we speak. Please, five more minutes.'

Malika considered this and as it fell roughly in line with her plan: it would enable them to get close enough to the Eastern seaboard, which in turn would only bring them closer to her target.

'Okay, I am reasonable, but do not take one second more than five minutes. Also, get ready to transfer five million dollars to a bank account at the same time. One million dollars for every minute I have given you. Get a pen.' A few seconds passed before Malika spoke again. 'The account details are 33012719177816, code 20-39-11.' After a short pause, she repeated them.

Malika had memorized the numbers and this was part of the false message of hope that this was indeed a simple hostage takeover. If there was money to be collected from a bank account in the Caymans, surely the terrorists planned to be around to spend it. She repeated the number and hung up.

What she didn't realize was that her message of false hope had actually set alarm bells running off on the ground.

Head of airport security, Todd Williams, was the first to respond… with his finger on the mute button that held the captain's line.

'Five million dollars. Is that all? Who hijacks a planeload full of passengers, that's worth one hundred million dollars and asks for just five? We have a serious and deadly problem.'

Paul asked the question to everyone, 'Are you sure the five million's not simply linked to the five minutes?'

Agent Harris chipped in before Todd could answer. 'Not a chance. These terrorists are extremely well prepared, well-educated and they wouldn't take a mission on like this for a lousy five million dollars. They must have known we would try and ask for time at some stage, and she had the bank account numbers well-rehearsed because when she repeated them, they were the same. Plus, have you ever heard of a terrorist who keeps asking for different amounts of cash?'

'Okay, but let's not alarm the captain, so stop discussing the subject matter immediately,' stated Todd forcefully.

He released his finger and immediately the captain came back on. 'Hello ground, hello ground…'

'We have you Mike. Just lost comms for a brief moment. We have the bank details and whilst I'm not authorized to agree to the payment, I am sure it's doable. Give us a few minutes to review the footage and we'll get back to you.'

'Will do, thanks Todd.' Captain Turner hung up.

'She gave in too quickly to the extra five minutes, didn't she?' Negotiator Paul Garcia said.

'Yes she did and that means we have a large object, flying at 500 miles an hour, 25% full of gasoline heading for an unknown destination somewhere close to New York.' Agent Harris grimly commented.

Chapter 44

Now I had established the rules of engagement, I asked myself 'Why me? Why not someone else on the plane?' Surely there were braver people on the plane than me. Maybe even ex-military or the police force. Why should it be me? There must be other passengers thinking what I was thinking, coming to the same conclusion as I had.

Surely, as soon as I rose up in rebellion, tens of other passengers would join me and we would easily overpower the terrorists. But I have seen the movies and nobody does that. Everyone sits there, not wishing to engage, fearful the attack won't work and the idiot is left at the mercy of the terrorists and gets killed.

Maybe the right question was 'Why shouldn't it be me?'

Why was I so special I could sit back and do nothing because I was scared? Why should I sit and hope and expect someone else to step up and save my life, whilst endangering their own? I was supposed to be a CEO, which stands for Chief Executive Officer, not Chief Coward. Yet I wanted to be a coward. I wanted someone else to save the day but couldn't ignore the simple truth; I had to take action. I had to step up like I ask my senior people to step up: 'Try and be courageous, don't back away from things that frighten you.' I've always tried to tell my children the same thing. To die with my fellow passengers, knowing more would die on the ground and I did nothing, simply wouldn't do. I closed my eyes and prayed again. 'Dear Lord my father, please forgive my sins and those sins I have committed against other people. You know exactly the situation I'm in. You know that hundreds of people are soon to lose their lives. Please give me courage and strength …and luck to help the situation. To overcome the obstacles before me. Give Bob the same courage; help us both. Please watch over us in our endeavours.'

I had more tears streaming down my cheeks; I was in a terrible state. I seemed to feel these were my last words I would ever speak to God.

Could I really do it? Could Bob? Bob seemed like a nice guy, smart... the sort of guy you meet at a business convention. But he wasn't a very big person. How the hell did I know I wouldn't bottle it... that we both wouldn't? I knew nothing about this man and he knew nothing about me, except I might be the person that causes the end of his life.

A plan was needed, but what about the explosives they carried on their waistcoats: could they be dummies? Could they have passed through security? Yes and no, and of course they could have been hidden onboard anyway.

I still had the niggling doubt that I might be bringing the plane down, killing everyone, when it could have ended peacefully.

I had seen movies where suicide bombers have triggers that they hold in their hands to set off the explosives, but I hadn't seen either of the two terrorists carrying anything other than the guns. Maybe there was a simple button on the waistcoats they pressed. But how could that be? It would have been very risky wearing the waistcoat all day and on a plane for seven hours in case somebody bumped into you and set it off by accident. Maybe there were remote detonators. But how could they do that 35,000 feet up? Maybe they were fake explosives?

I looked towards Bob. 'Bob.'

'Yep, what's the plan?' He replied.

'Those sticks of dynamite are fake.'

Bob's face lit up. 'How do you know?'

'Because how else would they have got through customs? The security screens, the sniffer dogs. And they couldn't have been hidden on the plane already before we boarded as the sniffer dogs check the planes out as well. Plus, where would they hide them? Their waistcoats, assuming the females got one on, are pretty bulky.'

'I've never seen sniffer dogs checking a plane out before,' Bob said.

'I don't know how, but I bet they were around somewhere. You don't think they want us to see lots of dogs sniffing around for explosives just before we board? It would freak half the passengers out.'

'True. Makes sense. But supposing you're wrong.'

I had no reply. I wasn't even convinced of my own bullshit. I was scratching around for positives and needed to convince both Bob and I, that we had a chance.

I looked at Bob; both of us looked like we'd been 10 rounds with Mike Tyson. Sweating, puffed up faces, hands trembling and bloodshot eyes from crying…we were in a right mess.

The lady to my right nudged me. 'What have you been talking about? Are we going to be alright? Are we going to die? The man with the gun said we would be safe and home with our families. Do you know what's going to happen?'

I considered telling her the truth for a few seconds, but resisted. 'Yes, it's probably going to be alright.'

I didn't think she could be *that* passenger who could step up and help. At that moment, she seemed so timid, so young and afraid. 'All we can do is pray we will be alright and that the authorities will work with them to release us,' I said in a soft voice.

'But governments never negotiate with terrorists,' came her reply. 'We all know that. So, what are they hoping to achieve?'

I had nothing for her. No words of comfort, no bullshit, not anything. I agreed with her 100%. She seemed to start to answer her own question. 'That's means…' but I interrupted her. 'That means we must pray that another solution comes up, or at the very least we get to land and hope the security forces rescue us.'

She took my hand. 'Please pray with me.'

It's amazing how we turn to God in our hour of need. Whoever your own God is or whatever you believe in, we get great comfort knowing there might be or is someone out there that we can reach out to.

Sometimes I feel embarrassed that I only seem to want to talk to God when I need help or I want something. But deep down I know it doesn't matter to God. Whoever we are, whatever we are, He loves us all.

This lady's hands were shaking and her eyes closed tightly. We sat there for 10 to 15 seconds before she opened them again and then I spoke. 'My name's David.'

'Elizabeth.' came the reply, as we both parted our hands and returned to our own little worlds.

At that very moment, I saw them. One grey object was about half a mile to our right and on looking to the left-hand side of the plane I saw the other. I had no idea what type of planes they were, but I could see from the one to my right that it had missiles attached to its undercarriage. 'Shiiiit' I muttered under my breath.

'Bob.' Bob looked across. 'We need to go. Time's running out,' I said as I beckoned him to look out of my window.

'Bloody Hell. Are they hear to protect us or…?' His voice trailed off and he never finished the sentence.

What a huge call someone, probably the President of the United States, would make or had already made. Blow up a passenger airline for the greater good of those on the ground or not. It would send a strong message to any potential future terrorists that America will take any steps required to protect the people on American soil. What else could the reason be for them being there? This actually helped reinforce my decision.

I had a window - albeit probably a very small one - to try and make a difference that day. Not only for all the passengers on board but for their friends and relatives on the ground. Yes, people obviously suffer when they die, but it's those friends and relatives left behind that can suffer for an eternity. If there were 300 people on board that flight that must mean 3,000 relatives and possibly 30,000 friends impacted by their deaths. I had to find a way to try!

Chapter 45

'Bob, when the guy from economy pops his head around our cabin, you put your hand up to grab his attention. Say something like you need to use the toilet because you feel sick. He'll refuse and walk back and that's when we both jump him. Full force, holding nothing back. We push him down and I punch him as hard and fast as I can, whilst you get his gun. Don't let him go for his jacket or do anything with his hands. If need be, stamp on then, and stamp hard enough to break them. Understood?'

'Really! That's your plan? And then what?' Bob asked, almost mocking my pathetic plan.

I continued. 'And then we rush the guy in business class and either shoot him or overpower him. Hopefully, at that stage, other passengers would have joined in.'

Bob responded. 'What other passengers?' The lady to my left is still crying to herself and hasn't spoken a word and you have another passenger a few seats ahead who will probably get up and help the terrorist.'

'I don't know, but what I do know, is that if we do nothing, we'll all die. That we are both agreed on, right?' I said.

Bob placed his head in his hands that were almost shaking uncontrollably. He looked up. 'Tell me the plan again.'

I repeated what I had just said and probably missed some points out because I didn't really have a plan and certainly not a fool-proof one. 'Just get his attention and I will jump him.' I repeated for the third time.

The moment of truth!

'Yes. Fucking yes,' Bob replied looking directly at me, trying to psych himself up.

As if my body was completely rejecting any idea of me trying to disarm a man who had explosives strapped to his body, I started to hyperventilate. I felt like someone was strangling me: I couldn't breathe and started to feel dizzy. I thought I was going to have some kind of seizure. I wasn't up to this and my body knew it and was going to make me pass out rather than let me go ahead. I started taking short breaths trying to calm myself down. Could I really do this? No, I couldn't!

I looked across at Bob and he himself looked as white as a sheet. We might mentally be able to go through with this, but were our bodies going to fail us? Much to my horror, he closed his eyes and then pressed the call button and the whole cabin heard the 'ping' as his overhead attendant light came on. With strained faces, everyone turned their head towards Bob's seat.

The terrorist, who I had named T3 popped his head around the cabin and then disappeared into the section between cabins. Every second felt like a minute and my fear left me shaking and nauseous. I lost control of my bladder and felt a wet patch forming at the front of my trousers. I tried to stop it, but couldn't. I undid my seat buckle and somehow managed to place the buckles on top of each other so as not to arouse suspicion. T3 walked up the aisle towards Bob's seat and dropped his head to Bob's.

'What do you want?'

'Can I... I need to use the toilet?' Bob stuttered.

'No-one uses the toilet. You have been told and will not be told again. Stay in your seats.' The terrorists replied.

As Bob lowered his head, T3 turned to go back to the economy and I leapt out of my seat. Unfortunately, I hadn't pulled my arm rest up and I caught it with my thigh and winced out loud and this mistake cost me a valuable second and reduced my element of surprise. I pulled the armrest up and steadied myself, but then pathetically threw myself at the terrorist, who had now heard me get up and turned back towards me. My arms reached, not his upper body as planned, but his waist as I tried to grab onto him. I pushed my legs forward to try and push him backwards, but he had the better stance and easily repelled my efforts. That lost second had cost me dearly! In an almost comical way, I was trying to wrestle a man with a loaded gun and failing miserably. He then managed to push me backwards nearly onto my seat, and just before I landed exactly back where I started, I saw Bob's face staring blankly straight ahead of him. My own expression said, 'Bob, please help me'. But Bob was frozen with fear and didn't move an inch. I put one last effort in and raised my left arm towards the terrorist's face and then there was a loud bang, as his gun went off.

Chapter 46

There was mass hysteria on the plane as passengers screamed aloud. T2 rushed into the cabin and shouted at T3.

'Are you alright, my brother?' Ahmad asked

'Yes, I am. This fool tried to attack me; I had no choice but to kill him. It was him or me.'

Dalmair looked down at the lifeless body. The posh lady continued to scream as she stared at her own blouse that now had a bright red spray across her shoulder. Ahmad slapped her face and she went silent.

Malika arrived seconds later, speaking to everyone in the premium economy section: 'This is what will happen to you all if you don't obey our commands. I have promised you will survive, but if you are foolish, you will die.'

Dalmair was shaking from the incident, horrified that his own actions had resulted in another man's death. 'Dalmair, look at me,' Malika demanded.

'You are a brave man. A brave solider. You have done the right thing. Our whole mission might have failed.'

Dalmair looked at Malika. 'I know, sister, I know.'

Chapter 47

Edward was shaking uncontrollably. Having first heard a passenger call out and now a gunshot, something had gone wrong and he had to take action. He nervously unbuckled his seatbelt and started to get up from his seat. Other passengers around him thought he was a hero, trying to help the situation and one even put their hand on his shoulder and tried to pull him back down. Edward tried to reach down to grab his knife from his sock. He reached for the knife and felt the warm handle, but for some reason couldn't seem to pull the knife out. The young child that had befriended Edward's name was Juliet and she and her sister were screaming and his mind was racing. Could he put the knife to her throat? Could he harm her?

He saw a lady running down the aisle from the far end of the plane. She was waving a gun and shouting. Another man had also appeared and was heading in the direction of where the commotion was coming from. Edward paused for a few seconds and the woman raised her voice and started talking. Someone had been shot and her confident and powerful voice reminded everyone of the severity of the situation.

She appeared to have things under control. The plane was relatively quiet again and the girl's mother in the seat in front of Edward held her arms over Juliet to smother her sounds. Edward slumped back into his seat, extremely relieved.

Chapter 48

Local time 12.01 pm.

The cabin quietened down but further along the plane in the cockpit, a horrified Captain Mike Turner was studying the inflight cameras. He had seen the passenger's actions and was reporting the incident back to the tower.

'And then the gun appeared to go off and the passenger was thrown back in his seat,' Mike commented.

'Was it deliberate, Mike? Could the terrorist have avoided it?' Todd asked.

'I can't tell… but what we do now know for sure it that they have loaded weapons. A tough way to find out,' Mike answered.

Trying to change the subject, head of security Todd Harris asked the Captain: 'How you guys doing on gas, Mike?'

'Are you kidding me? The terrorists have just shot a passenger' Mike responded loudly.

'Mike, you're in charge and responsible for all the other 300+ passengers, and you need to stay focussed. There's nothing you can do for that passenger. What do the fuel gauges show?' Todd asked. After a few moments, Mike responded.

'All good for now. Regulations state we must carry about 40 minutes more than we need, so add that to our planned fuel load, we have about 40 to 50 minutes, dependent on air speed. The female terrorist has just returned to the first-class cabin and I'm going to engage with her to try and calm things down.'

Before the captain could reach for the phone, it rang.

'Where is your superior? You only have two minutes left. And have you paid the money into the account yet?' Malika demanded.

'He's arrived at the airport and is rushing through the terminal to get to the tower to talk to you. More concerning is your actions towards the passengers. You told us you were talking hostages, not looking to hurt people. What the hell happened back there?' The Captain demanded.

'It's the passenger's fault. He tried to attack my brother and we warned you and everyone what would happen if you failed to follow our instructions. What should concern you more is the life of your crew member I am going to execute in two minutes and the rest of the passengers if I decide to blow up the plane. I must also give you one more instruction: the two fighter aircraft that have now joined us need to back away. They are too close. I realize they are part of your protocol, but I don't want to see them, so tell them to back away,' Malika said.

In a stronger tone, the captain demanded 'But what about the passenger whose been shot. Please let one of the crew assist him or make an announcement asking for a doctor on board and I need some reassurance you will not harm any more of my passengers and crew. I am trying to resolve this peacefully.'

Ignoring the Captain's question, Malika said firmly 'Then you need to follow my instructions now. I want you to turn the plane 18 degrees north, away from New York.'

'What about my passenger whose been shot?' The captain demanded again.

In a softer, but confident tone Malika replied. 'He does not need a doctor.' And not wanting to give the Captain time to react, Malika repeated her instruction again. 'I want you to turn the plane 18 degrees north, away from New York. Do as I asked…and tell those Jets to disappear!

Having regrettably understood exactly what this meant and with a heavy heart and after a sorrowful look exchanged between the Captain and his Co-pilot, the Captain responded. 'You have taken the life of an innocent passenger. You have destroyed an entire family.'

Malika's response was clear and very simple. 'Captain, there are no innocent people on this plane.'

'At the very least please give me the seat number of the passenger.' The Captain requested.

'This is not of great importance now. I will find out but this man brought this on himself. He tried to attack my brother and I told you and the passengers to sit quietly and that if they did they would all be okay. He chose to ignore these simple instructions.' Malika answered.

More thoughtful and not wishing to antagonise the terrorists the Captain asked. 'Where do you intend for us to land?'

'That is not your concern right now. What you should be concerned about is saving the life of your crew member. Do as I have instructed and turn the plane.'

The captain gradually turned the plane and reported back the instructions to the tower. 'At least that's a relief: now we're headed up the east coast, rather than into New York City. It ties into the hostage scenario.'

Special agent Harris intervened, trying to bring some form of positivity to the desperate situation. 'That's good news, captain. And we have more news: we have identified the lead terrorists from the footage you sent. She is an ex-school teacher from Yemen, who got into some bad company, which led to her joining a militant group. Last known location was a training camp in Pakistan. She's on our watch list but was not seen as a significant threat. This ties into her story of this being a hostage situation rather than a suicide, kill-everyone situation. Her name's Malika Al-Umari. You have the green light to call her by her first name.'

'That's great news, Harris. But I need to give her something in, well, less than 90 seconds, otherwise she's going to kill one of my crew. She already proved she is prepared to take life,' the captain stated firmly.

The negotiator Paul Garcia chipped in. 'Mike, try and engage her on a personal level. Definitely call her by her first name. Ask her if she would trade anything else for another five minutes. The fact you're now not heading directly for land is a good thing and any more time will allow us to come up with other solutions. Ask her about her list of demands and tell her if she gives you her first two or three, we can be working on them before she allows the plane to land.'

'Understood,' the captain answered.

Before his last discussion with the captain, Agent Harris had been on the phone to his own superiors at the FBI in Washington. The news regarding Malika and her two associates had come through two minutes earlier. They had been quickly identified by using facial recognition data and the news was not good. Agent Harris's own boss's boss, the Deputy Director James Addison was on the line, which gave Agent Harris great cause for concern.

'Agent Harris. Malika Al-Umari, Ahmad Suqami and, we believe, Dalmair Alghamdi, are the 3 suspects on board. We cannot be sure there are just three, but that's the Intel we are going on right now. Last known location for both Malika and Ahmad was a training camp in Pakistan. The 3rd person, Dalmair Alghamdi, is not on any of the watch lists and arrived in England in April this year and promptly disappeared. He's on the standard *yellow* list of people the local authorities would like to talk to, but nothing else. Malika is a definite a *Person of Interest* who quite honestly should have been picked up going through airport security. But that's for another day. She is seen as a black risk, meaning that she represents a serious and dangerous threat to life. Part of her training involved weapons training, but from what we can gather, not explosives. The camp she was located at was a low-level threat, which ironically is a greater cause for concern.'

Agent Harris cut in. 'Does that mean… or *could* it mean… the dynamite is fake?'

'Affirmative. In the short space of time, we've had to review this, that's our conclusion. No explosives training and we don't believe they would have got through airport security if the stuff was legit. Those dogs can sniff out semtex from 100 yards away,' the Deputy Director said.

'Which means they probably plan to bring down the plane, rather than blow it up?' Agent Harris commented.

'I've spoken to the director who in turn has spoken to the Whitehouse. The bottom line: unless someone or the Lord Almighty himself intervenes, in the next 10 to 15 minutes, operation *Gemini* comes into play,' states the deputy director.

With a distinct softness in his voice, Agent Harris responded: 'And that's bad news for the 300 or so on board, and their families on the ground.'

Operation Gemini was the code name agreed upon by all the NATO countries for the action that could be taken in the worst possible scenario in a situation where a significant number of civilian lives were threatened by a terrorist group.

Never before had an order been given by the commander-in-chief of the USA or any head of any NATO country to bring down a passenger airliner. After 9/11, over ten thousand man-hours were spent with experts from around the world discussing various scenarios regarding future terrorist plots involving airplanes. There are now over 200 no-fly zones in America alone and the general principle, which wasn't up for negotiation, was that if a genuine threat existed, no plane would be allowed to get within 10 miles of the coast of America. This meant any possible threat would be an analysed right up to the last minute, but also ensure no one from land could ever witness such a tragedy.

Being President came with great power but also a great responsibility, and whilst the American and worldwide public would take many years to forgive such a decision, the decision was already pre-ordained. Yes, the President had to give the final go-ahead to the attack, but even if he changed his mind or failed in this duty, protocol would follow and his Vice President would give the order.

Captain Mike Turner pressed the call button. Outside his cockpit both Debbie and Jenny sat terrified in their seats, both holding each other tightly. Debbie had almost run out of tears and was now looking back over her life. How much had she wasted? Why hadn't she tried out for a modelling career? Even though he ruined her life, her ex had mentioned how beautiful she was a thousand times, urging her to get a portfolio done to send to lots of modelling houses. She told herself what she would do if she managed to get out of this situation. She made many promises and vowed to keep them all if only God would intervene and save her.

Chapter 49

The phone buzzed and broke Debbie from her thoughts. The terrorists grabbed it. 'Have you got good news, Captain?'

'Malika, please call me by my first name: it's Mike.'

'No games, Mr Captain. So, you think you are very clever knowing my name. I don't know how you managed to get it so quickly, but it doesn't alter anything.'

'Not at all, but I thought it's easier to use our first names,' the Captain said.

'I am not interested in becoming friends *Captain Mike*, I am interested in you opening the cockpit door and letting me talk to your boss, as in less than 30 seconds you will have blood on your hands.'

'You want to discuss terms? You want to negotiate with me?' the captain asked firmly.

'Yes, and for the sake of your crew, it must happen now.'

Malika had already decided she would probably need to kill at least one passenger to convince this guy to obey her. She knew they were not supposed to open the cockpit door in any circumstances, but then maybe the arrogance of *this* American pilot would mean she could get in there before that happens. Maybe he wants to play the American *Tarzan* to rescue his *Jane*!

Unfortunately for the Captain, Malika's judgment of him was spot on, and his over-confidence and the fact that he had found Debbie to be possibly the most attractive woman he had ever seen, meant he couldn't simply sit back and follow the rules that those 'experts' on the ground had driven into him over the last 17 years.

The captain's idea was to also buy himself some more time. More time for what exactly, he didn't know. 'You say you want to talk, and I've done what you've asked. I've changed our direction and now you should work with me a little. Malika let me come out of the cockpit and we can talk face-to-face. If you move back to the business class cabin, I will come out so we can talk.'

Malika angrily responded: 'Captain Mike, I am in charge and you will do as I want. I have the gun; I have the explosives.'

'But if you're true to your word, it's all about focusing on your demands, not hurting people.'

Malika reasoned with herself for a moment. She had another 15 minutes or so before reaching Boston and she doesn't want the captain or the people on the ground becoming suspicions of her real intentions. 'Okay, I will do as you ask. I will take your flight attendant with me and if I see anything I don't like, she will be executed. You must come out with your shirt off and hands in the air. No games, Captain Mike.'

'No games, Malika. No games.'

Pleased with himself and happy to have bought the plane another few minutes, the captain looked through the security hole in the door to see Malika enter the business class cabin. He stripped his shirt off and opened the cockpit door, but looked at his co-pilot Dale Stanton. 'Dale. This is one hell of a mess. Under no circumstances should you open this door for anyone, including me, unless I am on my own. On my own means, you can see clearly that no other person, whoever it is, is within 15 feet of me, understood?'

'You know this goes against all the security protocols Mike, even if it works, they'll throw the book at you. We are not allowed to open the doors!' Dales said and went on. 'Don't you want to ask the ground about it?

'No Dale. They can't possibly appreciate the position we are in.' The Captain said.

'But this will be the end of your career, Mike.' Dale said desperately.

'I know Dale, and it's a judgment call. Right now, we need more time and she's already taken 1 life and my crystal ball says she'll kill some of the crew. Your views are noted but I'm the captain and it's my call. It's on the voice recorder. Understood?'

'Understood, Mike. And good luck,' Dale said and he shook Mike's hand.

After taking a few deep breaths, the captain keyed in the code and slipped out the cockpit door, quickly closing it behind him. He walked a few paces and was quickly met by Malika. His first impression surprises him: she is very attractive and much younger than he thought; the inflight CCTV cameras never give a perfect picture of a person's face. His second impression was very different. Stood before him on his plane, with over 300 passengers under his care and control, was a woman, probably as scared as he was, holding a loaded weapon and wearing a waistcoat with a very visible string of dynamite sticks strapped around the front. He tried desperately to control his nerves. 'Malika, it's good to meet you face-to-face.'

Chapter 50

As soon as a significant and 'live' situation arises anywhere around the world involving a possible terrorist attack, thousands of computers and hundreds of analysts spring into action. 16 minutes had passed since the takeover on board flight BA57 and already millions of pieces of information were busy flowing through computers around the globe. Getting a fix on the terrorists' names had been a very significant and timely breakthrough. It allowed the computers to search for all data associated with those names. Any sentence that had their first or second names in it was given an amber colour, which meant over a hundred junior analysts around the world followed up leads and anything that made any connections between the names or included their names or surnames together was handled as a top priority.

There are three *super* computers in existence: one in the USA, one in Russia, and one in China. Through extensive and painful negotiations at the highest level over the last six years, these computers now actually talk to each other. Capable of passing thousands of pieces of information to each other every minute, cross-matching keywords, names, or places… all trying to find clues to the activity of known terrorist organizations. 61 different nationalities were killed in the attacks on 9/11 and even the most stubborn leaders from the largest superpowers on Earth recognized the need to work together on terrorism. So far the information had led the director of the FBI and the head of the United Kingdom's MI5 to the conclusion that the plane was going to be crashed into the ground, killing all those on board, as well as likely causing a significant number of causalities on the ground. However, this wasn't clear-cut, and the likelihood of this conclusion being correct was rated at 85%. A high enough rating to action *Gemini*, but not conclusive. The latest move to redirect the plane had led to more doubt.

Decisions made in the corridors of power were rarely 100% 'slam dunk' obvious ones. Loads of historical and present-day data were used, but rarely did it make any big decision simple.

Because the flight's departure location was England, the President of the United States, Mathew Hughes was on the phone with the British Prime Minister, Anne Simpson.

'Madam Prime Minister, I fear we are in that situation that no human being would wish on another. The collective data, combined with both our team's own analysts, suggests we have no alternative but to follow protocol Gemini.'

A little annoyed at his formalities in using her full title, Anne replied: 'Matt, cut the crap, we've known each other long enough. How long have we got, or rather how long can you wait before acting?'

Unperturbed by Anne's sharp tongue the president responded: 'Anne. At best, another 10 to 15 minutes, maybe less. Their change of direction gives us a little more time, but it doesn't change any of the possible scenarios.'

'We believe the on-board marshal was incapacitated by one of the terrorists and now the captain has left the cockpit to try and give us more time.'

'Left the cockpit?' the prime minister asked firmly.

'I know that's against protocol, but the co-pilot confirmed it was done in a secure way. The on-ground negotiator asked him to get more time and the captain used his own initiative to help save the life of a crew member.'

'But still, the change of direction could mean they are really hoping to negotiate and that this is a genuine hostage situation. Doesn't that pretty significant turn of events mean anything?' the prime minster asked.

'Not according to both our teams, Anne.'

'But still, an 85% probability that the decision's the right one still leaves a 15% probability that we are just about to blow up a passenger airliner full of over 300 souls, when we could end this peacefully.'

Speaking softly the President said: 'Anne... we both know where we are right now. We both spent time with the collective agencies around the world. The American government made a very clear and important decision over seven years ago. You yourself agreed with that decision and have the same policy for the United Kingdom.'

'I know Matt, but it stinks, it really stinks. How can it be the right move?'

The President interrupted: 'Anne, it stinks to high Heaven, but it's the right call. Yes, it's confusing that they have changed direction and my team cannot understand what possible target they have on the ground, but we have to stand firm.'

'Doesn't the 15% probability that this is the wrong decision feels like too high a number to blow one of our own planes out of the sky?' the Prime Minister asked. Before he could answer, the president's chief of staff, Ross Barkley, entered the oval room holding a laptop.

'Mr President, we have an important breakthrough.'

'Anne, please hold the line.'

'Mr President, the FBI Director has just emailed through a short video believed to be from one of the terrorists aboard our plane.'

He set the computer down on the president's desk and pressed play. The president said: 'Anne, I am putting the phone next to the laptop's speaker.'

After an initial bit of interference on the screen, it was clear this was a homemade video, the type of which they had all seen many times before. Sitting crossed-legged on the floor with a large book in front of him was Ahmad Suqami.

'I pray, Sister, please forgive my actions in taking away your last living family member. Our parent's deaths must be avenged. We cannot sit back and let the infidels in the West destroy our culture and dictate our futures. Those governments around the world must sit up listen to the voices of their mourning people and stop killing innocent people in our county.'

Ross interrupted. 'It's a classic suicide video that we intercepted from Ahmad's personal email address that's timed to be sent to his sister in Iraq at 2 pm local US time. Our next step is to check for known associates and cross-check his travel plans and activities over the last six months against other known suspects.'

Reverting to their formal titles because they were no longer alone.

'Madam Prime Minister, that nails it. This isn't going to end peacefully. The 'hostage and demand' thing is definitely a smoke screen, and I guess this takes the probability way into the 90%.'

'I hate to agree with you on this Mr President, but you're right.' After a few seconds, she continued. 'We must inform and share all the facts with the other world leaders.'

The President responded. ' My chief of staff tells me that most of the key nation's leaders have been updated and I will ensure they all get the latest news. I will stay in touch, Madam Prime Minister.'

'God help everyone onboard that plane, Mr President.' Anne said as she hung up the line.

Chapter 51

Local time 12.05 pm.

I felt very dizzy and could smell something burning. I couldn't open my eyes, but I could hear myself breathing. I had a strong stinging sensation in my chest and shoulder. Oh my God, I've been shot! It was all coming back to me. I'm heading for New York. Terrorists have taken over the plane.

I remembered the lady sitting next to me and slowly I moved my head to my right and tried to open my eyes. I still couldn't seem to open my eyes. I recalled my pathetic attempts to overpower the guy with the gun. I remembered falling backwards and then hearing a crack, which must have been his gun going off. The burning I could smell was me. The smell from the aftermath of the bullet piercing my skin. But I was still alive! I tried to focus on the sounds around me. I could hear the light humming of the plane's engines. How long had I been out? I kept trying to open my eyes, but they felt so heavy. I moved my right arm to see if I could touch the lady, but I couldn't feel her at all.

Unbeknown to me, after the screaming stopped, they moved her to another seat so she wouldn't have to sit next to a corpse.

I felt the pain even more from my chest and from my back, so I must be alive. Why from my back? How long before I bleed out and die? I started to feel more conscious and started to assess my situation. Could it be possible that everyone, including the terrorists, thinks I am dead? If that's the case, what does that mean? Again I recalled the almost comical way I tried to wrestle the terrorist, but didn't understand why my back hurt. Come on David, think!

I suddenly realized what must have happened.

Yes, it's because the bullet went straight through me. That's why - and that was maybe why I was still alive. Could the close range of the shot actually have helped to cauterize the bullet wound? I had definitely been reading too many books!

I sat there for a few moments more and started to worry more about the possible loss of blood. This in turn meant I started to breathe more heavily. Would anybody notice? Knowing we were still going to die either by being blown up by our own government or because we crashed into the ground actually ignited some anger inside me. Could I use my death to my advantage? Could I try again to overpower the terrorists? Would I have the strength? Answers that all came back with either a 'no' or 'don't know'!

Firstly, I had to see if I could open my eyes and move myself. Slowly I forced my right eye open. I wanted to be discreet because if I aroused any other passengers, they would surely scream out that *the dead guy had woken up.* Sure enough, the seat next to me was empty. I slowly opened my left eye and tried to assess my wound. There wasn't much blood. The centre of the wound appeared to be more towards my upper left shoulder than in my chest.

That was good news. I tried to move my fingers on my left hand and they worked perfectly. Whilst around two feet away across the aisle, I could sense Bob's presence. I carefully moved my head to my left and opened my eyes fully. Bob immediately saw my movement and before he could make any noise, which would have been understandable due to my sudden resurrection, I winked at him. His face told so many stories. Shock, delight, shame. But after I gave the briefest of smiles, he smiled back and mouthed the words: 'Are you okay?' My wink had been a risk, so I responded with an okay hand sign to not bring any attention to myself.

'I'm so sorry,' Bob mouthed silently again. I repeated my hand signal. I felt sorry for Bob, but knew how terrified I was myself earlier and I knew it could easily have been me that froze. I surveyed the area around our seats and everything was the same.

I had to ask Bob how long I had been unconscious for. What was the situation? Had anyone else made an attempt to overpower the terrorists? Were they still in the same positions? I realized I couldn't get any of the four important questions answered without exposing myself. I also knew at some stage, without medical attention, I could bleed to death or go into shock of some sort. I chose to risk asking Bob one question, so I mouthed silently. 'Any changes?' Bob lip-read very well and shook his head. I continued. 'How long have I been out?' Where are they? Bob sat up in his seat and took a casual look to his left and returned to his normal position. 'About 4-5 minutes. Same place as before'. He whispered both answers. I then started to move as many parts of my body as I could. I wiggled my toes, clenched my butt cheeks, flexed my leg muscles… I had to make sure everything was working and that I could move properly.

I looked back at Bob and then asked him. 'Ready to go again?

Bob's face was a picture. Shock at first, then a warm smile appeared on his face.

Somehow Bob's own shame of his inability to act earlier, coupled with his own personal thoughts since the shooting, had galvanized him. Bob had gone through several emotions in the last five minutes. He had questioned his own self-respect, his own whole life, even his whole purpose on Earth. He had even promised himself if he got another opportunity, he would push himself beyond all reason and try and take down one of the bad guys. He wanted to be remembered as someone that stepped forward, someone he could be proud of. He told himself this, safe in the knowledge it probably would never happen, but at least it gave him a purpose. Bob now sat up firmly in his seat. He seemed to pause before whispering.

'You must be kidding buddy. You have a bullet inside you! I can't believe your still alive. Surely it's best to get you some medical attention. Let me call them over and ask for a doctor?'

'Bob, this is perfect' I replied.' No one's gonna expect anything from a corpse' Bob frowned and then managed a brief smile.

'You're not wrong, and you might even scare a few bad guys to death'.

We both sat them for a few moments.

'You okay to do this? Do you want to swap roles?' Bob asked quietly.

'I'm dead. We do exactly the same as before,' I whispered. Bob got it straight away. If the terrorist was surprised the first time, he was going to be in for an awful shock this time.

I was very conscious that time might be running out. 'Okay to go partner?' Bob mouthed at me.

'Let's do it.'

Considering I still wasn't sure if I could get up out of my seat and wouldn't know for sure until I tried, Bob's own apparent energy had also changed the situation. Somehow, the events of the last five minutes, coupled with our own animal instinct to survive, had given us both an inner strength we never knew existed. I kept flexing my hands and legs and checked to ensure my arm rest was still up. I noticed that I was soaking wet and recalled wetting myself before I stood up to challenge the terrorists. But right now, I didn't care.

Chapter 52

At that very moment, the captain Mike Turner was in one-to-one discussions with Malika. Something was bugging Mike: no matter how many times he asked Malika, he couldn't get one single demand from her. Other than entering the cockpit, she had no shopping list whatsoever. Yes, she had earlier demanded $5m be paid into a bank account, but surely that's not it? Whilst he was pleased the deadline appeared to have passed, he was fearful that this very clever woman was playing him like a fiddle. Whilst she kept threatening to, why hadn't she killed a crew member? She had repeated her explanation of the death of the passenger a little while earlier as an accident. She was just obsessed with the cockpit area and speaking to his superiors. He explained that he could forward the list of demands, but she wanted to do it personally.

'I am not allowed to let you in the cockpit. You must know that. Even if I beg, my co-pilot will not let me in, even if you threaten to kill me.' Mike said.

'I really don't care about your rules. I am in charge. Who is in charge Captain?' Malika shouted as she pressed her gun down on Debbie's forehead as Debbie squealed. 'You are in charge Malika, you are, but please don't hurt anyone. Please take me…let me stay with you as a hostage and let the air stewardesses go back to their seats.' Mike said. This angered Malika even more and she grabbed Debbie by the hair and brought her to a standing position. 'Turn around pretty one and pray to whatever God you believe in. Last chance to open the door, Captain.' Malika said as she stood there ready to execute Debbie.'

Before Mike could respond, he heard some commotion coming from further down the aircraft and within a split second heard the passenger's screams that followed.

Chapter 53

Local time 12.07 pm

Bob had pressed the call button again and we both took deep breaths. The same guy, T3 appeared, leaned his head down to Bob's, and very quietly asked what the problem was. Bob repeated his earlier request to go to the toilet and bizarrely (probably affected by the earlier incident) the terrorist said he would ask his superior and then started to walk away from us up towards the front.

I took a huge breath and sprung out of my seat as fast as I could and virtually jumped on the terrorist's back. My weight forced him downwards towards the cabin floor. The pain coming from the bullet wound had disappeared completely in the previous 30 seconds as adrenaline pumped itself around my veins. I punched T3 in the side of the head as many times as I could and much to my surprise he very quickly slumped into a state of unconsciousness. Bob had also got up immediately after me and, whilst there wasn't much room in the aisle, he had also managed to land a few good blows to the back of the terrorist's head.

Luckily for us, as he fell downwards with my own body weight on his back, his head had hit the armrest of the passenger seat one row in front of us and that contact had knocked him unconscious.

I felt alive but was panicking. I couldn't see the gun and I didn't want to set off any explosives by rummaging around his body. I looked up and saw it on the seat next to us. I instinctively grabbed it and pulled myself up to a kneeling position. It felt weird and extremely light at one end and heavy at the next, almost like a toy gun. Not how I would expect a gun to feel like.

I then remembered my own advice about the detonation of bombs, which panicked me even more. 'Step on his hands, Bob, hard as you can.'

Bob initially looked at me strangely and then appeared to read my thoughts. He then began to follow my instructions; however strange and unnatural it must have looked. Bob started to place T3's first hand on the floor in front of the body. At that very moment, a very startled T2 came down the aisle from the business class cabin. He had his gun in his right hand but didn't appear to be able to reconcile what he was seeing before him.

Thirty seconds earlier, Ahmad had heard the call button go off in the next cabin and assumed it was another female passenger asking to go to the toilet. Dalmair would deal with it as it came from his section of the plane. But no sooner had he heard some light conversation than all hell seemed to have broken loose.

He ran across the middle of the business cabin and turned right into the aisle towards the premium economy. What he saw astonished him. Dalmair was nowhere to be seen, but there was a man half standing over what looked like a body, but what confused Ahmad more, was the sight of a man on his knees, with his arms stretched out, pointing a gun directly at him. With his own brain refusing to comprehend the scene before him, he just kept on moving down the aisle.

Two female passengers in our cabin were screaming, whilst another shouted, 'Help them, somebody, please help them.'

I could hear my heart thumping. T2 just kept on coming. Did he think the gun was empty? Was it empty? Had they only managed to smuggle one bullet on the plane? I took aim. 'Please God, may there be some ammunition in this gun.'

About 18 years ago, we were visiting our close friends in the US and the husband was a part-time policeman who was certified to carry a weapon. He took us to a local firing range to use his 38-caliber handgun. I remember it because it was the only time I had used a handgun and I was rubbish. The noise and the power the gun gave off scared me and the thought that this gun could easily take a life gave me no appetite to try it again. I painfully recall my ex-wife Linda bettering my own scores easily. It wasn't until around 10 years later I had a sight test and realized

I needed distance glasses. Yes, I can drive easily without using them, but things are definitely much more defined with them on.

Fortunately for me, T2 was only 20 feet away and closing. I squeezed the trigger and fired off two shots. Both hit their intended target; the first in the terrorist's stomach and the second in his upper torso, close to his neck.

I still had no idea if he was dead and my overwhelming paranoia developed from watching those movies where the bad guys miraculously get up after taking 20 shots, which led me to pull the trigger twice more. But only one bullet came out, and as the terrorists were down on the cabin floor, it missed anyway. Unbeknownst to me, I had used up all the bullets in the gun as its unusual setup meant it could only hold four bullets and 1 had already been used on me earlier.

The whole plane had erupted and I glanced behind me to see Bob stamping on the terrorist's second hand as two other male passengers from economy ran up the aisle into our cabin. One shouted at me: 'Grab the gun, grab the gun.'

I stood up, still half crouching, and rushed towards T2. His body was twisted with his head on its side. There was blood everywhere, largely coming from the 2nd wound. Both eyes were wide open as if in shock. I looked for his gun and found it wrapped tightly in his hand. I peeled the fingers back and stayed crouched down. There was definitely at least one more terrorist who was armed and probably carrying explosives. I stayed still trying to catch my breath, but just became more frightened seeing a dead body that close up. Think, David. Think!

My chest and back were now starting to sting and my hands were shaking. I looked down and the blood leaking from my own chest seemed to have gotten worse, as most of the left-hand side of my shirt was red. The body is an amazing thing, as the more I had been pushing myself, the more my body compensated by pumping adrenalin around itself. At the same time, God gave me the strength and courage to carry on.

Chapter 54

'I must get up; I must do something,' Edward told himself. 'My time has come. Something has gone badly wrong'. Edward had his eyes closed but instead of seeing Allah or gaining any strength, all he saw was the face of Juliet, then his two sisters, and then Juliet again. His hands were gripping his arm rests and with his body straightened up, it wasn't obvious whether he was trying to get up or trying to stay fixed in his seat. His hands were shaking and he started to mumble parts of the Koran under his breath. Not understanding any specific words that Edward was saying, yet concerned for Edwards's welfare, the man in the window seat to his left put his own arm around his shoulders and held him tight to offer him some comfort. As a fellow passenger, he obviously felt Edward was terrified and in desperate need of support. He then brought his face towards Edwards and started whispering his own prayer out loud. 'Our Father in heaven, hallowed be your name. Your kingdom come, Your will be done…'

This man that Edward have never met, had not spoken to for nearly seven hours of a flight was now praying to God for protection for *Edward*.

Tears were streaming down his face and he heard the other passengers around them start to say the same prayer. Edward slowly relaxed his own shoulders and then said out loud. 'Please brothers forgive me, please forgive me.'

Chapter 55

Two minutes earlier, air marshal Brad Miller had come around with a thumping headache. He felt the top of his head and his hair had matted with the dried blood from a wound. It didn't appear to be too large and when he saw that the colour of the blood was dark red, he knew the wound had probably stopped bleeding. He had been sitting silently considering various scenarios that might help the situation. It hadn't taken him long to realize the position he and the 301 other passengers were in. The terrorists were not planning on taking a planeload of passengers for hostage. His own training for his air marshal's role included some time with Homeland security and a few sessions on anti-terrorism. The US government never negotiates with terrorists. He knew that and worse still, he was 100% sure the terrorists did too.

This plane was going down, probably in the sea, about 10 to 15 miles off the east coast of America... or worse still, into a hospital or school on the ground.

As he was busy considering the percentage risks associated with any attempt to attack the terrorists, he heard a huge commotion coming from the cabin behind him. The terrorist from his own business class cabin jumped across the seats and ran down the aisle towards the noise. What he heard next startled Brad and left him completely dumbfounded.

A shot ran out, quickly followed by another. Had the terrorists shot innocent passengers who were trying to start a rebellion or was there the minutest chance that a heroic passenger had overpowered the bad guys? In a millisecond after the terrorist had gone out of view from his own cabin, Brad had his answer.

The very same terrorist who had just passed him had been repelled backwards by the second shot that had hit him in the upper torso.

Without thinking and without concern for his own well-being, Brad undid his seat belt and rushed forward towards the first-class cabin. The female terrorist, on hearing the noise and the gunshots, had done the opposite. Two seconds later Malika came face to face with a charging Brad Miller. Much to Brad's surprise, she quickly reversed a few steps and took aim with her gun at the captain. Captain Mike Taylor reversed back into the galley that separated the cockpit from the first-class cabin. Malika fired off three shots at him: two missing him, but the third hit him point blank in the chest. If she was going to die, the mission wouldn't fail. Malika stepped over his body and rushed down the right side of the plane towards her brothers.

Chapter 56

Even though the noise was almost deafening due to the screaming and shouting, my thoughts were clear and I had made my decision. I would move forward towards whatever terror waits for me. 'Please God, you have brought me this far, please grant me the strength and luck to see this through,' I begged.

Still cowering so as to remain as small a target as possible, I moved forward.

Immediately one, two, and then a third shot rang out, coming from up ahead of me, seemingly from the first-class area.

'Come on David, you can do this,' I said to myself out loud.

No sooner had I left the business cabin and entered the first class one, the female terrorist entered my aisle some 25 feet in front of me. She had a very determined look on her face, steely eyes and was brandishing a gun.

At this stage, I had already made so many wild assumptions. I assumed the dynamite was fake, or I had been extremely lucky shooting T2 in the stomach as my shot must have missed the sticks of dynamite on his waistcoat. Unless only one or two of them had real dynamite and the only person carrying real explosives was now hurtling towards me. Her own apparent confidence and assured facial expression made me think she was invincible. She looked so powerful and confident and I felt a complete mess. For some reason, she didn't fire her gun at me which allowed me the chance to crouch down again and take aim. Unless of course… she only had one bullet left and needed to make it count!

Chapter 57

Earlier, having secured the air marshal's gun, Malika had decided to give her own weapon to Ahmad. At that time, she felt extremely confident everything was going to plan and despite her own misgivings about Ahmad's ability to use the gun against a fellow human being, the fact that all three members of her group were now armed made her feel better about maintaining control of the passengers and crew. A decision she was now regretting.

Malika knew she only had one more chance to regain control of the plane, and worse still, only one bullet was left in the air marshal's gun. She had to make it count. Her own gun wouldn't have been any good anyway, as it was only accurate at close range and this guy was too far away. He was now some 25 feet away from her and was crouching down to make himself a smaller target. Maybe an ex-military guy or even another air marshal. A mistake by her not to have identified him on her earlier walk around.

Chapter 58

In a panic and without thinking about how many bullets the gun probably had in it, I quickly pulled the trigger, completely missing the terrorist with the shot. Because she was so far away, I needed to aim for her head to ensure I didn't hit another passenger, most of whom had crouched down as low as they could in their seats. At that distance, her head made for an extremely small target and the first shot had gone way over her head into the roof of the plane.

She took four more paces forward, bridging the gap between us to around 12 or 13 feet, and then with her left hand reached to her waist and brought out a gun. Assuming this gun had the same number of bullets as the last, I fired my second-from-last bullet into the bigger target that the decreasing distance between us had created. Amazingly, and because I was aiming a little too high anyway, it entered the right side of her face, just above her eye and she immediately dropped to the floor as if she had no skeleton holding up her body.

As if I was taking part in my own movie, I ran forward and fired the last bullet into the side of her head. This was one terrorist that wasn't going to get up.

Immediately I realized the foolishness of my actions. Suppose there were more terrorists on the plane? I quickly grabbed the gun the female terrorist had dropped to the floor and, still crouching, walked forward towards the galley, where I saw the captain with his shirt practically covered in blood. Another passenger was holding his hand against an apparent wound, trying to stem the flow of blood. The other passenger looked up at me, seeing my own blood-stained chest. 'Are you okay? You've been shot…'

I ignored the question and instead asked. 'Are there any other terrorists on the plane?' The attractive air stewardess joined us and I answered the question. 'I don't think so. I heard the female telling the captain about her brother and sister being on the plane.'

'Who are you?' asked the man administering help to the captain.

'David. David Johnson.'

'I meant what are you?' The man asked. A question I didn't understand.

'What do you mean? Are we absolutely sure there are no other terrorists on the plane?' I repeated. We also need to ensure the first guy is incapacitated.'

'You're hurt,' the stewardess said.

'I know, but let's check on the other passengers first,' I replied and left the galley and walked down the plane. Several passengers were on their feet and asking questions. 'Is it over? Are we safe? Is there a bomb on board?' All good questions, but I ignored them and headed for where I had left Bob. Everyone seemed to be stepping aside and sitting down as I passed them, which was probably down to the fact that I still had a gun in my hand.

On reaching the premium economy section, I saw Bob was sitting across the first terrorist whose muffled screams were being drowned out due to the fact that Bob was sitting on his head.

I sat down in my seat.

'You okay, Dave?'

'Fucking Hell,' was my response: very happy to pay the £1 fine. I rarely swore until this moment in my life, but now felt like the appropriate time.

'Fucking Hell, Bob.' I repeated.

'You okay, buddy?' he said looking at my red-stained shirt.

'I don't know Bob, I really don't know.'

'You did great mate, really great.'

'We both did,' I replied.

'What about the explosives?' Bob asked.

I bent down to the terrorist's head and demanded 'Are these real dynamite sticks? Where is the device that sets them off?' His face was screwed up in agony due to his left hand being broken and his right severely swollen.

'They're fake! They're fake! I promise.' He begged me to believe him.

Like so many times over the last half an hour, I didn't have a clue what to do. Could we trust this guy? Would another terrorist on board set the explosives off remotely? Was there a small device somewhere on this guy's body that, if, pressed, would blow the plane out of the sky?

All these questions and the events of the last 5 minutes had exhausted me. I couldn't think straight. Why weren't the other passengers coming up with solutions? Why couldn't I sit back and get some first aid and leave everything else to someone else?

'Bob, can we believe him? And what if he's lying?'

'Not sure he'd be capable of doing anything with his hands the way they are?' There were now several people standing up around them.

'Any ideas, anybody?' I asked. Silence came and went. An idea suddenly came into my head. A strange one, but at least it was progress. 'Everyone back to their seats and get strapped in.'

With the terrorists' guns still in my hand, everyone seemed to obey my command as if pleased someone was in control.

'Bob, we need to strip this guy… fully.'

'What?' Bob replied. I repeated. 'Strip him naked. We need to know he can't hurt us. We have come too far to get tricked by him.' It was the only idea I had. 'Tie him up with his own clothes and strap him into a seat. Strap his shirt around his neck onto the headrest.'

'How?' Bob asked. 'Get another passenger to sit on his lower body and then take his waistcoat off, carefully. Then do the reverse. Shoes, socks and all. In fact, firstly, let's take his watch off.' I bent down to his broken hand and pulled at his watch. He screamed loudly, as I dragged the watch off his hand then placed it on the floor and stamped on it.

I looked across the seats and called out to a heavy-set guy I had recalled seeing when I first entered the cabin. 'Fella, please come over and help us with this guy.'

'No problem,' he replied. 'Only too happy to help.'

'Over to you, Bob.' I stood up and nearly passed out. I rocked over into another passenger's seat and flung my arms around the headrest. Trying to steady myself, I heard Bob's voice. 'Buddy, grab him.'

The guy in the seat pushed his arms up to stop my fall and together they managed to keep me upright. Then they assisted me back in my seat as I gathered my thoughts and tried to find some energy again.

Chapter 59

Local time 12.09 pm.

Debbie and Brad had pulled the captain onto a seat in first class and had him lying flat. Both first aid kits were out and they were struggling to keep him alive. The crew member who was the designated first aider on the plane had just arrived from the back of the plane and was going through the emergency medical kit they had on board to treat ill passengers. Laura was banging on the cockpit door trying to get the co-pilot's attention, but there was no response. He wouldn't answer the phone or respond to her shouts.

Unbeknownst to Laura or any of the passengers, the co-pilot Dale Stanton had taken a stray bullet in his back from Malika's gun that had been meant for the captain and was slumped forward in his seat. Maybe Malika would achieve her mission after all?

Seconds before the bullet had entered the cockpit through the side wall, Dale had been on the phone to the tower giving them a second-by-second update of the captain's movements. In the last three-to-four minutes, Todd Williams had been trying to re-establish contact with the co-pilot. 'Dale, are you there? Dale, please respond.'

The silence had completely thrown Todd, Paul, and Agent Harris. In the absence of the truth, they were making up all sorts of possible reasons for the silence, but the main one they kept coming back to was that the terrorists had somehow breached the cockpit and were now holding a gun to Dale's head. The bottom line was that the terrorists were now most probably in charge of flight BA57.

Two minutes from the start of the silence from the cockpit, the decision was taken to arm the rockets that were situated on the belly of both the F14s that were flying less than two miles on either side of Flight BA57.

Chapter 60

After drinking a bottle of water given to me by another passenger, I left Bob and went towards the front of the plane. Bob's voice was trailing behind me. 'Get some first aid, buddy. You need to be patched up.'

I gave instructions to anyone around me that would listen. 'Everyone must stay in their seats. Please pass the word down the plane.'

I entered the first-class cabin and the air stewardess who had been trying to reach the co-pilot was crying and the man I spoke to earlier approached me.

'David, my name is Brad Miller. I'm an air marshal and whilst I don't know who you are, we have one hell of a problem.' He pulled me to one side and lowered his voice and continued. 'For some reason, we can't contact the co-pilot. Maybe he's passed out or something, but he's not responding at all. I have had some basic first aid training, something they make us do every six months, but based on my experience the captain may not make it, and having looked outside the windows a little while earlier, there are two fighter aircraft somewhere close by ready to blow us out of the sky.'

'What! Have we any other way of contacting the ground?' I asked.

Brad replied. 'None that I can think of. The plane's transmitter will only kick in at around 10,000 to 12,000 feet and I suspect we are at the standard 25,000 right now.'

'Any other way of getting into the cockpit? Can we even see in there from any other part of the plane?' I asked.

'Like where?' Brad asked.

'I have no idea, I'm just clutching at straws. Was the co-pilot ill before the attack, or have we any idea what could have happened to him?' I replied. Brad turned and repeated the question to the other stewardess. 'Not that I was aware of.' Laura replied. 'We need to get you looked at. Is that your blood on your shirt?'

'Yes, I got hit a while ago, but based on the pain in my back, the bullet must have exited through me. I wouldn't mind some form of painkillers.'

'You've been shot?' Laura asked.

'Yes, by terrorist number three, the first time I tried to attack him.'

With a puzzled look on her face, Laura continued. 'You're not the passenger we thought had been killed…are you?'

'Yes I am.' came my casual reply.

As if galvanized by the realization that I had been shot, she grabbed my arm and tried to pull me towards the shelving that contained some first aid stuff.

'My name's Laura and you need to do exactly what I say. How long ago were you shot? How much blood have you lost?'

'Laura, my name's David and we have more serious issues than my wounds. We must contact the ground, and fast. She started to undo my shirt buttons and I grabbed her hand. 'Please just give me some painkillers.'

'But…' Laura said.

'Laura, don't argue with me. Look at my face, take me seriously. If we don't contact the ground and soon, we will be blown out of the sky by our own country aircraft.'

Laura gripped my hand and said softly. 'Protocol kicks in,' Laura said as she had suddenly joined up all the dots. Laura continued slowly. 'The government won't let us near the land in case we fly the plane into a building?'

'Correct,' I said. 'That's why we must get into the cockpit'.

I turned to Brad. 'Come on, if we wanted to break in there how would we do it?' Brad's answer wasn't good news. 'We'd try and bust down the door, but they're made of solid steel now, nearly three inches thick. Built to withstand a small explosion.' We both moved towards the cockpit door and Brad started to rub our hands around the edges as if looking for a weakness.

That's when Laura noticed it. Whilst we were focused on the cockpit door itself, Laura noticed a small hole to the left-hand side of it. Pointing at Laura asked. 'What's that?' Brad looked up and ran his hand over the area. A hole, about the size of a pea, was visible. Brad tried to put his finger in it, but his fingers were far too big. 'Can you get me a pen?' He asked Laura. Seconds later she returned with a pen and gave it to Brad.

'Oh my God!' Laura exclaimed. 'Could that be a bullet hole?'

'Could be,' replied Brad. 'Shit. That might explain why the co-pilot's not responding to us. He's been shot!'

'Oh my God!' Laura shouted out even louder than before.

Unfortunately, whilst the door and frame were made of solid steel and were bullet proof, the outer area was made of a hard fiberglass material that can be penetrated with a bullet. When Malika fired off the three shots at the captain earlier, one had hit the intended target, but the other two had missed. The first had lodged itself into the drinks trolley that was fixed into the galley, but the second had gone straight through the side of the front of the plane, narrowly missing the impregnable solid steel frame of the cockpit door. It had, however, penetrated the fiberglass wall and entered the cockpit and into the back of the co-pilot, Dale Stanton. Still alive, Dale was now slumped over the controls unconscious. While initially a disaster, the bullet hole was now possibly a way we could get into the cockpit. With every second passing, Brad made the whole wider, until the pen broke. 'Get me something strong. I need a strong stick or a knife, anything that's gonna help me widen this hole,' Brad called out in desperation.

Behind me a call went out over the intercom 'Are there any doctors onboard? Someone needs urgent medical help. Please come directly to the first-class area.'

Chapter 61

At the same time, Brad was desperately trying to open up the hole wide enough to somehow get into the cockpit; the President was on the phone with the British Prime Minister. 'Anne, we have approximately five-to-six minutes before I give the green light, and the decision may come earlier if they change course. And things appear to have become worse on board. We lost contact with the co-pilot a few minutes ago, which suggests the terrorists now control flight BA57.'

'How on earth did they get into the cockpit?' Anne asked.

'I don't know Anne, but people are fallible. Who's to say they didn't start killing passengers and the pilot gave in? No-one can blame anyone for their actions under those circumstances. The only thing that's still bugging our guys is the route the plane is taking.'

'It's still heading along the east coast?' Anne asked.

'Yes, and we are tracking it going in a straight line, suggesting it's on autopilot. Because they're still around 20 miles from land it's okay right now, but the way the east coast land mass is structured, on its current course, in less than six minutes it will come within the 10-mile radius that forces our hand. Despite being ordered to stay out of sight by the terrorists, we are doing a fly-by to see if we can see who's in the cockpit.'

'Have your guys come up with any other information on the group or any possible solutions?' Anne asked.

'We've been in close contact with you Brits and the Palestine and Saudi authorities who have a good record of providing good insight, but nothing,' the President answered.

'Can you give those poor souls every possible second, Matt?' Anne said.

'You know I will Anne, but the second they cross into the 10-mile radius, I have zero choice. That's the tough decision made by congress.

All we can hope for is some kind of miracle. On another point, the press has got wind of the story and wants a statement. Some junior reporter stationed at Newark airport saw an FBI car arrive and told his boss and now three different news channels have arrived demanding to know what's going on. All we are saying for now is that there's an incident that involves a flight from the UK, but we cannot comment any further as it may risk the investigation. That's not going to work for much longer, as another reporter keeps asking why two of our F14s left Stewart Air National Guard Base airport some 12 minutes ago. They're adding up all the dots and starting to build a story. Any thoughts from your end?'

'An impossible position to be in. The other risk is the public finding out because if that plane gets much lower in altitude, everyone on the plane that can will be phoning their loved ones. Experience tells us that, in these situations, it's better to be as open as possible. No-one will thank us for misleading them,' Anne said.

'So you think we should come clean?' The President asked.

'Not completely, otherwise, there would be mass panic surrounding *Gemini* as it's hardly a secret. But a simultaneous announcement from both governments to the press, saying a passenger aircraft has been taken over by a group who are holding the plane and its crew as hostages, should do it. That's pretty much the truth anyway. And it's currently heading up the east coast, with two military aircraft as its escort. Say we can't reveal any more specific information because it might hamper our attempts to find a solution.' Anne said.

'Makes good sense, but then you were always the wiser one.' The President said.

'Let's get it done it the next two or three minutes.' Anne suggested.

'Agreed. And Anne, let's keep this line open and live,' the President responded.

'Makes sense, Matt. And let's both pray for a miracle.'

Chapter 62

Whilst out of sight from the commercial plane at approx. 2000 feet above it, the 2 F14s were still very much tracking the plane's movements.

'Base to Tango 2, copy.'

'Tango 2, copy.'

'Tango 2, do a fly-by and see what's going on in the cockpit. Understood?'

'Affirmative. Tango 2 out.'

James Trent had been a pilot for seven years and had flown sorties in Afghanistan and Iraq. As a boy, he had dreamed about flying planes and initially thought he would go into the commercial side of things, but after 9/11 he was determined to make a difference and joined the air force. James had been married two years earlier to Veronica, who gave birth to their son, James Junior, 15 months ago. They would regularly laugh about the timing of the birth and how Veronica had made James wait until the wedding day before allowing him to consummate the relationship. Of course, this wasn't true, but it made for a fun story to tell everyone. The reality was that they had been making love since a month after they met and the fact that James Junior had been conceived on or around their wedding day, meant he was their very special son.

Most of his action had been blowing up caves in Afghanistan where named terrorists were supposed to be hiding, or destroying targeted buildings that were supposed to be of 'special interest'. All of this typically happened when he and his plane were over 1-2 miles away from the target. The missiles they carried now allowed for pinpoint accuracy, using on-the-ground and in-flight computer software.

Today was very different. When the base alarm fired off around 20 minutes earlier, both James and his on-standby buddy Ryan Coster thought it was another standard drill. Having both done three tours in hostile territory, they were now part of the homeland security force that protected the skies over New York and the east coast. Whether a drill or not, they had a target time of three minutes flat to get to their planes and take off. Because of the healthy competition amongst both men, they always tried to outdo each other and today had been no different.

James had got off the ground in 2 minutes 43 seconds and Ryan was only six seconds behind him. Only once airborne did they get their instructions. Both were told to fly to 20,000 feet and head 30 degrees south and wait for further instructions. James's rank was captain, which made him more senior to Ryan (second lieutenant) and normally James would receive the mission info first in case some discussion was needed.

In a change of protocol, three minutes later they were jointly given the news that would possibly change and reshape the rest of their lives. Both were given clearer co-ordinates, then the shocking news about the potential target from their Major Todd Taylor on the ground. After the Major repeated the instructions twice, he said: 'Take a moment to digest what I've just told you guys and I will respond in 30 seconds.'

But the Major didn't give James any time to absorb the mission and was straight back on the radio. 'James, this is a shit-storm: a no-win scenario. But I've gotta know you can handle the mission objectives if called upon. We have hundreds, potentially thousands of lives on the ground to protect. Understood and copy.'

'Understood and affirmative, Major. What the hell's going on?' James asked.

'All I know, and I had a short briefing from the pentagon less than two minutes after you were scrambled; is that some terrorists took over a plane arriving from England. There are over 300 people on board and our mission, if we get the green light, is to take it down. The Major waited a few seconds. 'I had hoped I would never have to give these instructions, but if I give the green, I need to know you will execute the order?'

After a few seconds, James responded.

'Affirmative Major. Understood. How long have we got?'

'Around five to ten minutes,' The Major replied. 'For now, just get to the plane's coordinates and then flank the plane on either side with Tango 1. Understood?'

'Copy that, Major,' James replied, as he switched off his comms.

'Wow. Shit. Oh my God,' James said as he plugged in the correct data into the plane's computer and headed off to intercept flight BA57. 'This cannot be happening. This must be a drill,' he said to himself out loud. Once level, he reached out to the picture he had in front of him of his new family. 'Guys. God, please help me. Make this a drill and if not, please help those people on the plane find another way out.'

Could he do it? He'd trained for it. Being part of the security of the state of New York, the biggest single target for terrorists in the world meant he had constant refresher training and regular simulated exercises covering loads of eventualities. He kept thinking that maybe this was another test. It had to be!

He didn't know the Major very well as he wasn't his direct superior, but the man wasn't known for his sense of humor, plus he was known as a 'by the book' guy, who was retiring soon. Hardly someone to take practice missions to this length! But surely this was a test? It had to be…

Completely out of normal protocol, the Major separately contacted the other plane. He had to know that if James couldn't press the button, he had another option in Ryan. 'Ryan. A tough one.'

'Yes, Major. A bloody tough one.'

'Ryan. We have done loads of training on this very type of mission before, but I've got to know you can follow the instructions if given?'

'Affirmative, Major. But Major, respectfully we get an average of 5 drills like this each month, surely this is just another one?'

The Major answered swiftly. 'If you have any doubts whatsoever, I need you to return to base and we will send someone else up.'

Having pushed it once and not wishing to challenge the most senior person he has ever engaged with, Ryan responded. 'Negative, Major. Whilst I certainly didn't sign up for this, somebody's got to do it.'

Four more minutes had passed as they flew a couple of miles from the passenger airline when Tango 2 (James) was given the instruction to check on the cockpit. He pulled his jet around and got to within 200 metres of Flight BA57. He steadied himself and looked into the cockpit and his desperate hopes that this was only a drill were dashed when he saw what looked like a man collapsed over the instruments. He reported this back and returned to his position at the side of the plane.

Chapter 63

Local time 12.13 pm, eight minutes after the scheduled arrival time at Newark airport.

In two minutes the President of the United States of America, the most powerful man on the planet, would give the green light that would instruct the F14s to engage in the attack to destroy the passenger plane.

The plane was heading directly for Boston, Massachusetts, and on route it got ever nearer to the ten-mile zone as it passed close to Portland.

Without warning a sudden burst of severe turbulence hit the plane and everybody was shaken a little. A few passengers in the economy section also heard a noise that could be mistaken for a small explosion, but as the sudden bout of turbulence also broke open several of the overhead lockers, they were distracted. Loads of items had fallen into the aisles and that in turn had caused a fair amount of commotion.

In reality, a small explosion *had* gone off in the undercarriage at the back of the plane and whilst the movement was felt by everyone on the plane, no-one suspected anything abnormal.

What they didn't know was that the front wheel arch was completely bent outwards and the shears - the metal rods that hold the wheels in place - were sheared off and the heat from the explosives had burnt through the cables that connected the complete wheel system, rendering the whole of the landing gear useless.

This had also been a lucky escape for half the passengers sitting in the left forward part of the economy class cabin. If, back in England, Andrew Shaw had attached the small package to the wheel arch facing *inwards*, which was his instruction, including the landing gear, the far-left side of the plane would have been blown apart. Instead, the bomb exploded outwards, causing relatively minor damage to the body of the plane. The fact that it had gone off approx. 12 minutes early was simply the result of Andrew Shaw's fake watch being incorrect when he set the timer on the package.

'WOW. Did you feel that?' I said to Brad.

'Yes, that was pretty severe turbulence.'

We steadied ourselves, but as the plane continued as normal, we brushed the incident to one side. A few passengers and the crew cleared the aisles of the plane and closed the overhead lockers. With a knife from first class, Brad was making a little headway with the hole, as the first aider on board administered a small injection into my shoulder, just below the wound. As this was happening, Brad had instructed two other crew members to move both the dead bodies into the first-class cabin and strap them in with blankets covering their bodies. This took a few minutes as he had instructed them to be very careful regarding the explosives. We weren't completely convinced they were fake, so didn't want to take any chances.

Debbie came through the cabin. 'The passengers have calmed down, but need to know what's going on. Can we make an announcement?'

Brad was busy with the hole that had now become the size of a fist. The trouble was it needed to be the size of a basketball to allow a small person to squeeze through.

'Good idea…' I said, not knowing her name.

'Debbie,' she said, as if reading my mind. 'David, isn't it?'

'Yes.'

'David, you have been brilliant. I saw the way you took down the terrorists; you were so brave. What part of the military are you in?'

'Military, me? None. But you should make that announcement. Just say the terrorists are dead and we are in charge of the plane. No, don't say that. Say they're *secure* and the plane is now in the control of the pilots, who will be making an announcement about our arrival shortly. Okay? No need to worry everyone. Okay?'

Debbie replied with a nod of her head and disappeared to make the announcement.

The two F14s had closed in again and were very visible to everyone on board. 'Brad, we have got to hurry. We have to make the signal soon. Let's use a trolley draw to batter a larger hole.' I grabbed one from the galley and Brad started trying to smash through the material, with some success.

'I hope you're in the air force, David, cos we're gonna need a pilot either way.' I ignored the comment, but it made me think: 'Why does everyone think I'm in the air force or military or whatever?' Anyway, we needed a small person, a skinny teenager, to slip through the hole. Any second now, it should be big enough.

I looked across to Debbie. 'Can you find us a skinny person to get through the hole, and it's pretty urgent. Do you know how they can open the cockpit door from the inside?'

'Laura has the code"

'Good. Can you get it off her and then can you deliver me a skinny person and the code?' Whilst I smiled with this seemingly ridiculous of requests, I was panicking inside.

Debbie scurried out of the first-class section and headed off on her rather unusual task.

Did we have five minutes or five seconds before the planes blew us out of the sky? I couldn't believe the situation I was in. Firstly, I try a pathetic attempt at over-powering a terrorist with a gun. Then I get shot, and then somehow I get lucky with the bullet not killing me. Then I don't bleed to death, and then I stupidly try it again and survive. Then I managed to shoot another terrorist without him blowing us all up, and then a woman came at me with another gun trying to kill me. Miraculously I managed to shoot her, but now, after all that, the United States government is probably going to kill me anyway.

Chapter 64

Sitting in his chair in the Oval Office at the White House, the President looked very withdrawn and hadn't spoken to anyone for 60 seconds. The room was full of people. His Chief of staff, The Head of Security at the White House. The head of the National Security Council and the government's own chief of council were also in attendance. Whilst the United States Congress had already authorized the use of *Gemini*, there were still procedures that had to be followed, otherwise, the President would leave the White House and the United States government open to all sorts of legal challenges and lawsuits, possibly from several countries from around the world.

Until you're in a certain situation, no amount of preparation can prepare you for it. In less than 60 seconds flight BA57 would breach the 10-mile zone off the Portland coast. The next steps were ingrained on page 182 of the 340-page document that had been put together by the government, covering what force or action was or wasn't allowed, when the US soil came under threat from an unknown enemy from the air. *The full force of the United States government can and MUST be used to stop a missile or plane entering the 10 miles radius of land.*

It wasn't a subject open to debate. All the debating had gone on into the two years following 9/11.

Every president was expected to follow the policy and there were no exceptions. The 340-page document had over 100 pages of back-up data covering the historic attacks on both American and foreign-populated cities. In over 75% of cases, the loss of life on the ground far exceeded the numbers of souls lost on board the plane.

That was before the report showed the huge financial and disruption costs of a large plane smashing into a target on the ground. Quite understandably, this additional data was only added in the index, as if only as an afterthought. The main focus had to be the people onboard vs those on the ground. A typical school or hospital would hold over

1000 people. Whilst an extremely tough decision, it was ultimately a very pragmatic one, based on numbers. However, in this instance, none of the researchers or people in the room could even think of an obvious target on the ground. Several 'places of interest' had been identified, but there appears to be no obvious target.

An added upside (if there was ever one in this type of situation) was the message it sent to other potential terrorists in the future.

The President was now holding the phone, and on the other end was Lieutenant General Adam Fitzgerald, the current commanding officer in charge of the Steward Air Force base. 'General, anything happening on board?'

'Negative Mr President. The fly-by report said there was a body slumped over the controls, but no-one else was in the cockpit.'

'Has the plane changed course in any way?' The President asked.

'Another negative, Sir. In 40 seconds, the plane breaches the 10-mile limit.'

The Oval Office itself seemed to hold its breath. 20 more seconds of silence passed.

The President cleared his throat. 'Please give your pilots the go-ahead. That's a green for go.' The President gave the worst order any human being alive could give.

The Lieutenant General Adam Fitzgerald replied. 'Sir, Mr. President. Can I respectfully ask that you repeat the order?'

Understanding the reason for the confirmation, the President somberly replied. 'That's a green light General.'

'A green is the order Mr President.'

The Lieutenant General looked up from his desk at Major Todd Taylor. 'Major, that's the order for a go. I repeat that's a green light for go.'

Chapter 65

The hole was now around two feet in diameter and was getting bigger with every blow from Brad. Debbie soon returned with a young girl about 15 years old (although it's impossible to tell how old children are these days). A bit younger than I hoped in case she was too timid or afraid, but nevertheless, very skinny. 'Hi, my names David, what's yours?'

'Mandy.'

'Okay Mandy, we have a small, but incredibly important job for you. Are you up for it?'

'Of course,' she replied almost offended by the question.

'We need to get you safety through that hole. Once you're in there; unfortunately, you are going to see an injured person. The co-pilot. He's just passed out, with an injury to his back.'

'You mean he's been shot.' Mandy Asked?

'Who told you that?' I replied.

'Everyone's talking about it.'

'Well, err... Yes, he's been shot.' A split-second decision to tell her the truth.

'Okay, is he dead?' Mandy calmly enquired.

'Honestly Mandy, we don't know, but what we do know is we are pushed for time. Will you do it?'

'Of course,' Mandy said casually.

Have you got the code? And where exactly is the key pad?' I asked Debbie.

'78612 and press enter. The key pad is just to the right of the door,' Debbie said to Mandy.

'Okay Mandy, here's your big moment. This is Brad and we are going to help you get through that hole.'

'No sweat. Pretty cool, actually,' Mandy replied. 'I think I can manage it myself.'

As cool as anything, Mandy stuck first her head through and then wriggled the rest of her upper body through the hole. 'You okay Mandy?'

This was sounding more like a great adventure for Mandy. Something to definitely brag about on Facebook. I only hoped she would be around to write that post!

'Yep, just need a push from you.' Mandy requested. I grabbed her legs and by pushing and turning a little, it wasn't long before she got all the way through.

'Yuk. Disgusting,' came from inside the cockpit.

Trying to keep Mandy on plan, Debbie said the code number again. 'Do you see the green keypad on the back of the door? It's 78612 and presses enter.'

Two seconds later there was a ping and the door opened and Mandy stood there staring at the co-pilot. Brad quickly forced his way past Mandy to assist the co-pilot.

'Great job, Mandy! Now if you could return to your seat and please do NOT tell anyone what you have seen. Do you understand?' I asked.

'But I can once we're on the ground, right?' she replied.

'Absolutely and our sincere thanks for being so brave.' I said.

'Whatever,' came the reply from a rather cool teenager, as she turned and wandered down the aisle.

Chapter 66

Both Tango 1 and 2's radios crackled into life at the same time. 'Tangos 1 and 2 receiving.'

'Tango 1, Roger that.'

'Tango 2, Roger that.'

'James, we have a go order. I repeat: a go order.'

'Jesus Fucking Christ,' Ryan responded.

'Acknowledge receipt of order Tango 2.'

'Is this a test, Major?' James asked.

'No test. Tango 2, acknowledge order.'

'Order acknowledged. Order is a go, it's a green,' James responded.

With tears in his eyes, James turned his F14 to the right for almost a complete circle, where he would end up some 1200 yards behind the passenger plane, which had now become his target. On his missions in Afghanistan and Iraq, when attacking targets, he never saw a single person on the ground. On today's mission, he could clearly see the passengers as they poked their faces out from their window seats to catch a glimpse of his plane. In less than 10 seconds he was in firing position.

Chapter 67

'Shiiiiit!' came the scream from Brad inside the cockpit. 'The plane on the right has disappeared. That might mean it's about to close into a firing position. I've attended the classes… that's standard protocol.'

'Bloody Hell! We have to make contact. Press some buttons; anything,' I said desperately as I looked around the cockpit. All I saw were hundreds of different coloured buttons but I started pressing them anyway, calling out: 'Hello, can you hear me? Hello?' I picked up a pair of headphones and shouted into them. 'Hello, hello... fucking Hell, somebody answer.' Sod the £1 fine!

'Jesus Christ,' Todd Williams, head of airport security said as he was sitting in the tower contemplating the fate of the people on board. He lept up and grabbed the microphone. 'Is that you, Dale?'

'No it's not, but tell those planes not to blow us up; we have control of the plane!' I screamed out.

'Who is this?' Todd repeated.

'My name's David Johnson and I'm a passenger. The terrorists are all dead. Do not shoot the plane down.' I shouted desperately.

'How do I know you've not got a terrorist's gun to your head?' Todd shouted back

'Just trust me. Fly past the cockpit. Please don't blow us up. I'm with a guy called Brad…Miller and he says he is an air marshal.' I begged as I gave the headphones to Brad, who repeated the desperate plea to save our lives.

1200 yards away, with tears in his eyes, James said into his microphone: 'Missiles armed.' And, three seconds later, 'Missiles locked on.'

'I cannot believe I'm doing this, Major. Please tell me it's a test?' Against protocol, James made one last attempt.

'Negative Tango 2, it's not a test. Complete mission as ordered,' came back the stern reply from his Major.

James Trent, from a small town called Newburgh, some two miles west of Stewarts air base, flipped the cap on the firing handle that would send over 300 souls to their deaths. The sky was blue and Flight BA57 looked as if it was stationary. Almost like it had been painted onto a canvas.

'Dear Lord my Father. I beg you to forgive me for what I am about to do. I pray for the forgiveness of those families of the people on board.' He looked down at the picture of his family once last time and placed his thumb on the firing button.

Chapter 68

'Tango 2, Tango 2: abort mission! Abort mission!' came the scream for Major Taylor.

Five seconds before, Todd Williams had contacted the Major with the latest news. 'I'm not saying it changes anything Major, as we have our orders and it could easily be a bluff. The plane is flying steady but is now 9.5 miles from Portland point,' Todd said.

The Major made a decision. A decision that would perhaps save the lives of everyone on board. He didn't want to retire knowing his last significant order had been that his own men attack a passenger airliner full of innocent civilians. And hell, he hated Portland anyway and for the sake of another 30 seconds, he could at least give those on board one more chance.

James could hardly see from the perspiration and tears rolling down his face. 'Mission aborted Major…you fucking asshole,' he replied, assuming now it had been a test and that he had been driven to nearly breaking point.

Ignoring the understandable outburst from James, the Major responded. 'Tango 1, do another flyby and check the cockpit out. Tango 2, stay in position and be ready to fire on my orders. This is not a test, Captain! Stay in position with missiles locked,' the Major ordered. 'Tango 1, I want to see that there are friendlies in that cockpit and no-one else.'

'Affirmative,' replied Ryan. An extremely long 15 seconds passed as both Major Taylor and James Trent waited anxiously for the report. 'Was this a drill?' James asked himself.

'This is Tango 1 reporting. I can see what looks like two friendlies in the cockpit. Both white males and one is frantically waving at me.'

'Is the cockpit door open?' asked the Major.

'I cannot see that far back, Major.'

'Tango 1 and 2, standby,' said the Major.

Almost standing with my face pressed to the windows in the cockpit, I continued to wave my arms around desperately hoping for someone to take notice. I held the earpiece up and screamed. 'I'm waving right at your guy now. Tell them to not attack us,'

'Close the cockpit door. We need to verify you're in charge,' said the guy on the other end.

I did as he asked. 'Are we good? Are we good?' I repeated. A few seconds passed. 'Are we fucking good?' I screamed at the top of my voice.

A few seconds passed and a crackle came over the ear peace, 'I think we are, put the air marshal on.' On hearing this amazing news I very nearly collapsed. The loss of blood, the near-death experiences, the sheer pressure of the situation. Brad stuck an arm out to stop me falling and I collapsed into the captain's chair.

Chapter 69

Lieutenant General Adam Fitzgerald nervously picked up another phone that was on his desk and spoke to the President. 'Mr. President, we have new intel and have aborted the mission for now.'

'What new intel, General?' demanded the president.

'Sir, it appears and has been confirmed by a flyby that the passengers, or one particular passenger are now in charge of flight BA57. We have seen inside the cockpit and Newark traffic control has spoken to a passenger going by the name David Johnson. He has confirmed that two terrorists are down and one has been disabled.

'How do we know he's legit?' the President asked.

'We don't know 100%, Mr. President, but our guy at the control tower feels certain he's a civilian and that they have taken the plane back. There's an air marshal on board who he's also spoken to and both are registered as being on board.

'Mr. President, it's our opinion that the plane is safe,' the Lieutenant General responded. The President sat back in his chair in the oval office and everyone clapped & cheered, including the British Prime Minister who was still on loud speaker.

In the meantime, Todd Williams was grilling Brad, who was struggling to answer Todd to his satisfaction. Unsurprisingly Todd had loads of questions. 'Who is this civilian? How do you know him? Where was he sitting on the plane before the incident took place? Why are you both in the cockpit? How did you get into the cockpit? Where are the Captain and co-pilot?

One at a time, Brad tried his best to give the answers, but many of his responses were simple 'I don't know,'

Chapter 70

Looking at the co-pilot I asked. 'Is he alive? Please let him be alive...'

Brad, who had taken the headset off, responded, sweating as much as I was. 'He's breathing, but only faint. Let's get him out of here and into first class. I think Debbie found a doctor who can hopefully help,' Brad said. We both, as carefully as the small space in the cockpit allowed, carried the co-pilot into the first-class area. 'Lay a seat down fully,' Brad demanded from another crew member.

'Where's the doctor? This guy needs help!' I shouted.

Another passenger, presumably a doctor, was working on the Captain. He spoke briefly to Laura and then came over to help the co-pilot.

'How's the Captain?' I asked.

'Not great, but we've stabilized him. We need to land in the next ten to fifteen minutes otherwise we could lose him,' the guy replied. 'They've got some half-decent equipment on board, but he is bleeding internally and needs opening up, which really needs an operating room environment.'

Brad grabbed my arm and pulled me to one side.

'How're you feeling, David?'

'How do I look?' I replied and Brad laughed. Laura came forward with a first aid kit. 'Now will you get some attention for your shoulder?'

'Yes Miss,' I replied as Laura started to unbutton my shirt and attend to my wound.

'Brad, please talk to the ground. Please make sure they're not going to do anything stupid. How much fuel have we got, and what's their plan?'

After giving the people on the ground an overview of the situation, a minute or two later Brad returned to the first-class area where I sat receiving attention from Laura. 'David, they want to speak to you.'

'Me? Why?'

'You've done great so far and whatever experience you have, military or not, they need to talk to you.'

I struggled up, with Laura's help. Now my upper body and shoulder were very painful. I guess my body decided I didn't need any more adrenalin or perhaps it had simply run out. I struggled into the cockpit and grabbed the headphones. I put then on properly for the first time. 'Hello. Who's there?'

'David? My name's Todd Williams. We spoke before. I'm head of airport security for Newark Airport, New York. Normally in these situations, we would have slightly different people on the line, but as this incident is only thirty minutes old, the on-site people are in charge. I am going to pass you over to a colleague of mine, Alan Peterson. Alan is the head of the pilot's association out of Newark.

'Hello David, its Alan here.'

'Hi Alan. We can still see the two planes on either side of us. I want a guarantee they're not going to attack.'

'David, currently you're in and out of Maine airspace and ranging from between 10 and 12 miles off the coast. Brad has given us an overview of things and everything is okay. You are in safe and friendly hands. I need you to calm down.'

'Calm down? How can I calm down? Both our pilots are in critical condition and I've got a bullet hole through my body and this is only the second time I've ever been in a cockpit.'

'David, you must calm down.' Alan said.

Deep breaths, David, deep breaths.

I took a couple of deep breaths. 'I am calm,' I lied.

'David, are you alright or do you need urgent medical attention? Brad told us you took a bullet when you overpowered the first terrorist?' Alan asked.

'I'm okay. Luckily for me and I cannot believe I'm using the word luck in this sentence, it went straight through me. I've been patched up and am okay.'

'You've done one helluva job onboard that plane. What part of the forces were you with in Britain?'

'Listen, I've never been in the forces. What are you going to do about getting us another pilot if we can't find one on board?' I asked.

'David, with respect, it's important we start our relationship off with total honesty. Whilst your personal file says you're currently the CEO of a decorations company, clearly in the past, and possibly the not-too-distant past, you were an active member of the forces?'

'Will you stop banging that drum and tell me how you're going to get us a pilot?'

'Don't bullshit me David, I've now seen the video footage of their takeover of the plane and your own actions in taking out three terrorists. What arm of the forces were you in?'

'I was not and am not in any type of armed services!' I screamed out.

'So you're not ex-military?' Todd spoke up.

'No, I am not.'

'David, how do you explain your activities of the last 30 minutes?' Alan asked.

'Dumb, stupid, lucky… very, very lucky and more stupid thrown in!' I replied.

Alan thought for a moment. For some reason, this guy didn't want to talk about his service background. Todd moved his hand across his own neck as if to advise Alan to move on from the subject. Whatever the truth was about this guy's background didn't matter right now, plus they had loads of resources on the ground that would eventually find out the information.

Understanding Todd's message Alan said: 'Okay David. It's all about the next steps. Brad's briefed us on the terrorists. Apparently one is still alive, but you have him tied up. We all got very luck with the explosives, as they appear to be fake. Just to make sure, we have asked Brad to place them all in the metal food containers in the galley at the back of the plane and move the passengers in those last rows forward as much as possible. What have you told the rest of the passengers?'

'Nothing yet, because they're likely to freak out when they realize both pilots are out of action,' I said.

'Then don't tell them,' came Alan's reply. 'No one needs to alarm them any further, but you do need to talk to them. Be a calming voice. Every five minutes make an announcement, just to keep them feeling like you're in control.'

'Why me?' I asked.

'Why not?' came Alan's reply. 'David, according to Brad, so far you've managed to take out three terrorists single-handedly despite being wounded. Brad says your actions since then have made him feel that you're the guy on board who's in control. Brad's near-to-retirement age and the senior cabin supervisors probably haven't stopped crying since the attack and hell, somebody has to step up and be in charge and that's you!' Alan's voice became louder as he finished the sentence. A few seconds passed as I tried my hardest to appreciate the situation I was in. Why shouldn't it be me? This is what I do for a living anyway, plus there's probably not much to do now except keep the passengers calm.

'Okay,' I replied. 'But the honesty thing works both ways. How and when are you going to get someone on board to land this plane?'

'Good. Brad's given us the fuel update and we just need a few minutes to review the various scenarios and will revert. Stay close to the cockpit. The planes on autopilot so you are in good shape.'

'Okay. Let's speak soon, real soon,' I replied. Alan responded quickly. 'We will come back to you in a minute or 2.'

I left the cockpit and found Brad and Debbie together. 'How are the pilots? Will either one be able to fly the plane?'

'Don't think so, David. Doc says they're both in a bad way. Loss of blood being an issue for both and internal bleeding for the captain. Both still unconscious and it's not looking good.' Brad replied.

''We need to make a passenger announcement. The guys on the ground reckon every five minutes, just to keep everyone calm and informed,' I said.

Debbie spoke 'What do we say? Both pilots are…'

'No,' I interrupted Debbie. 'That's the last thing we say.' I had no idea what to tell the passengers, my brain was frazzled. I needed time to think up something.

Five seconds passed.

I looked at Debbie. 'Please just say we are in total control and the captain's okay. Did the girl see him?'

'Don't think so. He was down the other aisle when she came up,' Debbie replied.

'Good, say the captain's okay. Also, no-one should get up unless they need the toilet, then only two people at a time for each toilet, so we don't clog the aisles up. Get all your staff to stay in each cabin to reassure people. Personally, go and chat to that young lady and again tell her to not talk to anyone else about what's she has seen.' I paused.

'And Debbie, a small drink for me would help.'

I had a terrible taste of bile in my mouth and needed something stronger than orange juice to get rid of it. My shoulder was also giving me a piercing pain. As Debbie made the announcement, she pulled out a drawer from the gallery and I grabbed a miniature bottle of whisky. I hated whisky, but I needed must. I then asked Laura to stay in the cockpit whilst I went to see my old friend Bob.

'You look a right mess,' Bob laughed when he saw me.

'I feel it too. How's our friend.' I asked.

'All tied up. You were amazing buddy. Real amazing.'

I leaned towards Bob and lowered my voice.

'So were you Bob. Without your help, we'd be sitting at the bottom of the ocean right now,' I said.

'I did nothing; you did. How you kept it together I don't know. What's the plan now?'

'All good. I just spoke to the guys on the ground myself and they're advising where we can land.'

'Why did *you* speak to the people on the ground?' Bob asked

I didn't want to lie to Bob. Despite only speaking to him for the first time a short while ago, I am sure we had shared so much of thoughts about the realities of life and death, plus without him, we would not be here. I lowered my voice to a whisper.

'Please don't react to what I am about to tell you.' I looked at Bob firmly in the eyes. 'Both the Pilot and co-pilot have been shot and are in a bad way. It's critical we don't tell the passengers as there'll be mass panic. Apparently, the air marshal on board has nominated me to be in charge of the situation, until they find a solution. Don't suppose you have any flying experience my friend?' I smiled with the question.

'No I don't and bloody hell.'

'I know, but they'll think of something, so mum's the word.'

'What does that mean?' Bob asked.

'Sorry, a British saying. It means don't tell anyone we have problem.' I smiled and patted my friend on the shoulder and left to return to the front of the plane. After a few steps, another passenger grabbed my attention. 'Is everything all right up front? Why hasn't the Captain told us what's going on?'

'I'm sorry, but you've heard the announcement and I'm sure you'll hear again soon. Everything's under control.'

The passenger grabbed my arm softly. 'Well done, by the way, well done.'

'Thank you,' I replied and headed to the front and into the cockpit.

Chapter 71

Local time 12.22 pm.

'Brad, the passengers are getting restless,' I said as I entered the cockpit. Laura handed me the headset.

'What's going on Alan? Talk to me.'

No answer. I waited a few seconds thinking there might be a time delay or something.

'Alan, Todd, anybody.'

'Hi David, it's Alan back. How you holding up?'

'The passengers and I are getting restless and worried. What's the plan?' I asked.

'We said we would be honest with each other David.' Alan replied.

'Correct,' I said.

'Here it is, and let me finish,' Alan said firmly. 'Airliners like yours carry just under an hour's excess fuel. As you may know, the flight's already over its expected arrival time. From the stats Brad gave us, you have 25 to 30 minutes' of flight time left. If we can get you to reduce your speed, we can increase this time by maybe five minutes. And yes, we are still evaluating options, but from your feedback and Brad's, neither pilot is conscious, so you need to find a passenger with some flying experience. Ideally without freaking everyone else out on board.'

'And how do I do that?' I asked.

'David, with respect, you've seen the movies. You make an announcement. Saying the co-pilot got injured during the struggle and the captain would like a co-pilot to back him up for landing. Don't make a big fuss about it. Just ask if anyone with flying experience would come forward. Take the opportunity to introduce yourself as an air marshal and that will help calm people down. We don't have lots of spare time, so do it now please David,' Alan said.

'But what about you getting us a new pilot?'

'David, please just do as I said,' Alan replied.

After a brief pause and very nervously as if I was about to speak at some business convention in front of a few thousand people, I took the cockpit phone from Laura. The very phone the Captain had used earlier. Laura gave me the instructions. 'Just press the grey button and speak. Any time you don't want to speak, release it again. David, you can do this. *We* need you to do this,'

Shit and double shit. Here goes. I pressed the grey button. 'Hello everyone. My name's David. You've probably seen me wandering around the plane. I am with the Captain and he's asked me to update you. All is well and shortly we will be turning the plane around and heading back to New York. Unfortunately, the co-pilot got injured in the struggle to overpower the hostages and the Captain has requested, for both security and safety, that he has another pilot sitting in the cockpit with him for the landing. Could I therefore ask anyone with flying experience to come forward. As we are struggling for time, could you do that immediately, please? I will keep you updated in a short time.' I released the button and wiped my sweaty hand on my shirt.

I looked a Laura and said. 'I hope we now get trampled by a load of flying instructors, like a herd of elephants.' Laura smiled and clasped my sweaty hand in hers and pressed gently.

Chapter 72

On hearing the announcement by the air stewardess, Larry Anderson's heart started racing. He also became breathless and wondered whether he was imagining a sharp pain in his left arm and shoulder. Betty saw her husband's reaction to the announcement and quickly opened her purse and opened a bottle of medication. 'It's going to be okay husband, just take some medication.' He started to shake and the medication got spilt down his shirt. With her arm now firmly around her husband's shoulder, Betty forcibly pressed the bottle to his mouth and poured. 'Drink slower, dear, and you will be okay. Try and be calm, my love.'

Whether the medication worked that quickly or not, gradually Larry stopped shaking and buried his face into Betty's shoulder. A few seconds passed and he gradually looked up and saw Betty's face. Larry wondered where his wife got her strength from. She was so in control, and whilst the tears had left several small lines on her face, she smiled as if everything was okay. Yet he was in a pathetic state. Gripped with fear about flying. Scared to death the plane was going to blow up any minute and worse still, the Captain now needed someone with flying experience to help him land the plane and he was so terrified he could hardly speak. *Pathetic* described perfectly how Larry Anderson saw himself. And worse still, it was all happening right in front of his beloved wife.

'Don't worry dear, your flying days are over and I'm sure someone else will be able to assist the captain,' Betty said. Almost as if she was reading his thoughts, she added. 'You have done your bit and more for your country and we are all very proud of what you have done'.

Lovely and very kind words indeed, but Larry knew the truth. He was a coward. A man so frozen with fear that he probably couldn't manage a trip to the toilet right now, let alone leave the safety of his seat to go into the cockpit. There was a second request for a pilot a minute later and Larry just closed his eyes and prayed for forgiveness.

Chapter 73

We waited. 30 seconds passed, then another 30.

I picked up the phone. 'Hello again, it's David here. Could anyone with flying experience come forward to assist the Captain? Thank you.'

I contacted the ground. 'Alan, can't you check the passenger lists for people with flying experience? Perhaps people don't want to put themselves out there or only would if it was a real emergency?'

'David, trust me when I tell you that for the last 35 minutes, we have been screening passengers as fast as we can, but there are over 300 on board that plane and it takes time. We started off from first class and are moving down the cabin. The theory being that current or ex- pilots would be regular flyers and would use their reward points to upgrade, plus ex- pilots don't like economy travel. That's the view from us on the ground.'

'Understood, but nobody's coming forward right now!' I stated.

Alan replied. 'Okay. In the meantime, let's save some time and fuel and at least change the course of the plane so it's heading back to Newark. Are you sitting in the pilot's seat?'

'Yes. Why?' I said.

'Good. We want you to perform a couple of simple tasks which means you will have to take over the controls briefly.'

'What the...?' but before I could finish, Alan shouted at me.

'David, shut up and listen!' Believing he had my attention, Alan continued. 'Reducing speed is a very simple task and only involves two things. I promise you it will be dead easy. The other key thing that I need you to do is turn the plane around. That's a little more challenging, but again only involves two instruments. Got it?'

I responded and my speech quickened in panic. 'You are kidding me. When I look at the number of knobs and buttons and screens in front of me, it all turns into a blur. Some of the buttons are already flickering on and off and there's a buzzing noise coming from somewhere, but I don't know where.'

Alan shouted at me again. 'David, get Laura back in.'

I called Laura back in.

Alan was hoping my own pride and ego as a man would kick in.

I was hoping she was going to fly the plane.

Laura came in and sat down in the spare seat, which was slightly behind the co-pilot's seat, meaning she had no plans to fly the plane.

'Ask Laura to put on the co-pilot's headset,' Alan asked.

Now we were both sitting there involved in what felt like a very bizarre conversation. 'We want you to help David with the two key tasks. Understood, Laura?'

'Understood,' came Laura's reply.

'David, firstly, we need you to turn the plane around a little. There is a fairly large screen in front of you, about 20cm wide that covers the autopilot and its functions. In the middle of the screen, you will see the altitude indicator.' I looked down on the dashboard and couldn't see any labels or headings with any writing on them.

'The indicator... altitude?' I shouted.

'Forget the name David and stay focused. This smaller screen shows you how level to the horizon the plane's flying at. You will have seen these before?'

I finally found a large screen with a smaller one inside it.

'Yep, in films I've seen, but not in real life. Anyway, I think I have got it.' I said.

Ignoring my comment Alan continued. 'Anyway, currently, the plane is being flown by autopilot and if required it will continue to do so, and that includes landing the plane in most circumstances. On that large screen, you'll see several other panels that have abbreviations on them. What we're going to do is press a couple of these to influence the autopilot, which will turn the plane around. Standard procedure means that the pilot takes over the control wheel at the same time to ensure the turn is made cleanly. That involves holding the wheel, very, very lightly and not actually putting any pressure on it. It's almost as if someone else is doing the driving, but you're watching over them in case there's a problem. This should take about 45 seconds to make the turn we want you to make. As long as you don't force the wheel, the engines will do the rest.'

Alan and his colleagues in the tower had discussed this. They were having no luck finding a pilot on the plane and knew they didn't have enough time for other options. Whilst everyone has seen the movies where people are ferried midair from another plane into the cockpit, it's a very specialist job and there are only 3 trained teams to do this in the US, 2 of which over 30 minutes away, and it would take another 30 minutes to get their kit and a plane rigged up and in the air for the exercise. The 3rd team was out of the question as it was situated on the west coast of the US. One of the teams were on their way, but they knew it was hopeless as the plane would run out of fuel and fall out of the sky 10-15 minutes before they could reach it. The autopilot should easily land the plane on its own, but it was normally only used in poor visibility conditions, such a fog. Autopilots are not 100% failsafe and even when being used it's good to have a pilot on hand to adapt to any problems. Having said that, this was looking like the only option. Most major airports (which fortunately included Newark) were fitted with an Instrument Landing System (ILS) and that communicates with the same system on the aircraft and effectively lands the plane. It positions the aircraft correctly on its descent to ensure it is gliding straight on the runway, and then it amends the onboard autopilot flight speeds and the plane's speed of decent.

Right now, Alan felt this change of direction and reduction of air speed would be an excellent opportunity to give David a feel for the plane. Without him realizing, he was having his first training session on how to fly a 777.

'Why can't the autopilot do all this on its own?' I asked in desperation.

'David, it practically is, you're just supervising. You won't be switching it off whilst you make the turn.'

'Are you crazy? Suppose I press or grip too tightly and it turns too far and we go into a dive. Suppose I turn too slowly...'

'David. Get a grip. You have come so far and can do this. It's a simple maneuver.'

I couldn't do it. I remember some 20 years ago, at an air force base about an hour outside London, my friend, who knew someone on the base, had got us a free go in an aircraft simulator. I can't remember exactly how many times I crashed the plane, but I didn't win any prizes and was never invited back.

'What about the speed reduction?' I asked.

'Once you come out of the turn we will discuss this, but for now, follow my instructions for the turn,' Alan answered.

'See the button marked HDG? That's the button that allows you to change your direction. Don't press it yet, but when I tell you to, press that and type in a three-digit number into the pad below it and press the ET button on that pad. Do this with one hand still on the cockpit wheel. Once you have pressed the number, place your other hand on the wheel. Are you ready?'

I wasn't sure I trusted what Alan was saying. Autopilot means the plane fly's automatically, so why risk me holding the steering wheel? What happens... 'oh shit,' David. I said to myself and then I decided to stop questioning things.

5 seconds past, before I said, 'Ready,'

Alan called out the three-digit number twice and, keeping my left hand on the wheel, I typed it in the pad and pressed the ET button, and quickly grabbed the wheel with my right hand. The plane seemed to go straight into a dive and I panicked.

'Shit, what's happening?' I screamed.

'David, calm down. All that's happening is the plane is doing a turn. It may feel like it's dipping slightly but that's just a sensation. Keep hold of the wheel. Can you feel it turning?'

'Yes, it's almost slipping through my hands.'

'Grip a tiny bit more,' Alan suggested.

'Okay, I'm not sure I'm actually doing much. Which suits me down to the ground.'

Once I'd gripped it a little tighter, I almost gained the sensation of flying the plane. My own body and shoulders turned, almost as if I was on the back of a motorbike and moving around a bend. The twist of my shoulder should have bought back the pain from the wound, but I guess the good old adrenalin was kicking in again.

'David, check your airspeed. There's another dial in the center column and it's like a dial in a car, which shows you your speed. It should show about 500 knots right now,' Alan stated.

'Can't see it. Can't do three things at once, Alan.'

I couldn't bear to take my eyes off the horizon dial and steering wheel.

'Laura, please can you check it out?' I asked.

'No, Laura. David, you find it. Look to your right and you'll see it,' Alan demanded.

'Bloody Hell. Where is it? I thought Laura was going to help me?'

Again, Alan chose to ignore me and said calmly. 'It's at about 2 o'clock for you,'

At first, I took a few glances to find it, then I saw it clearly, only it was saying 500, it was closing in on 550. 'Shit, it's at 550!' I cried out.

Alan quickly responded. 'You're going too fast in the turn. Loosen your grip on the wheel a little. As you're turning, because you're facing a little downwards it means you automatically speed up.'

'I thought you said the autopilot was in control?'

'It is, David, but you're overriding it a little by gripping too hard and almost forcing the turn. Don't force it.'

I eased up a little and the engine noise also quietened a little. I hadn't noticed it had got louder. I glanced at the dial and it was reduced to 540, 530, 520…

'It's reducing okay,' said Laura.

'Good work David. How's the horizon dial? It's been 35 seconds and you should be looking to straighten up now. David, very slowly, slow down the wheel as if you were coming out of a bend.'

I think I understood: whilst the autopilot could get me to turn unless I did something, we would just go around in circles. I followed the instructions and looked at the horizon ball. All I could see was blue sky all around, but the ball looked pretty level. Half blue, the top half, and the bottom brown.

'Looks good,' I said, relived we had stopped turning. The plane seemed to settle itself.

'Now re-type in a new three-digit code and press the ET button,' Alan said, then he proceeded to give me the code twice.

I peeled my right hand off the steering column and I followed his instruction.

'You should now be heading for Newark airport, New York. Congratulations. Now let's reduce your speed to save on some fuel.' Alan said.

My whole body was washed in sweat. My hands were soaking wet. Laura saw the mess I was in and pulled a small towel out of a flight bag that was down the side of the co-pilot's seat and handed it to me.

'Thanks.'

Alan piped up. 'David, see the thrusters in the middle section? They're the same on all planes and I'm sure you've seen them in some films.'

'Very funny. Now we have time for jokes?' I replied.

'These are very straight forward. You push them forward, and the speed increases. You pull them back, you go slower. Remember the speed dial. What's your speed?'

'501 knots.'

'Good. Again, very slowly, pull back on the thrusters. Very, very slowly. You're doing great buddy. Keep an eye on the speed. You want to reduce down to 400 knots.' I slowly pulled back on the thrusters and nothing really happened.

'How are we doing, David? What's your speed now?' Alan asked.

Nothing had happened, so I pulled a little more. The engine noise reduced slightly and the dial started to move.

'David, what's happening?' Alan asked almost aggressively.

I responded with some enthusiasm. 'It's happening now. When I first did it, even though I could swear it was moving back, it clearly wasn't. When do I stop and do I just leave it in that new position?'

'When the dial gets to around 400, take your hand away and leave it,' Alan instructed.

I once again followed his instructions and the dial slowly moved down to 400 and I released my hands and sat back in the chair, exhausted. As wet as my hands were, I was gripping everything so tightly that I left had imprints on both the steering column and thruster grips.

'Bloody Hell,' I said.

'David, you were magnificent.' Laura said.

I looked at her with a serious face and with a firm but polite tone said, 'Laura, we need to find a pilot on board this plane!'

Laura knew that it wasn't a suggestion or a polite request, I was being deadly serious.

Chapter 74

Local time 12.29 pm. Approx. 20-25 minutes of fuel left.

I sat there in the pilot's seat staring at the controls. I've seen the films and read the books. Autopilots can practically do anything and most certainly can land. How do we think pilots land planes in really foggy conditions?

I tried to guess what the controls were for, but there were so many of them I gave up. The buzzing I had heard before felt like it was getting louder although I doubted it actually was. It was probably my own senses were getting clearer. My shoulder and upper chest were certainly stinging a lot more. My mind drifted to my children. I couldn't believe what had happened to me.

What would my son James be doing right now? I checked my watch and it was about 12.30 pm local time, which meant it was 5.30 pm back in the UK. Probably on his PlayStation, either shooting some bad guys or playing football. I allowed myself a smile.

A loud voice from the radio broke me from my trance. It was Alan. 'David, are you there?'

'Yep,' I replied.

'We need you to change the plane's coordinates and log in some other data that will allow the plane to pilot itself to land. You're now about 10 minutes from New York and we need to get you and the passengers ready for landing. You have done a great job so far and now we need to get you all down safely so everyone here can buy you a beer. Can you get Laura back in please?'

Laura had already heard the radio and had re-entered the cabin. She calmly placed the head set over her head. 'Laura here.'

'Hi, Laura. We need to prepare the passengers for landing. Can you go through the normal drill again, only do the mini version? We know the Captain's in need of urgent attention, so want to make this happen as fast, but as safely as possible. Once done, please come straight back to the cockpit,' Alan instructed.

As if having a couple of minutes to kill whilst he waited for Laura's return, Alan casually asked me about my family. 'David, I understand you have three children. How old are they?'

'13, 15 and 18,' I replied. 'What about you?'

'I've got four and another one on the way. Getting set up to have a whole basketball team,' Alan replied.

'Wow, I thought three was a lot. You're going to have five. Good luck with that.'

'But they *are* amazing, David,' Alan said.

For some reason, the conversation about my children had weakened my grip on things and the floodgates opened and I started crying and soon became a sobbing wreck. All the things that had happened in the last 40 minutes. Being alive and very, very scared. Being shot, so close to death, yet surviving. Only to try all over again and then take someone else's life. For some strange reason, I blurted out to Alan. 'I wonder if the terrorists all have children?'

Countless times over the horrifying few minutes of my desperate attempt to stop the terrorists, my children's faces flash through my eyes. Was I risking them having no father when the terrorists were always going to let us go free?

There was no reply from Alan. I spoke again. 'Alan, have I risked the lives of everyone on the plane by being some foolhardy idiot that tried to save people, when they didn't even need saving?'

Laura returned after instructing the other crew members and saw me huddled in a ball. 'David, David, it's all okay. You've saved us all, it's all okay.' More embarrassed than anything, I managed to half pull myself together and Laura gave me some tissues from her pocket. Alan, having heard my sobs, came back on the line to try and get me to pull myself together.

'David, you have every right to let go. You have been through so much and achieved so much. Let me put someone else on the line.'

Agent Harris, from the FBI, had been listening to every single work David had said. Largely to understand first-hand what was going on, but also to get a full appreciation of the state of mind of this guy who appeared to be the only hope for the plane load of passengers. He decided I needed a boost to try and get me back in the game.

'David, this is Agent Harris, we briefly spoke earlier. I am going against all protocols when I tell you this but I think you've earned it. I can confirm we have identified three terrorists on the plane from the video footage. One was on our *black list* and in the last 30 minutes we intercepted a video from another that had a time delay. It was your classic suicide video that one of the men was sending to his family. Rest assured, what you have done today has saved lives, not risked them. Without your intervention, you and the whole plane of passengers would be dead right now.'

A pretty blunt statement, but nevertheless it made me feel instantly better. All the soul-searching I had done earlier, whether to get involved or not, appeared to have been worthwhile.

After absorbing the information for a few seconds, I replied. 'Thank you, Agent Harris,'. Somewhat re-energized, I sat up from the seat… but quickly fell back into it, as my wound sent a piercing pain through my body. I blurted out: 'Alan, tell me what buttons to hit, and let's allow this plane to land.'

Chapter 75

Both Laura and I took more instructions from Alan, and whilst I asked him to reconfirm every task at least three times, he remained patient throughout. There are many people I wanted to have a beer with when this was all over and Alan was at the top of my list.

After a brief pause, Alan came back on the radio again.

'Good work, guys. So, the plane's now heading straight towards Newark Airport, and, all things being equal, you should be on the ground in 6 to 7 minutes. Next step is to bring the landing gear down. Laura, there's a large button to the left of the co-pilot's seat... roughly where your knee would be,'

'The one that's flashing Alan?' Laura asked.

Alan's heart sank. His memory bought him back to the buzzing noise David mentioned earlier. Surely not? 'Laura, yes, press the button. If you get closer to it, it has two small letters on it: LG.'

Laura pressed the button, but nothing appeared to happen. Not that that alarmed me or Laura - at least not yet. We had seemingly pressed loads of buttons on the dashboard and nothing much ever appeared to happen anyway.

'Was there a loudish noise indicating the landing gear was coming down?' Alan asked.

'Nothing our end. All we can hear is that continuous buzzing noise in the cockpit.' I replied.

'Press it again please, Laura, but a bit firmer this time,' Alan instructed. Linda pressed it again, in fact, she kept pressing it, and still, nothing happened.

'No noise at all,' Laura said.

'Alan, are you sure we are pressing the right button?'

'Is it red and by your knee and does it have the letters LG on it?' Alan responded.

'Yes on all counts,' Laura replied.

Releasing the intercom button on the radio, Alan shouted. 'Shit, shit, shit' Everyone else surrounding him in the tower stood in shock. He continued agonisingly. 'Surely it's not possible? After all, they have been through... no fucking landing gear? How? Why, when?'

As the radio had gone silent, both Laura and I became a little alarmed. 'Alan, is that a problem? Don't bullshit us, is there an issue?' I said firmly.

Todd was already on another radio and speaking to the Major in charge of the two F14's. 'Major, can you do a casual flyby, underneath the plane to check the status of the landing gear?'

'Affirmative,' replied the major and passed the instructions on to Tango 1.

Alan replied to my question. 'David, give us a minute; we are just checking something.'

'What could they be checking?' I asked Laura.

'Did you hear any noise whatsoever, when you pressed the button?' I asked her.

'Nothing... nothing at all. And I do recall the crunching noise you can normally hear when the landing gear goes down. Although I am always in the cabin, so maybe it's not something we would hear in the cockpit,' Laura replied.

Seconds passed and the Major came back on the radio to Todd. 'Todd, negative, there is no sign of any landing gear whatsoever. Worse still, there are some black marks on the undercarriage, indicating some sort of fire or small explosion may have taken place.'

'Jeeesus Christ,' Todd said slowly as he dropped the radio onto the desk and sat down.

Todd continued. 'Those bastards. They've disabled the landing gear to ensure the plane comes down and now we're two minutes over land, it's gonna come down in a heavily populated area. We can't even blow it out of the sky without some casualties on the ground. What a complete shower of shit the security must be at Heathrow airport. Firstly, they allow known terrorists to pass through security, with possible explosives and handguns… and now they had given access to someone on the ground to plant a device to disable the landing gear up'.

Agent Harris responded almost defensively on behalf of the different security services.

'Let's not make too many assumptions. We all know how sophisticated the terrorists are these days and how far-reaching their resources are.'

'None of this matter right now,' Alan interrupted. 'We have over 300 people to try and save. Let's focus a hundred percent of our energies on that!'

This information was immediately fed back to the White House on a line that was now permanently open and the President called the British Prime Minister back. 'Anne, after the amazing news a few minutes ago, things have turned bad again. Whether by a mechanical fault or whether its sabotage, the plane's landing gear will not come down.'

'Oh my God!' replied the Prime Minister. 'Are they going to get any luck? What are the options now Matt?'

'Anne, the team are working on solutions, but you know as much as I do and I can't immediately think of any.'

Chapter 76

'What's going on Alan?' I demanded.

Alan, quickly thinking on his feet replied. 'David, I'm not going to lie, but we have a serious problem with the landing gear. For whatever reason, it's falling to engage and it's too late to try and do it manually. Normally a plane brings its gear down some 10 minutes before you did and that's enough time to solve any problems that arise.'

'Problems that may arise? Are you fucking kidding me?' I screamed. 'This isn't a *problem*, it's a bloody nightmare!' I had completely forgotten about the family swear jar.

'David, Laura… I need both you to listen carefully. I want to give us more time, so you will need to amend the flight's data.'

'Someone give me the co-ordinates for the Hudson,' Alan shouted without realizing he mistakenly kept the radio line open. A couple of controllers quickly searched the map and looked up at the screen that showed the flight path of flight BA57. One of them shouted some numbers across to Alan.

Alan came back on the line. 'Guys, you need to plug in some new numbers into the autopilot. The same buttons and process we did a few minutes ago to get us heading towards the airport. Okay?'

I shouted my reply. 'No, we are not okay and why do you want us to go towards the Hudson River?' Slightly confused as to how David knew this information, Alan replied.

'David, just do as I instruct. Nothing more, nothing less. I need to create some time to think. Type in 423, then 835.' I typed the numbers into what I now knew to be the autopilot and the plane slowly veered to the right. As the plane had already started its descent, it was at approximately 12,000 feet and both Laura and I could see the city approaching. And now, even though it was a long way down, we started to see what could easily have been a river and we both guessed it was the Hudson, a couple of miles or so away.

After a few moments, the plane steadied itself and carried on in a straight line. My heart was racing again and I didn't have any words to describe how I felt. We were going to die all over again. Having survived being shot and being blown up, we were now going to crash into the murky waters of the Hudson River. God, why are you doing this to me? How can you get me through the last hour and now put me through this? I want to see my children. I must see them. I never got the chance to say goodbye properly. To hug them for the one last time. I must tell my girls what to expect when they get older and what to watch out for. I need desperately to hold my James. I was crying again.

'Good work, David. Now hold on for a few movements whilst we come up with some options.' Alan said.

Laura and I looked at each other. We didn't speak but were probably thinking the same thing. What possible options could there be? I also wondered whether they would blow us out of the sky rather than have us crash anywhere. Surely not?

Laura had tears in her eyes and reached out a hand to me, which I just saw through the tears that filled my own. 'I'm scared,' Laura spoke quietly.

'You're not alone, Laura,' I replied.

'But if anyone can get us out of this, you can.' She added with a level of false determination in her voice to try and get me to pull myself together. I had a terrible feeling of complete despair. What possible options could there be? Even if we had a pilot on board, we hadn't got any landing gear to land anyway.

Another minute passed as our pathway now flew pretty much in line with the river.

At the control tower, the last two minutes had been surreal. Agent Harris was on the phone to his superiors. They were in turn, in touch with the White House. Todd and Alan had moved to a corner of the tower and were in deep discussions. It was as if time had stood still.

'Is it possible to repeat 2009, Alan?' Todd asked.

'With a 777, you must be kidding,' Alan responded.

'Is it possible?' Todd firmly restated.

After a brief pause, Alan said: 'Everything's possible Todd - practically everything.'

In January 2009, US Airways passenger airliner number 1549 flight made an emergency landing on the Hudson River. All 155 passengers and crew exited safely off the plane and there were no serious injuries. The plane had flown into a flock of geese and both engines had been lost. There have been other recorded incidents of planes landing safely on water, but never with a plane the size of the 777.

'You're also missing the obvious, Todd.'

'I know, Alan: flight 1549 had a very experienced pilot on board.' Todd responded.

'But Alan, what other options do we have? I cannot see the President giving the order to blow the plane up. Isn't it better we lose the plane and its passengers at least trying to save them? Don't they deserve a shot? David's performed miracles already. Can we desert him now?'

'What about the risks to the people on the ground?' Alan asked.

'If we find a wide enough section, then it's just a ditch. If we get lucky, maybe a few people on board will survive. There's loads of places that are over one or two miles wide. Hell, I think the widest part is over three miles wide,' Todd said.

'But in his situation, the autopilot will be no good, which means that David is going to have to land the plane. Is he up to it?' Alan asked.

After a few moments, Todd gave his answer. 'So far he's been magnificent... almost superhuman. You didn't see the video footage of his actions on the plane. I know he says he was very lucky but no normal man gets that much luck. If anyone has a chance of saving just one passenger, he would be the guy I would ask.'

I picked up the headset again. 'Alan, what happened to the review of the passenger list? Surely there must be some feedback on it. We need a pilot'

'Nothing yet, apparently they're about halfway through. There just hasn't been enough time. Now's the time to make the passenger request again, and this time I would stress the importance of someone coming forward. And remember they don't even have to have to be a fully-fledged pilot - even someone with training would do right now,' Alan said.

How do I ask the passengers if anyone can fly a plane? It's an announcement that sounds ridiculous, even as I thought about it. Something out of a B-rated movie. But then the whole situation *was* ridiculous. Like a very bad dream. Only an hour or so ago I was complaining to myself I hadn't enough time to finish the in-flight movie. I considered my situation for a moment and then I made my desperate plea for someone with flight experience to come forward.

I picked up the intercom. 'Hello again, this is David again, speaking on behalf of the captain. You may have noticed we have made a slight turn and have been asked to circle a little whilst they organize things on the ground. In this type of security alert, they want to clear a runway and terminal to allow us to disembark separately to other planes, as they're bound to want to interview all the passengers.' What a load of rubbish I was talking, but it sounded credible enough and hopefully there were no smart-arses on board that would add two and two up and realize we were in desperate trouble.

I continued. 'Unfortunately, we are still looking for that passenger with some flying experience to come forward. We are only five to ten minutes from landing and need some help from someone.' I was getting desperate. 'Anyone with some flying experience, however insignificant you may feel it is, is required to come forward and assist the Captain.'

Chapter 77

Larry Anderson was now completely drenched in his own sweat. Hearing the second request for a pilot was like receiving heavy kicks to his abdomen. Worse still, he heard something in the voice of the announcer that made him more certain of their impending doom.

Larry knew full well the autopilot could land this plane. The conditions were almost perfect for a landing. Clear blue skies and he recalled the wind strength was only light to moderate (an old habit of Larry's, checking the travelling conditions on any journeys he took). Newark airport and the plane would be fitted with the necessary electronic landing equipment. Something else was definitely wrong. Plus, any pilot with experience of a large plane would be able to land the plane safely. All commercial pilots had a minimum of 10,000 flying hours before they were allowed to take charge of a plane this size and most had more than 30,000. The trouble was, Larry was so frozen with fear he could only sit there feeling pathetic. He knew that even if he could gather the strength to stand up, he wouldn't last twenty seconds inside the cockpit. The feeling of claustrophobia would be crippling. He also knew his wife's life may be in his hands. If there was a genuine problem with the plane, he could possibly be the difference between Betty seeing her new grandchild or not. He hadn't opened his eyes for the last two minutes. He was unable to face Betty; he felt so ashamed.

He heard the voice of an air stewardess coming down the aisle asking passengers if anyone had flight experience. Larry opened his eyes and she seemed to look straight into them, almost knowing he was hiding something. He quickly looked away, only to come face to face with Betty. She was smiling, but also had a look of fear across her face.

He had never seen the look before. Betty was always the optimist, someone that cared for others. Being an ex-pilot's wife meant Betty had a good understanding of the workings of a plane and Larry sensed she had gone through the same thought process as he had about their need for a pilot.

Chapter 78

The headset crackled and Alan was on the radio again. 'David, are you there?'

'Yes,' I replied.

'David, you have shown an amazing set of skills so far, saving the lives of all the passengers and crew, and most probably several hundred other people on the ground. I now have one final thing to ask of you. The teams on the ground have been considering 2 possible options, but one of these was dependent on us having more flight time. We think you are going to run out of fuel in less than ten minutes, so that option is off the table. The only remaining option is for you to land the plane on the surface of the Hudson River.'

'What?' I asked. I simply couldn't absorb what Alan had said.

'David, with Laura's support, you are going to land the plane on the surface of the Hudson River. It's been done before, and all the passengers survived and you can do it.'

'What did you say?' I repeated. 'Did you just say I had to land the plane? Me, land the plane, and on a bloody river? Are you fucking mad?' I shouted at the top of my voice. I was hysterical.

I repeated: 'Are you fucking joking? Me, fly a plane and land it on water? Are you out of your fucking minds?' I was screaming at the radio and poor Laura just looked on in disbelief. She too had a headset on and could hear the plan. She slumped back in her seat, with the feeling of complete and utter despair.

'David, get a grip of yourself. You're the only hope,' Alan shouted.

'Only hope? Me? What do think I am a bloody cat? Do you think I have nine lives? I am going to kill everyone on board!' I was so scared and shaking so badly I thought I was going to lose control of my bladder again.

Alan shouted again. 'David, what we know for sure is that unless you pull your fucking self together, everyone on board is dead. Everyone. Mothers, fathers, children... everybody. No-one will see their children again and that includes you.'

My head was spinning; it felt like it was going to explode. No, no, no. No way could I land a plane!

'Why me? God, why have you forsaken me... why are you doing this to me?' I cried out pathetically.

In a calmer voice, Todd spoke. 'David, I have no idea why this has happened and why you are sitting in the captain's chair onboard a 777 airplane. But what I do know is that whatever your background, you are an extremely resourceful man. And to stop the risk of an argument about your background, let's just say you're an extremely lucky man. Lucky to still be alive after being shot. Lucky to have overpowered and killed two terrorists and captured another. And I would much rather we have a lucky person to bring this plane home than an over-confident, smart-arse pilot. Yes, you are going to have to dig deep. Deeper than ever before. The fact is that the Lord of our world has chosen you to be in that seat right now. Nobody else but you, and I will say it again: there is nobody else that I would rather have sitting where you are now. Having read your resume, I understand you run a company. That means you're in charge of lots of people. You're a leader of men and woman. We are...' He corrected himself. 'No, in fact, all the passengers are asking you to try and save their lives just one more time.'

A good and timely speech that at the very least calmed me down a little. I have given many of the same to irate employees and managers over the years and every single one of them was completely incidental right now: managers arguing over the fact they were paid £250 less than their colleagues, employees accusing managers of being tough on them - all just silly, insignificant things. Everything that kept flashing before my eyes or was going through my brain meant nothing anymore. For some bizarre reason I thought about my fear of spiders and thought how pathetic I was. Linda woke me from my thoughts. 'David, you can do this. We can do this together.'

I was still struggling to breathe and could hear my heart pounding against my chest, seemingly trying to get out. My mouth was so dry, yet my hands were soaking wet with sweat. I looked across at Laura. 'Laura, how can we land a plane on water? Really, truly? How can we land a plane on water?' I repeated. Her own facial expressions didn't give me much hope. A few moments passed.

I gathered my senses, sat up a little and sarcastically asked.

'Alan, pray tell me, without giving me loads of information about dials and knobs and aerodynamics, exactly how and why this plane can land on water.'

A few seconds passed and with a tiny fragment of hope in his voice Alan spoke.

'Did you see the video footage of the plane that landed on the Hudson a few years ago?'

'Yes, I saw it,' I replied.

'It's pretty much the same way *we're* gonna land your plane. And I say 'we' because we are in this together. We just go for a normal landing with the auto-pilot in play until the last few seconds, then you will take over the controls and pull the plane up slightly as if you were taking off again. You cut the thrusters and effectively put the plane into reverse and it should land tail first, then the body and then the cockpit.'

'So all pretty straightforward then,' I replied and found my mouth forming a small smile.

'Yep, pretty straightforward.' Alan agreed in a polite voice as if we had just agreed on travels plans to meet down the pub.

Chapter 79

For some reason, there was a brief sense of peace or relief that seemed to come over all of us. For me, I don't know whether it was because, at that moment, I realized I was going to die and somehow felt a small amount of peace about it. There was no genuine way I could land this plane on water. I started to cry again. I would never see my children again. Never hold them, never witness them growing up.

Todd, Alan, and all the team on the ground had witnessed my screaming and Todd's intervention, and for some bizarre reason, the complete feeling of despair had been replaced by a faint sense of hope. At that stage, did we have anything to lose by trying? With slightly different amounts of knowledge and clearance levels, they each knew the history surrounding planes landing on water. Rarely do the public find out all the facts surrounding flight disasters, but what everyone did know was that in 2009 flight 1549 did land safely on the Hudson River…of that there was no doubt.

Probably with the rest of the whole world, both Linda and I had seen the dramatic footage of the plane landing safely in the Hudson, and that knowledge alone gave us some hope. However small or ridiculous it was, it was hope.

'David and Laura, you do need to prepare the passengers for landing on water and need to try and do it without causing mass panic,' Alan requested.

'How long have we got? I asked.

'Give us another reading from the fuel gage, but it cannot be more than eight or nine minutes before you're flying on fumes,' Alan replied. Laura read out the numbers again and I sat there trying to imagine what we were going to tell the passengers and how they would receive the information. What if it was me? Would I want to know I was going to most probably die, either as the plane broke up or by being drowned in the river. Most of the passengers would have been speaking to their loved ones on the ground for the last ten minutes. At below 15,000 feet the mobile phone signals had kicked in and from what Debbie had reported a short while before to Laura, the whole plane was on the phone.

I had calmed down a lot and was breathing easy again, still at twice my normal heart rate, but at least I didn't feel my heart was going to fly out of my chest at any second now. I needed to talk to my children just one last time. I felt a real sense of panic, and had to speak to them.

'Alan, Todd,' I called out over the radio.

'Yes?' Todd replied, almost panicked by my tone. 'What's up, David?'

'I need to speak to my children and I don't want any excuses or reasons why it cannot happen. You need to make it happen and right now!'

'Can you give us a number and we will call them.' Todd replied, but then corrected himself. 'Actually, we have their home number anyway, so will call them and patch them through when we have them.' The FBI had done a thorough background check on me and had every conceivable number and address I had lived at for the since my birth. The local time in New York was now 12.39 pm, meaning it would be 5.39 pm back in England and all the children should be home from school and college. I hoped they were all together.

My thoughts came back to the reality of the situation. Could I really land the plane? Surely not. I knew I would panic, just as I had earlier just with the thought of it. I had very little energy left. Yet again my shoulder and upper chest were on fire again. I needed a drink. Another disgusting scotch to help take away the fear I felt in the pit of my stomach.

I called out, 'Debbie, please can I have another drink?' Moments passed and an outstretched arm appeared inside the cockpit with another miniature bottle of whiskey for me.

'Many thanks. Laura, what shall we tell the passengers?' I asked.

Laura, rather calmly responded, 'David, just tell them the plan: tell them that it's been done before and there's no need to worry.'

'But we both know that's not true. We both know what's happening here, we both know that.' I said.

Linda interrupted me with a calm, but firm tone. 'David I don't know what to say or what to do. But you'll think of something and I trust it will be good enough.'

I sat back with my thoughts. 'What would I want to hear?' On hearing about plane disasters on the news, I had always felt sick on hearing the instances where passengers had known a few minutes before the crash that they were going to die. The personal horror and anguish for themselves on board and their loved ones they were travelling with must be horrific. Surely it's better to die instantly, without warning, or is it fair to give people hope… where there wasn't any? Or would people like to prepare themselves, say their goodbyes to loved ones, pray and maybe make their peace with whatever God they believed in.

I made a decision, but briefly before I switched on the plane's intercom I prayed again. 'Dear Lord, I cannot fathom why you have brought me to this place. Why you have helped me so much, only for me to probably be responsible for so many lost souls. Please give me the words and courage to speak to the passengers, my brothers and sisters. Words that will bring some hope. Some sort of confidence that we would or could survive. I don't want them knowing they're going to perish.'

I switched the intercom on. 'Hello passengers. This is David again and I am speaking on behalf of the Captain. We are going to be landing in approximately seven or eight minutes and unfortunately have another challenge that we must overcome. For some reason, the plane's landing gear has not released, so we are going to land the plane on the water.' I hadn't expected to stop talking, but the roars and screams of passengers took my breath away.

'Ladies and gentlemen, we must stay calm, I need you to listen to me,' I shouted. 'When the captain was a co-pilot in his early career, he and his captain successfully landed a plane on water and is very confident he can bring us down safely. He says it's been done 5 times over the last eight years and on every occasion, it's been without loss of life.'

It took 20-30 seconds before the passenger noise has ceased somewhat and I went on. 'Please listen to me: The Captain's done this successfully and has every confidence of a safe landing.' The plane went almost quiet. 'I know it sounds scary, but we will be okay. You will have most probably heard about the plane that landed safely on the Hudson river a few years ago, well that's exactly what we are going to do.'

I finally had their full attention. 'An important part of a safe emergency landing is preparation.' I was on a roll. 'We must clear the floor in front of our seats. Quickly but calmly place everything in the overhead lockers. If you are unsure or unable to do this, please pass any loose items to a crew member. This must be done immediately and then seat belts fastened. Please do this now and I will speak to you shortly.' Linda had already left the cockpit and with Debbie, was instructing the other crew to ensure the passengers were getting on with the task of preparing the plane and themselves.

Chapter 80

Larry Anderson now knew they faced certain death. Yes, by some amazing miracle a small 40 seater airplane had landed on the Hudson a few years earlier and yes other similar sized or small planes had also landed safely on water. Hell, there were even planes especially designed to do it. But a 777 is over 60 metres long and 60 metres wide, and on impact there was no way a pilot could handle the controls of something this big and Larry was 100% sure there were not 5 examples of planes landing safety on water. He recalled the number was closer to 2 or 3. Plus, he knew there must be something wrong with the pilots otherwise this guy called David, (who was probably an on-board air marshal) wouldn't be talking to them at all. The Captain always spoke to the passengers; it was the protocol. He was the calming and controlling voice, always had been and always will be. It would take a huge miracle to land the plane and for it not break up into thousands of tiny pieces. Both he and Betty were going to die. He knew it and, worse still, he knew Betty knew it. The only thing that remained uncertain was whether Larry could get himself out of his seat, walk the 100 feet or so to the cockpit and maybe, just maybe, give the passengers and his dear wife a 1% chance of survival. Would it all be in vain and even if he could walk, would he pass out as soon as he entered the tiny cockpit?

Chapter 81

In the meantime, back in the tower, Todd and Alan were going through the plan. They were reviewing the landscape of the river and looking for a best-case scenario of the plane crash landing. They had to assume it would crash because they knew the chances of a half-decent landing were near impossible. The plane was coming down in less than ten minutes and it was coming down hard. They needed a place that was lightly inhabited, but where the emergency services to get to relatively quickly. There were a number of options, but they also needed time to get David and the passengers ready. They figured that three or four minutes should do it. Anymore and the pressure of the waiting might tip David over the edge.

They identified a spot some 20 miles away. The river was two miles wide and it looked like there were no towns within two miles, and whilst that meant there may not be easy access to the river, they had to take the chance that the emergency services would find a way through. Anyway, most of the action would be on the river. Todd marked the spot on the map.

'Everybody listen now!' Todd shouted to get everyone's attention in the tower. 'We have a plane coming down hard in the Hudson in around seven minutes time. Location is approximately 20-22 miles along the river at this point.' He marked a larger map that someone had put up on a wall. 'I need all, and I mean all possible emergency services: divers, boats, helicopters, fire crew, ambulances - the full force of all emergency services to this point in less than five minutes. I know that's not possible, but I expect a bloody good turn out as soon as people can get there. Us getting help to this point is crucial, especially boats and divers.' He pondered for a moment. 'Somebody should even ask civilian boats to head for the spot. Every boat is needed, however large or small.' He pointed at the map. 'There must be boat mooring or fishing clubs along that stretch of the river.' He indicated to a couple of familiar faces he had previously seen in the tower. 'You guys find them and make the calls.'

There were several representatives in the control tower covering most aspects of the government, both local and national. Everyone jumped into action and within less than 90 seconds practically all the services were either packing or had left for the expected crash site. The Mayor of New York had previously been instructed to have everyone on standby by the President and now they had a target area, at least they could do everything they could to get there in time.

Chapter 82

I sat back in my chair, or should I say, in the Captain's chair and put my hands over my face. 'Good work David, good work'. Trying to give myself some a quick pep talk.

The radio crackled with Todd's voice. 'David, your daughters on the line.'

'Dad? Is that you, Dad?' came the voice of my eldest daughter Sarah. 'I started sobbing. 'Yes Sarah, it's Dad. Very quickly darling' I blabbered, 'Get Abigail and James together and put me on loudspeaker.'

'Dad, what's wrong?' Sarah asked.

Pulling myself together, and speaking more firmly I repeated. 'Sarah, just do as I say and do it now please.'

As I always call the children on their mobile phones, their mother Linda grabbed the landline phone. 'What's the problem, David?'

'Linda, this is very serious and I don't have much time. Have you heard the news about a hijacked plane?' I said.

'Yes, I'm watching the news right now and they're just saying the hijackers have been overpowered and it's currently over New York getting ready to land,' Linda replied.

'Well, I'm on that plane and whilst we don't have a terrorist threat anymore, we also have no bloody pilots and no bloody landing gear. The bottom line is, we are going to try and land on the Hudson River somewhere and I don't think we're going to make it. I need to have one last conversation with the children, so please put me on to them together, all on loud speaker.'

'You're joking, right? Although the kids did tell me you were flying to the states again...' Linda said. Before she could go on anymore I interrupted. 'Linda, I am not joking and I need to talk to the children. I don't have much time.'

'So who the hell's flying the plane?' Linda asked.

'Linda, for Heaven's sake, just put me onto the children.' I shouted.

Linda appeared to get the message as the next voice I heard was James. 'Dad, where are you? What's going on?' Then Sarah spoke, 'Dad, you're scaring us now. What's happening?'

'Where's Abigail?' I asked.

'I'm here, Dad. What's up?' Abby said, casually.

'Listen guys, I have got myself in a bit of a pickle. I'm still in the air flying to the US and we are having to make an emergency landing.'

Unconvinced, Abigail interrupted. 'Dad, you can't be speaking to us from the plane, it's not allowed.' Something we had discussed on our last family trip to Europe. Then Linda, understanding the situation clearly, spoke. 'Kids, this is your Dad and he is on a plane and shortly it's going to try and land on water. Listen to him.'

I spoke again. 'James, Abigail, Sarah. For some reason, God has chosen me to be on this flight, with loads of other people, on this very day. We will never fully understand why God does things and what his purpose is, but here I am right now and I'm in a spot of trouble. I want you all to know how very much I love you and how very ver...' I broke off, sobbing, not able to control myself or get the words out.

'Dad!' James called out. I could hear Abigail crying. 'Dad, are you there?' James repeated and somehow I managed to gather myself.

'Yes, I'm here son. I have been so lucky and probably very undeserving to have three amazing kids in my life. You have brought me so much and I love you so much.'

'Dad, what are you saying? Mums been watching the news about a plane that's in trouble,' Sarah asked. I had so many tears streaming down my face, I could hardly see anything.

'Sarah, darling, and the fact is there is chance the plane won't survive the landing. I want you to be strong and remember all our amazing times together.'

'No Dad, no, please don't talk like that, pleeease,' Abbigail screamed out.

'Abby, darling, be brave now. Sarah, hold your sister tightly. Listen, all three of you have great futures ahead of you and you are already growing into fine human beings. James, you have been an inspiration to me and so many others, I love you all so much.'

Todd interrupted, 'I am so sorry David but we need to make final preparations for landing.'

I spoke my last words to my three wonderful children. 'Guys, please always look after each other and make sure you tell Haley how much I love her. That's so important.' I felt guilty for not speaking to her myself. I continued, 'Family is so important and just because we don't understand why things happen, never turn away from God. He loves you all very much. I love you so...' The connection went dead.

After a few seconds, Alan came back on the line. 'Sorry David, I know it's brutal, but we must try and land this plane and get you all home.'

I didn't hear him. I wanted to throw up. My grief had overpowered me. I wanted to curl up into a ball and have my mother cuddle me. I needed her to tell me that everything was going to be alright and I didn't know why, but she was the only one who could make it better... make it all be alright.

Laura had just returned into the cockpit when I heard a voice that sounded familiar. It was Alan again and his voice brought me back to a horrible reality. 'David, can you hear? Laura are you there?' Alan was panicking a little at the silence.

'Yes, we are here,' I replied, softly.

'Right, we have identified a landing area of the river that's around two miles wide and you will reach the destination in around four minutes' time. All the emergency services will be there to assist you and the passengers. All we need to do now is go through the landing protocol.' Somehow, I had calmed down in just a few seconds. I almost felt some sort of humor in the situation. Was this really happening? Yes! What I going to attempt to land a plane?

I interrupted Alan. 'Alan, will you stop with the long words like protocol and keep it simple, please?'

'Sorry, David. Laura, are you *both* listening carefully?'

'Yes.' Laura replied.

'Right. As you both know, the autopilot is currently flying the plane and will be able to pretty much until you get to about 200 feet, and then it will need to be switched off and David will take over. All in all, it should be about 30 seconds from switching it off, to you landing. You will be going at around 180 knots on landing. If you go below 165 knots, the plane will stall. Now that's not a serious problem here, as long as your nose is up slightly when it happens. What's your current speed?'

It was a good question from Alan, timed perfectly to see what information I had retained from the earlier turning maneuver. I looked at the speedometer (I couldn't recall the correct name for the dial). 'We are going around 400 knots right now,' I said.

'Good,' came Alan's reply. 'Now you both know how to reduce the plane's speed with the autopilot, by imputing the target speed into it, and David you also know how to reduce or increase the speed manually by moving the thrusters back or forwards. The other important dial is the horizon dial. That's got to stay level, with the blue above and brown below. These are the three key instruments that we need to focus on. Laura, I would like you to move the wing flaps just to ensure their working okay… just as a precaution. These will need to be raised slightly on landing to create some down-force.'

Whilst Alan took Laura through this, I was wondering what else to tell the passengers. We had maybe three minutes or so until we would crash land into a huge river.

I grabbed the intercom. 'Hello everyone, this is David again with more instructions from the Captain. We have approximately three minutes to land and now need to go through the evacuation process.' I felt an urge to communicate to them, to reassure the passengers and take their minds off the fact that we were going to crash headfirst into a river, and if the impact didn't kill everyone on board then the subsequent explosion or risk of everyone drowning must have been obvious.

I continued. 'On landing, I will need the aircrew to man all the emergency doors, plus an additional passenger to help them.'

In the unlikely event the plane didn't explode into tiny pieces on impact I thought that there was a fair chance that several of the crew could be killed on impact and needed to have a backup plan of passengers willing to take over the responsibility of getting anyone off the plane. I continued. 'Air crew, please nominate a passenger or take volunteers from the emergency seats areas. Remember, whilst we are landing on water, the plane cannot sink. It has buoyancy aids on all sides of the plane to stop this happening.'

I realized I was waffling but I almost felt as if I wanted to talk to them all personally, to try and help ease their fears or maybe I was just trying to concentrate my own mind away from my impending death.

I went on. 'This is important for you to listen to because once we land there must be no panic and rush to the exits. Apparently, on previous flights passengers have been injured because there was blind panic and everyone was trying to get off the plane at the same time.'

Linda grabbed a life jacket from under my seat to remind me. I nodded and continued.

'Everyone must now put on their life jackets.'

Then I remembered the instruction I felt like I had heard hundreds of times before. 'But do not inflate them inside the aircraft.'

I had been on over thirty commercial flights in the last six years so the drill seemed to come easy for me to say. 'It's so important to follow the evacuation procedure and carefully follow other passengers down the aisles towards the exit doors. Do not over take any fellow passengers. Please take off any footwear that has heels. Everyone must stop using their mobile phones and focus on helping yourselves… and their fellow passengers. Please look around you and if you feel there are vulnerable passengers that may need some help evacuating, please help them.'

I instantly thought of James, which immediately brought more tears to my eyes. As a family, we had flown several times with James and on every trip, I couldn't help wondering how I would handle an emergency like this. My mind was wandering again, but I had to stop feeling sorry for myself and try and focus on the task at hand. I wiped my arm across my face to clear the tears.

Chapter 83

For the next 60 seconds, Alan tried to explain, in very simple terms, how I was going to land the plane and not kill everyone in the process.

There were three main things to remember and Alan was trying to make it sound so simple:

1. Switch off the autopilot at 200 feet (Laura would perform this task to ensure I had my hands firmly on the wheel). Then Laura had to push a lever to ensure the flaps were up on the wings.

2. Reduce the speed down to 180 knots and once contact has been made with the river, bring it down gradually to zero.

3. Hold the plane steady and land almost horizontally, with the tail first. Then lay the plane on the river.

Alan mentioned each part and made me repeat it back. He did this three times and each time I got it wrong. How could I perform the part about reducing the speed when I had my hands on the steering column? When Laura switched off the autopilot, how was I going to stop the plane from nose diving straight into the river? I couldn't seem to clear my head enough to take on board his instructions.

'David, it's simple. Laura does stage 1. When she does that, you will have both hands on the steering column. Yes?'

'Yes, I guess so,' I stuttered. I was feeling dizzy and thought I was going to throw up. I couldn't concentrate.

Alan was getting increasingly frustrated.

'You 'guess so'? What do you mean you 'guess so'?' Alan angrily responded.

'Yes, I will have both hands on the column.' I replied.

'Good.' Alan calmed a little. 'Then you hold the column for a couple of seconds and then, with your right hand, you pull the controls by your right leg, slowly back, reducing your speed further.'

I slumped back in my seat. I still couldn't hear him properly. I just heard words being spoken over the headset, almost like the sound of a radio in the background. I was staring forward with a blank look on my face. I was never going to see my children again. I loved Hayley and wanted us to have a new life together in the new house. I wasn't supposed to be in a cockpit. This must be some horrible dream. A sick horrible dream that I wanted to wake up from. I muttered under my breath: 'Please God, forgive me for killing all these people.'

The plane continued its descent.

Chapter 84

I heard some screams and initially thought they were coming from me, but then it grew louder and it became clear that it was coming from the passengers. I glanced behind me out into the first-class area to see Debbie coming up the aisle with a male passenger. He was an elderly gentleman, maybe in his late 60s, and he looked in a bad way.

Debbie was shouting, 'I've found us a pilot!'

The older guy reached the cockpit door but didn't enter it. 'My name's Larry and I haven't flown for 15 years, but will help if I can.'

'Larry, you may well be a lifesaver. Do these controls look familiar to you?' I asked.

Larry peered inside the cockpit. 'Yes, they're all pretty much the same as I remember, but with more fancy dials.'

He stayed in the doorway, holding onto the cockpit door and I didn't understand his hesitance to take over. I stood up and motioned him into the captain's seat. 'Larry, over to you, we only have 90 seconds before we hit the river. The autopilot's still on,' I looked across at the dial. 'We are at 1320 feet, and they reckon we need to switch it off at 200.' He still didn't move. I noticed his hands were shaking and that his knuckles were white as he gripped the cockpit door. He was sweating so much it looked like he was crying.

'Larry.' I raised my voice in my own panic. 'Larry!'

He then appeared to close his eyes for a couple of seconds, released his hand from the door and wiped his forehead. He then slowly and carefully entered the cockpit and replaced me in the hot seat. Laura got up out of the co-pilot's seat and sat in the spare seat behind.

I passed him a headset, but he fumbled as he tried to put it on. 'Alan, Alan, we have found ourselves a pilot. Larry is now in the captain's seat,' I shouted.

'What the...?' Alan exclaimed and came back. 'Pilot? Where from?'

'Does it fucking matter?' I shouted in reply. Alan quickly got it and spoke with a very professional and authoritative voice.

'Larry, my name's Alan, and I'm your guy on the ground who's been helping David thus far. Can you tell me your airspeed please?' Alan was quickly testing Larry's knowledge. A few seconds passed as Larry's eye surveyed the vast instrument panel. '229 knots and we are now at...' Larry searched for the dial. '650 feet and descending. Where's the autopilot switch?' Larry asked.

Before anyone could respond, Alan answered. 'Larry, leave the auto switch to David. Laura's already checked the flaps and they're all working. The plan is for David to switch it off at 200 feet and then for you to bring her down. You need to be at a speed of around 180 knots and at around 165 knots you will stall, but not a problem in this situation. Have you landed a plane in any type of similar circumstances?'

Then was a few seconds delay then Larry replied 'Firstly...' He looked around at Laura. 'Please keep the cockpit door open at all times.'

Then he responded to Alan. 'Yes, but it was the size of a Cessna and had sea boats attached to it instead of landing gear. And anyway, landing a small seaplane on a calm lake at some 65 knots is a whole different ball game.'

'Agreed Larry, but the principles must be the same,' Alan said. 'The key action is almost hovering the plane about 50 feet above the water, then laying the tail down gently first and then the rest of the body. The challenge is that when the tail hits the water, the shaking will cause a possible loss of control. That's the single most important factor between success and failure,' Alan stated.

'You mean life and death,' I piped up. Alan chose to ignore me and kept going.

'Larry, can you handle these controls? It's gonna be absolute hell trying to keep the plane steady.'

'I can only do my best. I have nothing else, but my Betty's back there and I've got to try and save her life,' Larry replied.

I looked back at Laura and also Debbie, who had stayed at the cockpit entrance. 'Is everything on the plane strapped down?'

'Yes, pretty much so,' Debbie replied.

'Then please secure yourself safely and cross those fingers. We are going to need every slice of luck to survive this,' I said.

For a few moments, Debbie and Laura embraced each other tightly and then looked at each other in the eyes before Debbie returned to her seat.

Chapter 85

Todd and Alan were delighted by the fact a pilot or retired pilot had come forward. At the very least, when the plane did crash and break up, it should now be in the middle of the river, meaning any debris scattered shouldn't reach land putting the lives of civilians on the ground at risk. Prior to this news, and after the earlier burst of activity sorting out the on-ground emergency services, they also had to brief the President on the situation. Given the history of planes landing on water, the size of the plane, the wind conditions, air temperature and fact that a so called civilian (or at the very least a guy with no flying experience) was at the controls, the President had asked the obvious question of Alan. 'What were their chances?'

'Mr President,' Alan began. 'The chances of *anyone* surviving the landing, or crash, as we expect it to be, are very slim.'

The President responded quickly. 'I don't need words, I need numbers. What does slim mean?'

Todd responded. 'Sir, we believe it's as low as five or six percent.'

'And is there any genuine risk to anyone on the ground?' the President asked.

Todd continued. 'Mr President, based on the expected landing location of the plane and locality to any built-up industrial areas or towns, we again think the risk to anyone on the ground is again less than five percent. Most of the area around that part of the river is farmland and the nearest towns are approximately three miles away. That's our best fucking guess with the information we have, based on the time we have had to put the plan together.' Todd's voice had inadvertently raised a fair bit as he said the last bit and the President picked this up, but appreciating the hopelessness of the situation and the stress the guys must be under, chose to ignore it.

'I understand some of the pressures you guys have been under and together with that guy on board, have done a sterling job so far. What I am asking you to do now is reach down into your very souls and convince that guy that he's a superhuman. A man so confident that he has the ability to walk on water, let alone land a plane on water. Do you understand? Be his hands, be his heart, be his eyes.'

'Yes sir,' Alan and Todd replied at the same time.

'Good luck, and may God be with you all,' The President said as he cut the line.

'Fucking Hell, Todd. Are you trying to throw away your career?' Alan asked Todd.

'Couldn't help myself... just came out that way,' Todd shrugged.

'I know what you just told the President about percentages, but what hope do you really give David to land that plane and save the lives of any of the passengers?' Alan asked, laboring the 2nd half of his question.

Looking very serious and sad at the same time, Todd replied. 'Less than two percent.' He went on. 'Even with an experienced pilot, a 777's a huge plane and the pilot would struggle to even feel the tail hitting the water until it's too late. The immediate friction and shaking it will cause will most certainly mean the pilot would panic and lose control. The plane will probably flip over and break up. The only upside I can see is that there's hardly any fuel left, so the plane won't blow up, which means very little fire. People not killed outright by the impact or break up will probably drown within a minute or so.'

'That's our best hope,' Alan said. 'Getting to the people as fast as humanly possible and trying to save even a handful would be seen as a success.'

Now, only three minutes after the conversation with the President, with an actual pilot at the controls, the mood had improved. Sarcastically, Alan leant over to Todd and whispered. 'I do believe our percentage has just doubled from two to four. Whilst it ain't much, it's a start.' Todd smiled.

'Over to you Sir, and good luck,' Todd shook Alan's hand and left him alone to focus completely on trying to help both Larry and David land flight BA57.

Chapter 86

In approximately 60 seconds flight BA57 from London, England, would land on the Hudson River in New York State.

It was very quiet in the cockpit and on the plane. Most passengers were in the brace position and any that were partners, relatives, or even work colleagues were holding hands. A good number of the passengers were also praying: prayers of desperation, payers of hope, and even prayers of forgiveness. Parents with children on the ground were asking that their God look after their children for them.

I looked out of the cockpit window and felt the factories and cars I could see were almost within touching distance. I could even make out a few boats on the river. I wondered what dying felt like. Would I be knocked out immediately on impact and die in an explosion, or drown still strapped to my seat? I was scared of dying and I certainly didn't want to drown. Why do I have to die right now? Why me? It's not fair. I saw my children's faces, then Haley's; I had been so lucky to meet her. I felt my eyes welling up again. David, I told myself, pull yourself together.

Betty Anderson was sitting alone in seat 22B and whilst she was scared and filled with immense sadness that she would never see her granddaughter, she felt extremely proud of her husband Larry. They had shared so much together and despite his own desperate fear of even moving from his seat, he overcame everything, and would now be sitting with the captain trying to save her and everyone on board. Betty knew it was a hopeless task. Did they even have a captain or other pilot? She had heard the shots being fired earlier and the desperate requests from the cabin crew for a pilot. Now there wasn't even any landing gear. Something had gone badly wrong. Yes, Betty was frightened, yes, she was physically alone, but she prayed to God just one last time and asked him to be with both her and Larry. A strange sense of peace had started to come over her. She had had a fulfilling life and 35 years of marriage to the most wonderful man. She knew very few people would ever be as lucky as she had been.

Chapter 87

Debbie was now sitting in her crew seat about four feet away from the bodies of the two dead terrorists. She had just pressed the automatic announcement to advise the passengers to get into the brace position. This was followed by a prerecorded message in 2 different languages.

She too noticed the quietness of the plane. How could so many people make so little noise? After all the drama, gunshots, and screams of the last hour, all she could hear were the engines of the aircraft and her own heartbeat. Debbie thought about Laura and how wonderful Laura had been today. So calming and in control. Nothing at all like Debbie. When that lady grabbed her hair, she remembered the piercing scream she let out, which was immediately followed by the screams of other passengers. Then she was dragged by her hair all the way into the first-class section. Worse was to come as the terrorists constantly threatened to kill her. She felt there was no way the captain would open the cockpit door and felt huge relief when he did. Of course, that relief soon turned to complete despair and she felt herself scream once more as the terrorists shot the Captain.

Could their lives really be over? Could the guys land the plane safely? Why not? It had happened before and that David guy is amazing. And now they had another pilot helping out.

'Yes, please dear God, let us be safe,' she whispered as she sat there trying hard to give herself a confidence boost. She would be going to Radio City tonight and she and Laura would be singing their hearts out to Queen's Bohemian Rhapsody.

Chapter 88

'Larry, please tell me exactly when you want me to switch off the autopilot,' I said.

Larry wasn't up for any small talk. His hands were gripping the steering wheel tightly and he stared straight ahead and began muttering to himself. 'Come on Larry old son, you can do this. Come on Larry you are a trained pilot.' Without turning his head to face us, Larry piped up. 'David, we all need to strap ourselves in tightly. When the tail makes contact with the river, the turbulence will be very powerful.' Both Laura and I checked our seat harnesses and pulled them as tight as we could. My shoulder didn't seem to mind at all… I guess the last ounce of adrenalin was flushing around my body. I looked again out of the window and saw the river fast approaching. The whole scene looked so weird. All signs of civilization seem to have disappeared. There were no houses or roads visible just a wide river with trees all along it. We could have been anywhere in the world. Why couldn't I see any rescue boats or roads for any cars or ambulances?

Did that mean they didn't need any, that this would be a clean-up operation, rather than a rescue? I had no idea that for every 10 to 12 seconds that went past, at our speed of around 200 knots, we were travelling just under a mile.

'Alan, can we make it?' I cried out. Why, I don't know, but I guess any sort of reassurance would have been greatly appreciated and I was desperate for something, anything. Alan chose to ignore it to keep the focus on the landing.

'45 seconds to touchdown, guys.' Alan said. 'You're at 300 feet, David; in seven or eight seconds, release the autopilot and soon after push the flaps upwards,' Alan instructed.

'Please God, help us and be with us now. Help us just one last time.' I said this out loud and Laura reached forward and grabbed my shoulder.

Clearly, my body didn't have enough adrenaline left as my shoulder did hurt and I winched in pain. Laura apologized, 'I'm so sorry, David.'

The seconds passed so slowly and then Larry took command and said: 'Switch off the autopilot and hold on tight.'

I flicked the switch and the plane suddenly dropped, as if we had hit one of those air pockets people talk about. I could see the water rise up as if it was coming towards us. Larry was now controlling the Boeing 777 aircraft. Larry now had the fate of 314 souls on board in his trembling hands.

Alan's voice came over the radio. 'Nice and steady Larry, nice and steady. Just slowly lay the belly down. Reduce your speed gradually.' And I saw Larry push the wheel forward and a few seconds later all hell seemed to break loose inside the cockpit.

Chapter 89

We had slowed to 160 knots the plane stalled and a loud voice came from nowhere.

'Pull up, pull up. Engines are stalling. Pull up, pull up.' It kept repeating itself. Alan, Todd, and the rest of the team heard the same automatic voice through the radio. Alan decided to keep silent so that Larry had no distractions from the ground. Then, as if almost deliberately synchronized to start at the same time, I started to hear the air stewardess shouting and repeating the words 'Brace, Brace.'

With these noises ringing in my ear, at that moment, right there and then, if I was flying the plane, I would have surely panicked and nose-dived straight into the river.

The words got louder and louder.

'Pull up, pull up. Engines are stalling. Pull up, pull up.' Then to add to my own panicked state, another, more robotic voice started repeating 'Terrain, Terrain, too low.'

I looked across at Larry and he had somehow managed to ignore all the noise and gently continued to lower the plane. He then sternly looked at me and he appeared to ask me to follow his gaze, as his eyes pointed towards a flashing red light above the controls. I hope he meant for me to press it because that's exactly what I did. The horrible noises stopped and for a few fleeting seconds, there was silence. The engines had stalled and we were effectively gliding.

I had seen this scene before, either in a movie or in a dream. It may have only lasted three or four seconds but the silence was surreal. The last seconds of my life were very calm and I felt surprisingly peaceful. I felt like I was surrounded by my James, Sarah, and Abigail.

I felt as if I was in God's hands, that he was holding me as if he had the whole plane in the palm of his giant hands. I saw the river come up to meet us and even caught the light ripple of the surface glistening in the sun.

Chapter 90

Then all hell *did* break loose; as the plane's tail and the river made contact, the whole cockpit seemed to shudder out of its casing and Larry's arms started moving up and down as he struggled with the wheel. I tried to tuck myself into my knees but I was being pushed forward and side to side and felt Laura's body battering into my back. The screaming from the passengers was drowned out by my own 'Jesus Christ! Fucking Hell!' as the plane shook from side to side. Laura was screaming behind me and I could see the right wing almost hitting the water, then the left wing. I looked ahead and saw what looked like a couple of helicopters hovering a few hundred yards away. As Larry laid the plane down, water rushed up over the nose of the plane and we lost visibility.

I felt myself falling forward as the nose of the plane went underneath the water. We're going to die!

But then, a few seconds later, I was thrown upwards and through the water-covered cockpit windows, I suddenly saw the sky again.

The same thing happened again and again. We were effectively bouncing, like a stone, skimming across the water. On each bounce, we went forward into the river and then back up again. The noise was deafening. The plane groaned as if it was screaming out as the power of the river shook her structure.

For fear of having my head ripped off my body, I tried to curl up into a ball, but the plane wasn't having any of it and I couldn't seem to keep my arms close to my body.

Larry's body was completing the same maneuvers and I briefly caught sight of his face and he appeared to be unconscious, with blood trickling from a cut to his forehead. All of a sudden, out of the corner of my eye and with a huge noise, I saw the right wing tear off and the plane seemed to turn around towards the left. The nose went high into the sky as if we were taking off again and then plunged again back into the murky waters of the Hudson. We were going to drown. Seconds seemed to pass and everything was dark again. Water was about to smash through the cockpit windows and death would surely be only seconds away. In preparation, I tried to inhale to get a decent breath, but I couldn't.

Then much to my amazement, with almost a popping sound, the plane's cockpit rose out of the water for the very last time. After a few more seconds, we came to a stop, facing the side of the riverbank. The plane still rocked from side to side, but slowly this stopped and we appeared to come to a standstill. Were we alive? Had we made it? It hadn't seemed possible.

I heard several noises from the passengers. Some of them were screaming, some were cheering and I thought I even heard someone clapping. I turned my head and Laura too was unconscious, most probably from hitting the back of my chair. I thought I heard a moan from her and some eye movement. She slowly managed to open one eye. 'We've made it. We've made it,' I said, softly.

I repeated it and she smiled the most beautiful smile I had ever seen. I looked around and could see several boats coming towards us and at least five helicopters landing on the nearside river bank. I then panicked a little. I didn't want to drown and whilst I had told the passengers the plane couldn't go down, I had no idea if this was true. I had to think fast. Before I could do or say anything, Laura spoke, almost as if she was reading my mind, 'Tell them to launch the evacuation procedure and open the exit doors.' I had lost my own headphones, so grabbed Larry's and pressed the open button. 'Ladies and gentlemen, please follow the evacuation procedure that has been discussed. It must be done quickly, but calmly.'

The plane didn't feel like it was moving at all. I felt a sense of joy. Larry started groaning and opened his eyes. I grabbed his arm. 'You were amazing. You have saved us all. Are you okay?'

Larry managed to mutter a few words. 'Are we okay? Have we landed okay?' He seemed to come around and then tried to get out of his seat. 'I have to get out of here, I have to find Betty.' Larry said and I helped him unbuckle his seat harness. As he got up he fell forward onto me and then righted himself.

'Larry, you've got a head injury. The plane's not going down; we're safe.' Ignoring me, he pushed past me and left the cockpit. Laura put her arm around my right shoulder. 'You did it. You and Larry did it.'

'We did it, Laura, we did it.' She flung her arms around me and for a brief moment I forget about everything that had happened; that I had been shot, that I had killed two human beings, that I had felt like I was going to die so many times, that I wouldn't see my children again. But then I had a bizarre thought and pulled out of the embrace with a mischievous smile on my face.

I pressed the open button on the headphones.

'Hi. Speaking again on behalf of the captain, this is David signing off. Thank you so much for flying British Airways and whoever you are, and wherever you're going, please have a great onward trip and we look forward to welcoming you on board again in the near future.'

Epilogue

The evacuation of the plane went incredibly well. Fortunately, as the plane had lost its right wing and spun left, it had moved into shallower water and the fuselage was only 20% submerged.

All of the passengers and crew exited the plane alive and only 23 people were treated with relatively minor injuries. Bizarrely, the person that fared the worst was the captured terrorist number 3, as he had been so trussed up by Bob that he couldn't get into the brace position, and both his arms and one of his legs were broken.

After the initial panic to get off the plane in case it sunk had subsided, it took around ten minutes to evacuate everyone and as I followed Laura off the plane into the emergency slide, I could see four people entering the plane from another slide. I assumed these were either US Special Forces or the emergency services to deal with T3. A few minutes before, I caught up with Bob halfway down the plane and I had suggested that we leave T3 on board.

Unbeknown to me, back down the plane near the tail, a young girl was sliding down an emergency slide in the arms of an unshaven young man. They were not related and had only met a few hours before. Whatever their own stories were, they were both grateful to be safe. Before the young man reached the river bank, his hand fell over the side of the emergency craft and his hand released an object into the dark waters of the Hudson.

A year later, around the anniversary of the landing, at the enquiry, all the aviation experts were still baffled how Larry had held the controls on impact with the Hudson. They said the pressure on the plane and steering wheel would have amounted to nearly 250 pounds per cubic feet. Even the fittest and strongest man would have struggled to keep control. (I wonder where Larry got his strength from?).

As for me, things were pretty weird for a while. I was transported straight to the hospital and then put under an armed guard. Whilst I looked a mess with my torn, bloodstained shirt and with a bruised eye from the impact when we first hit the water, I hadn't actually lost too much blood. After relatively minor surgery where they stitched up the two holes where the bullet had passed through, I was placed in a private room.

After being 'politely' interrogated at my hospital bed by a number of different people for a couple of hours, I seemed to convince them (or at least they gave up) that I was indeed a very normal citizen. Before I agreed to speak to anyone, I insisted on calling home, only to find Hayley and Sarah were already boarding a plane for New York and would be with me a less than eight hours. I did speak to both James and Abigail and after a very emotional ten minutes, I managed to convince them I was okay and would see them soon. After a couple of hours of sleep (supported by some sedatives), I just sat there reflecting on the most bizarre, frightening, incredible day, trying unsuccessfully, to make some sort of sense of what had happened.

As the evening drew near I had three visitors. Todd Williams and Alan Peterson came together and it didn't take long before there were more tears, mainly from Alan and myself, but I swear I saw a few in Todd's eye as he shook my hands again before they left. They explained the magical moment when the plane came to a standstill and apparently the whole control tower erupted in celebration. I did ask them if there had been a good or strong chance that our own jets could have blown us out of the sky, but they both either chose to ignore the question or didn't hear me.

I guess I knew the answer.

The third visitor was the President of the United States, who had decided to fly in from Washington. It was very surreal. Initially, he entered my room with two other guys who had that stereotypical look: smart dark suits, white shirts, and black ties, who looked like they had come straight off the set of Men in Black. But the President insisted they leave the room, so we could have a private moment. We chatted about many things and he insisted on me calling him Matt. He said I had earnt the right and that he was humbled in my presence. He seemed like a genuine guy.

I didn't really know what to say to him. He asked me if there was anything I needed and repeated a few times that the American people were indebted to me. What do you say when the President of the United States asks you 'if there's anything you need?' I just wanted to see Hayley, my children, my Mum and Dad, my Sister and Brother... my family.

Hayley and Sarah arrived very late that night and yes there were more tears. I only needed to stay in the hospital for two nights and then we all returned home, first class of course, courtesy of British Airways.

My experiences on flight BA57 left me with a number of scars and in particular it took me a long time to get over the fact that I had caused the deaths of two fellow human beings. Everyone told me that they were evil people and that I had nothing to feel bad about, but I couldn't help wondering what had brought them all together and what had made them into the people they were. In the eyes of their families, were the terrorist's heroes?

I struggled to carry on working a full-time job with my company and, despite them being very flexible with my hours, I resigned six weeks after the incident. I couldn't face the endless questions and publicity surrounding the flight. Understandably, everywhere I went, people wanted to know the details and, as I couldn't seem to come to terms with it myself, I struggled to explain what had happened.

Hayley and I had previously discussed setting up an internet company that would help people with disabilities find work and also find places that had decent facilities for them to socialize in. This became the perfect solution for me, as we could do a lot of the work from home.

Six months after the incident, I took Hayley, my brother, and my children to meet Larry and Betty Anderson. For me, I think I was also looking to talk to someone about that day that was there, someone that knew what had happened firsthand. They were a wonderful couple and we split up the trip with four days in New York. It was Christmas time and New York had a wonderful dusting of snow on the ground which, added to the amazing Christmas decorations and lighting that the shop owners had put up, made for a spectacular sight. We did some shopping, saw a couple of shows at Radio City and everyone had an all-round fun time. Personally, I felt like I was just going through the motions, as my last trip to New York had been so traumatic, plus I had previously visited the city a few times before. And, if I am honest with myself, I also just wanted to meet up with the Andersons.

Larry and I didn't discuss the flight at all until the very last evening when we were alone together. Hayley, my brother, and the children had left us alone, and for over five hours we sat in his backyard together, admiring his garden. We talked, we laughed and yes, we cried a lot. I learnt about his fear of flying and how difficult it had been for him to leave his seat on the plane.

By the time we went to sleep that night, I felt some closure was happening. I felt some peace in my heart, something I hadn't felt in a long time.

Whether you believe in God or not, try telling the 314 passengers and crew AND the 20 people who had been sitting in the air traffic control tower that day that a miracle didn't happen.

What was witnessed by hundreds of people on board flight BA57 were incredible acts of human endeavor where, despite all the odds, despite the almost insurmountable personal fear, people displayed genuine courage.

The End

Printed in Dunstable, United Kingdom